# For the Love of Alison

# Sahlan Diver

# For the Love of Alison

ISBN: 978-17-87233-70-6



Find out more about the author and his novels and plays at the publisher's web site
https://www.businessassistant.biz/novelsandplays.htm

Disclaimer: The fictitious political party, "Making Sense", characterised in this novel, is not intended to be a representation of the similarly named real-life UK political party, "Common Sense". As a resident of the Republic of Ireland, the author was not even aware the latter party existed until halfway through writing the work. Any resemblance between the real and fictional party is therefore purely coincidental.

# Preface

## Unusual Mysteries

*Unusual Mysteries*, the series of three novels, and a book of stage plays, presents mystery stories like you have never encountered before. Unusual settings, unusual characters, unusual plotlines, with multiple misdirection and startling reveals.

### (Mystery 1) The Secret Resort of Nostalgia
Shortlisted for The Yeovil Literary Prize 2017

A graduate is sent to document a remote Irish island community. What he discovers there may mean the difference between life and death.

" … unlike any other mystery novel I have ever read." *Sefina Hawke for Readers' Favourite*

### (Mystery 2) For The Love of Alison
Finalist 2020 Indies Today Award

A journalist receives an invitation to visit a woman who was the object of his obsessive mental illness thirty years ago. That same evening, a murder occurs. Can the journalist prove his innocence, and his sanity?

"… very different from the countless other crime/thriller books that I have read..." *Reviewer at LoveReading.co.uk*

**(Mystery 3) Sixty Positions with Pleasure**

In the year 2050, a suspicious hit-and-run accident sets off a chain of deaths, each more puzzling than the last. A vision in a cave prompts a stampede of pilgrims. An Irish town declares its independence from Ireland and the EU. And twenty-something English engineer, Charlie Gibbs, is co-opted by fifty-year old Dutch company boss, Ilse Teuling, to assist in writing a sex manual.

"… a fun read … with an enormous cast of characters, most of whom are not what we think they are … Very enjoyable." *Lucinda E Clarke for Readers' Favorite*

**(Mystery 4) The Chapel in the Middle of Nowhere
(and three other stage plays)**

Members of a fading and obscure minor cult hold a party in an isolated location. None of them are prepared for the disruption that will be caused by three uninvited guests, one of whom may be hiding a dark secret.

All mysteries in the series available from leading online sellers. Further information and video reviews etc at: https://www.businessassistant.biz/novelsandplays.htm

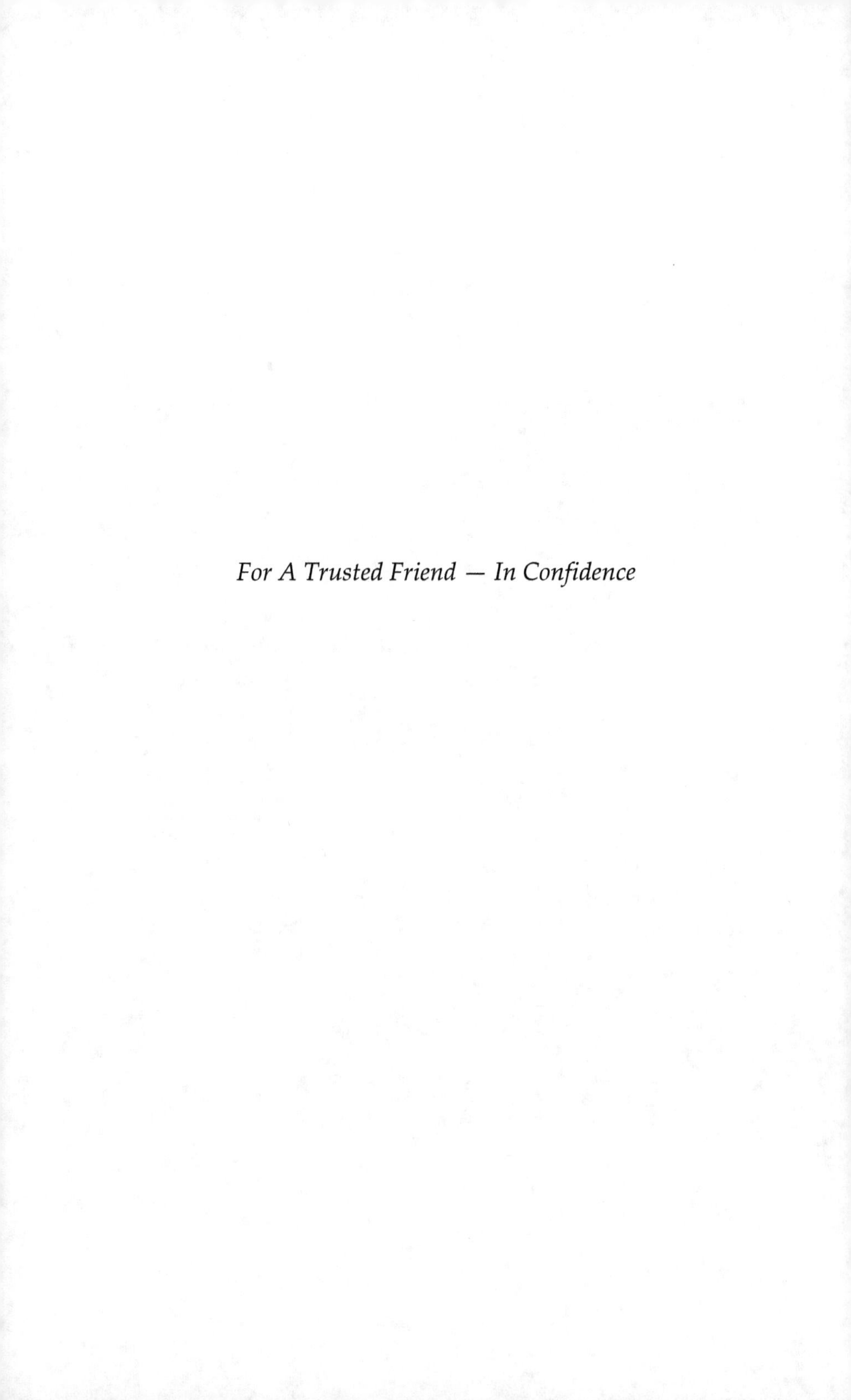

*For A Trusted Friend — In Confidence*

# TABLE OF CONTENTS

# PART 1

# TRAPPED

# Chapter 1

## Not Guilty,

## by Reason of Sanity

Question: What's the perfect way to commit murder?
Answer: Get someone who doesn't exist to do it for you.
Firstly, they don't exist, so there's nobody for the police
to catch.
Secondly, if the police did, by some miracle, manage to
catch them, well they don't exist, do they? So they can't
tell on you.

Does that sound a bit mad? Does it sound like I'm mad?
That's what they want me to admit, that there are serious
questions regarding my sanity; that these things did not
play out as I describe.

I had to write it down, just as it happened. Maybe then
I could work it out. Maybe you can work it out. Perhaps
I'm insane and witnessed only an illusion. Perhaps I'm
sane but taking everyone for a ride. Or perhaps I'm the
unfortunate victim of someone else's business — in the
wrong place at the wrong time. Or, perhaps the whole
thing is a trick and none of what took place that evening
can be relied upon.

The problem is only I know what is true. But that is the
problem. I don't know the truth. I only know what I saw.
Even that is too strong a statement. I only know what I
*thought* I saw.

And don't say it could never happen to you. Exactly
what I would have said a few months ago. An average

citizen, leading an ordered life. How could I find myself trapped in such a preposterous situation?

# Chapter 2

## Alison

The end is as yet unknown. The beginning is not. It started with Alison, with her phone call to my office. Alison, who had shaped my youth and abandoned me, I thought forgotten me. Alison, whom I had not seen for thirty years. Alison wants to meet up.

I almost didn't go to work that day, feeling shaky, a recurrence of my old illness. It comes every so often, then passes. If I'd done the sensible thing and called in sick, I wouldn't have been there to receive the phone call; I wouldn't have been there to fit in so neatly with the diabolical plan apparently being devised for my future.

I have to assume timing was critical. That day. That time. The window of opportunity. Another day? Too late! She even told me herself on the phone: "Tomorrow's out. I'm going to Paris for a week. Come this evening. We'll have a good few hours to talk before my husband comes home. Then you'll have to go. I don't think you and he should meet."

Early morning: my regular weekday Bromley commuter train to London. Early afternoon: an express racing up north. Nothing regular about that: because of Alison.

The train's only just started off and the ticket inspector's already doing his rounds. I offer the ticket apologetically. "Is it OK? I intended to get the three o'clock but saw this one would get there thirty minutes earlier. Do I owe any money?"

He scrutinises my ticket. "No, that's fine, sir. You can use it any time you want, including the last train back to London at midnight."

I thank him, saying I'm planning to return by the ten o'clock.

How did Alison know I can't drive? Most people assume I'll be visiting by car and immediately launch into a mass of directions relating to motorway names and exit numbers, which might as well be a foreign language to my ears. I'm obliged to hastily interrupt and ask what's their nearest train station and how far are they from it. I didn't need to with Alison. She'd even found out the times. "Get the three o'clock. Don't bother with a taxi — they go round the one-way system, which they use as an excuse to rip you off. We're literally walking distance. Take the hill directly opposite the railway; ignore two right turns; next right, past the evangelical church, is us. We're the third cottage along, the only one with a gnome outside the front door."

I laughed. "You won't believe this! I also have a gnome outside my front door! So it's third right, third cottage, gnome. I'll be there."

I hear the clatter of the buffet trolley approaching from the next carriage. Normally, on a longish journey like this, I'd order something but my thoughts are elsewhere. I hardly notice the steward asking, "Any drinks or snacks?"

It's funny; I can't remember the occasion on which I met Alison. I mean, I remember the occasion. I could tell you the date precisely. I have a clear impression of the room as I entered but, much as I try, I can't recall the actual moment of seeing her, nor of how we were introduced.

Perhaps because we became such good friends, shared so many good moments together, my recollection of that first time faded by comparison. Or maybe my illness blocked it out, a memory too painful to keep in view of what subsequently occurred.

We met at the opening session of the student drama society. I went along as potential scriptwriter. Alison attended as a performer, though not as an undergraduate — she worked as a student nurse at the nearby hospital. Because of the proximity of the university to the medical school, the drama society offered membership to both institutions. I do remember her audition. She did a skit, playing members of the royal family, including the male members. Hilariously funny. She was a first-class mimic, very good at voices. At some point, we found we had common ground politically, though she even more left wing than I. We went arm in arm on protest marches, sat together at political rallies, joined expeditions sticking posters on lamp posts.

I don't wish to denigrate nursing in any way but I felt Alison to be wasting her talents. I once told her there were any number of careers in which she might be successful *and* make more money. She replied by mocking me, saying she hadn't noticed me putting a high priority on earnings, with my sole ambition of becoming a published poet and playwright.

An hour out from London, we're pulling in to the first stop. Two hours to go. I'm nervous. More than that: turned on. I'm remembering the time I'd planned to bed her.

Alison slept around and didn't mind anyone knowing. Nice-looking, with thick blonde hair and a pleasant personality, you might even say gorgeous. She worked through an easy succession of short-term boyfriends. Not difficult with the university's ready supply of randy young males, living in halls of residence, unfettered by the behavioural constraints of living at home. Only once did her supply dry up. I took my chance. Our hall had a dance on — we used to call them "discos" back then. Naively, I mistook Alison's delight, when I invited her, as confirmation she too wanted what I wanted.

Eight o'clock they came down the corridor together: Alison and the guy. I'd seen him around but hadn't twigged anything going on. She asked could they borrow my room. An hour later, at the disco, they gave back my key. I went back upstairs, too peeved to stay. Whatever precaution they'd taken, it wasn't quite enough. On my bed sheet, a small yet tell-tale stain, still sticky, the nearest I'd ever get to sex with Alison.

The train speaker announces the final stop, reminding us to ensure we've taken all our belongings. This is it! At least this time, I can raise no false hopes. Well, she's married, isn't she? What are the chances she's invited me for sex?

Things went from bad to worse. At a party, I introduced Alison to my English Literature professor, Laurence Thompson, the well-known author. They began a passionate affair, difficult to organise due to the inconvenience of his having a wife. When Alison worked nights, they'd meet during the day, squeezing out our friendship. We drifted apart.

After my graduation I moved to London. If you're writing for theatre, that's where you need to be, making contacts, making connections. Alison's affair couldn't last forever. When my star as writer arose, I'd invite her to live with me, to share in my glory. The news of her wedding put a stop to all that. A university friend told me. Alison had settled down and got married: to a solicitor. Extraordinary! Such a confining, respectable act for a former left-wing activist and sexual libertine.

The train doors beep at me. I press the button and breathe in the decidedly bracing air of this north-eastern town. Through the ticket barrier, out of the station into the forecourt and there, beyond the taxi rank, the long steep hill of terraced houses, just as Alison had described on the phone.

Should I attribute my breakdown to the news of Alison seemingly lost to me forever or to the fact of my writing going nowhere? Whatever, that's when my drug dependency started. First a welcome palliative, a temporary escape from misery, then total immersion in an alternative world. I hallucinated constantly, unable to distinguish fantasy from reality. Luckily, police were called to "the incident", before I did harm to myself or others. Committed for treatment, I became a national health service success story, fully rehabilitated, though not without consequences — even till a few years ago I would get the occasional mental white-out where for five minutes I wouldn't know who I was, where I was, or what I was doing. That's why I'm barred from driving, and why I needed a job that would surround me with people, to keep me grounded in reality, also to raise the alarm and care for me if I had one of my episodes. The bustle of a newspaper office seemed ideal, as the job offered contact with my first love — writing. I worked my way up from the menial position of storekeeper given to me out of charity and sympathy, becoming a copy editor, then a features editor, finally their chief political columnist whose comments are read nationwide daily. The newspaper even provided a social life: receptions, cultural events, political dinners; the only thing not provided, a female companion. I'd go home at night to sleep alone in my Bromley flat, the life of a recluse, talking to nobody till back at work the next day.

This place isn't Bromley. No denying I'm in the industrial north here, though most of the old industry has either gone or been moved out to green-field enterprise parks. In the damp cold foggy gloom of an early January evening, as I pass by the glow of the street corner pubs, it's as if they're still attended by ghosts of workers past. Two pubs, two right turns — this hill is longer and steeper than Alison led me to believe. Should have got a taxi.

The phone call came after lunch. I'd been away from the office all morning for a briefing on *Death Means Death*, the new populist obscenity announced with a big fanfare by minor political party, *Making Sense*. The receptionist told me a woman had rung several times. Another call came in as she was telling me.

"Shall I take her number?" she asked.

"Tell her if she doesn't mind hanging on while I catch the lift, I'll be back at my desk in two minutes."

I felt in no mood to rush. The persistence of the caller made me suspect an ardent campaigner, or a right-wing troll seeking the opportunity to abuse me.

I picked up the office phone. "David Buckley here."

An unfamiliar voice, the voice of a middle-aged woman asked, "Is that David Buckley, the well-known columnist?"

I confirmed, bracing myself for the expected barrage.

"David, this is Alison. Alison Johnson. Sorry! Stupid habit! I mean Alison Tindell."

For a moment I thought this might not be happening, that I might be experiencing another whiteout. "Alison, is it you? It doesn't sound like you."

The voice on the phone said, "You don't sound like you either. We're a lot older than last time we saw each other. Sorry to remind you of that unpleasant fact."

She told me she knew of my column but never thought the writer might actually be me. The David Buckley she'd known had insisted on dedicating his life to poetry and plays. Compromise for that David was not an option. My recent article, confessing my drug addiction and rehabilitation, had connected the dots.

"Why don't you come and see me tonight?" she said. "The train gets in at six. Last one back to London is at midnight. You'll have to leave at nine anyway, before my husband gets home."

I pass by the looming Victorian façade of the evangelical church. The billboard slogan in the spirit of "Prepare to meet thy doom" seems apt, considering the house I am about to visit. It was when I asked whether there might be a problem my being there without her husband's knowledge that Alison dropped the bombshell. The solicitor she had married all those years ago was the man now notorious as "Honest Jack", my political nemesis, Jack Johnson, founder of the "Making Sense" parliamentary party and all-round foul-mouthed pub bore, stirrer of political trouble, a man whose opinions I had often lambasted and ridiculed in my daily column.

I reach the third turning right, cross the road and count the houses. Alison had said to look for the third cottage along, the only one with a gnome. Could Jack Johnson and I actually have something in common? Both garden gnome fanatics — the irony of the situation a temporary antidote to the shock of discovering Alison was his wife, shared his bed, presumably allowed herself to be regularly penetrated by that specimen of an extreme right-wing monster.

The gnome stands proud but the cottage is in total darkness. I'm beginning to suspect a malicious impersonator has sent me here on a wild-goose-chase. Surely not! How could they have found out about Alison? Then I realise: I caught a different train; I'm half an hour early. I could have forewarned Alison. Why didn't she give me her number?

As I walk up the garden path, I hear a crash, like furniture being knocked over. And an exclamation: "Shit and Blast!"

I ring the bell and wait. No reply, so I ring again. The cottage remains in darkness. After pressing the bell for a third time, I hear soft footsteps inside. The door's opened by a blonde in her early fifties. "Come in, David! Lovely to see you again! Well, it *will* be lovely to see you, when I can find the light switch!" She laughs, the sexy Alison laugh I remember so well.

# Chapter 3

## The Cottage

We've been talking now for almost an hour and a half. I'm amazed and touched by Alison's vivid remembrance of shared times past, coming out with story after story, most of which had totally gone from my recollection. Were it not for the stories and her sexy laugh, I wouldn't have believed myself talking to the person once a student with me in Birmingham, that with the passing of three decades she could so completely change in appearance and manner — I could have been talking to her mother. Well, of course, the one occasion I met her mother, she would have been ten years younger than Alison is now. Funny, isn't it, when you're in your early twenties, how your parents and your friends' parents seem ancient? Later in life, as you age alongside people, you don't think of them as growing noticeably older. Only when you see someone you haven't seen for years does age hit you and you see its effects with the clarity of your younger self.

Reincarnated as a mature lady, Alison remains gorgeous. Attractive, taller than average at five foot six, the same thick blonde hair, the same tiny beauty spot blemish just above her upper lip (something else I'd forgotten). She's wearing a cardigan and a skirt (which pleases me, because I'm a legs man and Alison's still showing good legs. She has on black tights, no shoes on her feet. Right now, she's curled up on the sofa, informal and relaxed. However, I sense a nervousness, like she's putting on an act. Is she leading the conversation away from controversy because the uncomfortable truth is we are no longer comrades-in-arms, she's fully gone over to the other side?

This room is obviously part of an old cottage that has been modernised. Oak beams, timbered walls. The front door opens directly into the living room. No space for a hallway because of the building's age. The only illumination the flickering of an artificial coal-effect electric fire and some wall lights turned down on a dimmer to a cosy, intimate light. The décor hints of a homeowner who enjoys success and standing in the community, with a suggestion of big money tainted by vulgarity. I'm surprised. I could understand Johnson showing off but I would have thought Alison a stronger restraining influence against the bad taste that is apparent. Really bizarre is a stuffed ferret mounted on a stand placed on a corner table. Ugly. Menacing. I comment on it. Alison merely laughs, exclaiming, "My husband!"

I ask, "Do you remember Hibbert?"

"Our marching colleague. How could I forget!"

"What happened to him, do you know?"

She sighs. "Prison, I expect."

"You're referring to his 'Robin Hood' tendencies, robbing from the capitalist rich to feed the poor, in every case the poor being himself."

"What was that story about the second-hand books?"

"He'd shoplift from the university bookshop, then take the book back later to sell to them as a second-hand item. He'd have the cheek to haggle over the money they offered, saying 'Look! It's in nearly-new condition!'"

Alison laughs. "Remember the porter at your hall of residence, the one who always got his opposites the wrong way round. He hated Hibbert being so vocal with his left-wing views. He used to say 'That Hibbert! He's a real *reactionary*!'"

I reply, "Even funnier what he said about Stephen, the gay guy. He didn't like him either. He whispered in my ear once, all intimate and confidential, when Stephen was standing nearby, 'I'm a *homo*-sexual and proud of it!'"

Alison says, "Lucky for him, you didn't take him up on the offer!"

In another room, a telephone rings. Alison tells me she's not answering — a bossy neighbour pressing her to do volunteer work. "It's not that I mind. It's a good cause but the woman keeps you hostage on the phone. She's a non-stop talker."

Alison asks whether I have news of Laurence Thompson.

I say, half-joking, "We none of us stood a chance against the professor, did we?"

She laughs. "I always did have a thing for successful men."

The phone rings again. Alison makes a face. "Some women! Think they have a right to demand your attention. Can't stand being thwarted. I'm not answering. She can stew!"

I'm pondering whether Alison's self-confessed attraction to successful men explains her present situation, in every respect at odds with the Alison of her youth. I say, "When we heard you'd married a solicitor, we all said what a weird conventional thing for Alison Tindell to do. Your affair with Professor Thompson I can understand. A brilliant man. But Johnson! Alison, I don't want to be rude about your husband ..."

She interrupts me "Why not? You're making a career out of being rude to him."

Now she's thrown down the gauntlet I'm determined to press my point. "Sometimes I think the world's going bloody mad! Look at the pattern of history: religious bigotry superseded by the enlightenment, the exploitations of the industrial revolution mitigated by social reforms, then the labour movement, leading to the national health service, free education for all, then the moral freedoms and sexual revolution of the 60's; women's rights; gay rights. A guaranteed steady liberalisation and progress of the human condition. Now look where we are! I saw a picture at work, a group photo op of American politicians, all middle-aged, all men, signing a proclamation to tear up a vital climate-change deal. They had smirks on their faces like a bunch of irresponsible teenage schoolboys whose teacher was temporarily absent from class and who were determined to create as much chaos as they could while they had the chance."

I expect Alison to engage me in a battle of words. She wasn't shy of giving political opponents a battering in the past. Instead, she gently touches my arm. "David, let's not start on an argument. I hope we can still be friends. I need time to explain my newfound philosophy. Next time we meet?"

She gets up from the sofa and goes over to a writing desk. "I've got a surprise for you!"

From a drawer she takes out a pile of foolscap papers, yellowed with age, precariously held together with a rusted metal fastener through one corner. "Remember this?"

She hands it to me.

On the first page is typed:


<u>HERE BE CLOWNS</u>

<u>A PLAY</u>

<u>BY DAVID BUCKLEY</u>

"You wrote it for me, remember? Though, considering the erotic content, I'm not sure it wasn't simply a ruse to get my clothes off."

I look at my old forgotten script with sadness. "Pity we never had a chance to perform it."

Alison laughs. "The professor banned it! David, here's the good news. We're putting it on in the town next month. The amateur dramatic society."

I leaf through the pages, so unfamiliar they could have been written by a stranger. "I haven't seen this since I wrote it. I hardly remember the plot."

Disappearing into the kitchen, Alison says, "You can read it while I make coffee."

Is this the reason for the sudden invitation, the reason why, underneath the pleasant bonhomie, she has seemed so nervous and apprehensive all evening?

17

# Chapter 4

## Here Be Clowns

The phone's ringing again. Must be an extension, because it sounds further away than before. I'm puzzled to hear Alison answering this time.

"Oh! Hello! ... Not now... I've got somebody with me... What does it matter to you? ... A man ... No, I can't ask him ... He might be embarrassed ... You're far too pushy! Has anybody ever told you that? I'll call you back."

She comes in with two mugs of coffee and a jug of milk on a patterned tray. "If I remember right, you don't take sugar in coffee."

"Was that her, the bossy woman?"

"David, this is awkward. I hope you don't think I'm taking advantage. The actor who's playing the part of the clown says he wants to come round and rehearse a scene. We need you to take part. Do you mind?"

I say, "How can I refuse, when it's my play!"

She leaves the room and I hear the push button beeps of a telephone, then a pause.

"He says he'll do it ... Do we have to? ... Can't you make an exception just this once? ... Now it's *me* who's going to be embarrassed ... All right!  You win again!"

Alison comes back into the room. "I have to get changed.  He insists we do it in costume."

"What's the guy's name?

"Mister Clown, like in the script."

"His real name."

Alison looks at me strangely. "You're going to have to humour him.  He told me not to tell you."

"Is he OK?"

Alison sits down close to me on the sofa. She's talking in a subdued voice, as if she doesn't want to be overheard. "He fancies himself as a method actor. He thinks he has to live the part. He's been running around town for weeks in his clown outfit. Somebody complained to the police. They called him in for an official caution, so he had to stop that tomfoolery. Tonight, he's insisting we play it for real, like in the script. You're only allowed to know him as 'Mister Clown'. If you remember, your corrupt politician character doesn't know Mister Clown's true identity, only that he's being blackmailed by him over a shady business deal. The clown turns up, just as you and I... "

I ask nervously, "Is it the sex scene?"

Alison takes my hands in hers. "David, promise me you won't feel embarrassed or awkward. Otherwise I don't think I can go through with it."

From an alcove in the corner of the room she fetches a plastic bag containing a heavy object. "It's OK. It can't fire. We'll be using sound effects in performance."

I take out a handgun.

Alison thumbs the script till she finds the page. "We're going from here. I'm your secretary but I'm secretly in league with Mister Clown. He's tried unsuccessfully to blackmail you, so he's set me up to seduce you. He breaks in on us to take compromising photographs. You try to grab his camera; he produces a gun; he doesn't know you also have a gun; you fire, wounding him; then he runs off."

I read the page and wince. "This sex writing is really dated. It'll never hold up with a modern audience. They'll fall about, laughing."

Alison says, "We've changed it. You don't have to play the super-stud any more. Just sit passively on this chair and leave me to direct the action." She pulls over a dining chair for me to sit on. "Go over your lines while I get changed."

I turn up the dimmer on the wall and read the relevant pages a few times. A dramatic moment in the play. On the other hand, straightforward. Why Mister Clown has singled out this relatively easy bit for special rehearsal, I can't imagine, though from Alison's description he sounds highly eccentric, which may explain a lot.

The lights turn down low again. I look up. Alison Tindell is standing at the entrance to the room. She's changed into a translucent mini nightdress, sufficiently see-through to reveal the outline of her breasts and her protruding nipples, and she's removed her tights, so her legs are bare.

"Wow! Alison, you're like a vision of Venus."

She smiles. "Come on! Let's get on with it!"

"What about Mister Clown?"

Alison looks over her shoulder. "I left the back door open for him. He'll be spying on us at this moment, just like in the play."

From somewhere inside the house comes the slow throbbing music of a seedy striptease club.

I say, "You'll forgive me if I think this is a little creepy."

"Relax!" she replies, "It's only a play. It's *your* play. Enjoy it."

She starts to dance, like a lap dancer. In character, she says," Mister Barclay? You seem tense. Let me help you unwind." She dances towards me, alternately sliding her nightdress up her body, then lowering it, teasing me with brief glimpses of her panties. She's good: very good. I feel myself getting rock hard. This isn't a rehearsal. It's a seduction.

"Waaaaaaarrrrrrggggggghhhhh!!!!!!!!!!!!!!!!!!" Mister Clown leaps into the room with such volume and force he startles us both. He's prancing round the room in clown face mask, bright scarlet wig, baggy check suit, ridiculous black rubber flipper feet and outsize white gloves, taking flash photograph after flash photograph with his infernal camera. "Pay me! Bastard! Pay me! Bastard! Pay me! Bastard!" The voice is brilliantly unpleasant. Mister Clown isn't rehearsing either. He's for real.

# Chapter 5

## Killing Time

I walk back downhill in the direction of the railway, trying to get a grip. Alison Johnson — Alison Tindell — wants to have sex. Tonight, when her husband is on the way to Paris. Am I hallucinating? Has meeting her revived old traumas, old psychological wounds, such that I'm imagining she propositioned me?

In my mind, I re-live what happened from the moment the clown leapt in. We spoke the lines in the script, leading to the argument where he gets his gun out then I pretend to shoot him with mine. In lieu of sound effects, I shouted, "Bang!" whereupon he shrieked, overacted I thought, and went limping out of the room. Alison, who had by now put her cardigan back on to cover herself, followed him out, returning a few moments later. "That's him done!" she said.

I looked at my watch. "It's nearly nine."

Fetching my coat, Alison said, "I don't want you to go."

I asked, "Could we meet again soon, or would that be difficult?"

She turned off the lights and opened the front door. In the darkness, hugging me tight, she said, "David, if you want, you can come back later, after eleven, when my husband has left for Paris. I'm not leaving till tomorrow. We can spend the night together."

I've been wandering around town for an hour, aimlessly killing time. Eventually, to escape the cold damp air, I came back here, to the railway, to wait in the warmth and brightness of the station buffet. A few passengers, fellow refugees from the unwelcoming night, are sitting huddled at tables, sipping mugs of hot tea. I desperately need normality, to get back to journalism mode, the only environment in which I feel truly safe. I notice the buffet has one of those pay-as-you-go Internet access terminals, so I sit down at it and google Jack Johnson. Wikipedia comes up top. The entry for Johnson is substantial, apart from the "Personal Life" section, which merely claims that, outside of his strident public persona, he is a quiet man who values his privacy and his close friends. The article adds that, in his business, "he enjoys the full support of Mary Johnson", though it makes no mention of Alison. I assume Mary is Johnson's sister, that they are in partnership, a family business, with the father a solicitor before them.

Next, I find newspaper articles on this morning's briefing in London, at which I was present. There's an election coming up. It will be a close-run thing, with the horrifying prospect of Making Sense's tiny band of MPs holding the balance of power. If this happens, they say they will press for a free vote on the restoration of the death penalty. Their campaign, under the slogan, "Death Means Death. It Makes Sense", contains the usual obfuscation of the truth, seizing on the scare opportunity afforded by recent serial killer murders to conveniently ignore the more mundane fact that the murder rate has been consistently falling for several years running. Johnson says they will demand the sentence of death be retrospectively applied to any murder committed from today onwards.

I have to hand it to Johnson. He may be a total sod but he's an accomplished political manipulator. Backdating the threatened law to the day of the announcement, is a *coup de maître*, a way of serving notice to any would-be murderer: "Better not chance it. If we do get our law through parliament in a free vote, that's your head in the noose. Guaranteed!" And should such a threat turn out to be effective, Johnson will point to the statistics: "See! We've proved the death penalty is a deterrent. Look how the number of murders dropped dramatically as soon as we announced our intention to backdate the law." Even should the backdating be ruled untenable by parliament or by the courts, in the mind of the general public he'll still have a powerful argument in favour of restoring the ultimate punishment.

Nearly eleven. The appointed time approaches. I quit the Internet and the station. In the cosy environment of the buffet, I felt assured I had not imagined the events of this evening. Now, as I make my way uphill along the deserted foggy street, doubts are coming back. It seems inconceivable Alison decided on sex spontaneously: the urgency with which she summoned me to the north, the premeditatîon of working out train times, all suggest the sex has been planned. How did she know she would want me? It's not like she were reviving an old intimacy. She'd never wanted me when we were young. Why now?

Perhaps I'm wrong. Perhaps her desire *was* spontaneously aroused. If I think about it there was no hint of sex until the phone call from clown man. Even then, she didn't want to do the scene, embarrassed by the erotic content. Only at his insistence did she perform it for real.

The moment of truth. The cottage ahead. That's funny — no gnome! Actually, it's very funny. Johnson must take in his gnomes overnight, worried they might get stolen. And the cottage is in darkness again.

I'm about to press the bell when I see the door is ajar, confirmation, if still needed, of the illicit purpose of our rendezvous.

I push the door open.

The silhouette of Alison is standing at the far side of the room.

The main ceiling light comes on, momentarily dazzling me.

The woman standing there, in a skirt, has Alison's figure, is Alison's age. On the floor in front of her, what can only be the body of a man, covered by a sheet.

The woman has black hair. She's not Alison.

"David Buckley?"

"Yes. What's going on?"

"I'm arresting you on suspicion of the murder of Jack Johnson."

# Chapter 6

## Interview

I'm being held for twenty-four hours at the local police station. Considering they arrested me on suspicion of murder, the treatment has been remarkably civil. They took fingerprints, got me a solicitor, got me a meal, then locked me in a cell overnight, Spartan but not uncomfortable. My few personal belongings have been temporarily taken from me. Now we're sitting at a table in an interview room: myself, my solicitor, and the lady detective who arrested me. There's an extremely tall policeman standing at the door — I assume for security. They've already done the usual caution and my solicitor reiterates that I don't have to comment if I don't want to. I say I'm innocent, I've nothing to hide and therefore I'm happy to answer their questions. In response to my urgent enquiry, I'm assured they have found no other dead bodies at the cottage, nor do they expect to find any.

The detective does bear an uncanny resemblance to Alison. Same age, same height, same build, same hair, except for the colour. Similarity of features, minus beauty spot on upper lip. No wonder in the darkness of the cottage I'd mistaken her for my friend. Her voice shatters the illusion. Hard northern vowels. Obviously, a local lass. "Mr Buckley, I'm Detective Inspector Jane Magee. The purpose of this interview is to get your account of the events at Jack Johnson's house. You don't deny visiting his house last night?"

"How can I? You arrested me there."

"Did you visit the house any other occasion, yesterday or any other day?"

"Just the once. Early yesterday evening. I stayed about three hours and left before nine."

"And what was your purpose in visiting Mr Johnson?"

My solicitor shuffles awkwardly in his seat. I've already told him the story in a private interview. He's not happy with what I'm about to say.

"I wasn't visiting Johnson. I was visiting his wife. She's an old college friend."

DI Magee seems confused by my reply. "But when you arrived, the wife wasn't there? Only Johnson?"

"No. Alison was there. Johnson wasn't. She told me to leave before he came home, so I never got to meet him."

The detective gives me a puzzled look. "There's something here that's not adding up. OK, we'll come back to that. You're saying you didn't see Johnson. Is it possible he was elsewhere in the house? How many rooms did you go in? Take a moment to remember the events as they happened."

I close my eyes, imagining walking up the hill, turning into the road, observing the gnome, opening the garden gate, walking up the path. Now I'm remembering something I'd totally forgotten. "There *was* someone else there! As I approached the cottage, I heard the loud crash of an object being dropped. Somebody called out 'Shit and Blast!' A woman's voice."

"Not the woman you came to see?"

"Understand I hadn't seen Alison for thirty years. It's only now, thinking back, I know it couldn't have been her."

"Three words heard through a closed door isn't a lot to go on."

I laugh. "It is if you'd known Alison as I did. If she'd hurt herself, tripped or dropped something on her foot, her spontaneous language would have been a lot richer than 'Shit and Blast', a phrase she'd never have used in a million years!"

DI Magee sighs. "So now we have two people in the house: Alison, and a mystery woman who you hear but don't see. Any other characters you want to tell us about?"

"Not unless you count the silent witness: the stuffed ferret."

My solicitor asks could we have a word in private. The detective and policeman leave the room. "A piece of advice, Mr Buckley. Don't joke with the police, especially with a serious charge hanging over you. Either way, whether you're innocent or guilty, it won't help your case."

DI Magee returns. I apologise for the ferret joke. "In bad taste. Like the ornament itself. What a thing for Johnson to keep in his living room!"

The detective gives me her trademark puzzled look. "Mr Buckley, you're sure you went in no other room in the house? There's no ferret in the living room." She calls in the police constable and asks him to go to the house and locate the ornament. "If forensics have finished with it, bring it back here."

I ask, "Detective Inspector Magee, could you tell me, how did you come to be there when I returned to the cottage? Who contacted the police? Was it Alison? I assume she wasn't present when her husband was killed, or she'd have already told you I didn't do it."

Magee replies, "We'll come to that in good time. First, I'd like you to tell me everything that happened. You can call me Jane, Mr Buckley. Not strictly by the book but it's a lot easier."

"OK...Jane. Alison let me in. The cottage was in darkness. She was having trouble locating the switch. The wall lights came on. We embraced and hugged. Then we sat together on the sofa and reminisced about old times. While we were talking, a telephone rang in another room. Alison said she wasn't going to answer; a bossy neighbour, a non-stop talker; she'd never get her off the phone and it would spoil our evening. We carried on talking. The phone rang again. Alison ignored it; said it was bound to be the woman. Sometime later, she went to the kitchen to make coffee. The phone rang a third time and I was surprised to hear Alison answering, considering what she'd said earlier."

I carry on, giving a full account of the strange incident of Mister Clown. I know my solicitor isn't happy. He's heard the story before and is convinced it's a clumsy attempt at a cover-up. I told him I have to tell the truth. However, I'm not telling the absolute truth. I say nothing of the invitation for sex, only that I came back to chat with Alison for another hour until the last London train at midnight.

# Chapter 7

## Questions

They had to let me go. My solicitor pressed them on the evidence. They admitted they had insufficient to bring charges. He wasn't so happy when I dismissed him. I told him only a guilty man needs to retain the services of a solicitor.

The police have requested I stick around, "to assist with their enquiries"; so here I am, ensconced in a modern hotel room with good wi-fi, my laptop having been couriered to me from work. I explained on the phone to my astonished editor, impressing upon him that my name is being kept out of the news so as not to prejudice the ongoing enquiry.

Normally I'd prefer a smaller, more intimate hotel but the impersonal nature of this one is welcome in the circumstances. They have put me on the top floor, a contingency, anticipating the windows may need to be out of range of prying paparazzi. My bedroom is decorated in the modern style, elegantly furnished, having down one side a long wide low shelf with plasma TV, the shelf functioning also as a desk where I can sit and work at my laptop. All my meals are eaten at this shelf also, delivered by room service. I never eat in the hotel restaurant — I don't want to draw attention.

Jane will be here in a few minutes. I'm anticipating her visit like a date with a new girlfriend. No doubt being too cosy with my interrogator could be used to trap me. I don't care. I'm innocent. Why shouldn't I enjoy it? I have only felt this comfortable with one other woman before.

I wonder where Alison is now, what she's feeling, what she's saying. I've been obliged to refrain from phoning her — a condition of my release is I contact nobody outside of work colleagues, also that I stay well clear of the crime scene. The local and national TV news are full of the murder, with rampant speculation on the motive — Johnson was the kind of man who made enemies. No pictures of Alison, though, just a statement read by a solicitor asking the press to respect the privacy of the family at this difficult time.

A knock on the hotel room door. I open it, to admit Jane accompanied by PC Forster, the policeman from the interview room. She asks am I satisfied with the hotel; do they need to find me another? I say it's fine; the important thing is I have good wi-fi. I sit at the shelf with my laptop while Jane sits on the bed, opening her case, methodically arranging various reports and papers across the bedspread. Forster stands at the door, maintaining an inscrutable silence.

Jane finds the piece of paper she's looking for. "According to this statement from a neighbour, he took his dog out for a walk last night at ten to six. He says he noticed a man who fits your description waiting outside Johnson's house at that time."

I answer cheerfully, "I expect that was me."

Jane Magee gives me a searching look. "Why only 'expect'?"

"I didn't look at my watch. The station clock said half past five and the walk took about twenty minutes."

"Why didn't you take a taxi? Last night there was a cold mist and a light drizzle. Not pleasant for walking."

"Alison didn't tell me her address. She said the taxis ripped you off. Better to walk. Her directions were straightforward, though the walk turned out to be longer than I'd expected."

"If she didn't tell you the address, how did you know which house?"

"She told me to look for the only house in the road with a garden gnome outside."

Jane smiles. "Another ornament?"

Forster lets out an involuntary snigger. Jane gives him a disapproving glance. She tells him sharply, "Ask them to locate the gnome." He leaves the room and I hear him in the corridor on his walkie-talkie.

Jane says, "I have to warn you, we haven't found the ferret. Do you wish to amend your statement?"

I reply, "Obviously it's been taken. It was on the small table in the corner. Why would somebody commit murder and then steal an ornamental ferret? There's no chance of it being a valuable antique?"

Jane laughs. "Mr Buckley, you're taking 'cooperating with police enquiries' to a new level. You're required only to answer my questions, not try to do my job for me. Before I chase round the country for a stolen ferret, I need to be sure it was there in the first place. The table you describe has a TV on it. We've checked with Johnson's social set, people who've been often in the house. They say they've never seen a ferret ornament."

Forster returns and resumes his position as inscrutable door sentry. No doubt the gnome request is causing him considerable amusement but he dare not risk a second lapse in front of his superior.

Jane continues, "Going back to your journey, let's suppose you'd planned to murder Johnson. It's not likely you'd take a taxi direct to his home, is it? Walking the back streets, as you did, would be a far better way to arrive incognito."

I say, "Even better for the murderer to drive to town. Why risk being spotted on the railway's closed-circuit TV?"

Jane stares hard at me. "In your case, Mr Buckley, we know you don't drive. We also know *why* you don't drive."

# Chapter 8

## Fact v Fantasy

Jane is here again with Forster. Same routine as yesterday. Forster stands at the door, though this time he's holding a leather briefcase. Jane sits on the bed, surrounded by paperwork. I rather like the sight of her sitting on my bed. She's wearing a skirt again — with legs as good as hers, why wouldn't she? She looks up from her documents, catching me ogling her. She crosses her legs and tugs at the garment to pull it down a little.

"Mr Buckley, I'd like to go into your relationship with Johnson. Would it be correct to say you hated the man?"

"I hated all that he stood for. I've attacked his ideas many times in my newspaper column. I can't say I hated him in person. I've never met him."

"But you would have seen him on TV?"

"Yes. Often. Not a pleasant character. Supercilious. Rather too pleased with himself."

Jane reads from one of the papers on the bed. "We've examined CCTV footage from the railway station. We see you returned there at ten. The buffet staff told us you used their Internet terminal and left the premises before they closed at eleven. We find particularly interesting the subject engaging your attention. We've had the machine analysed by a computer expert. Apparently, you spent all your time surfing web sites about Jack Johnson. Isn't that a little obsessive? You're more than three hours at Johnson's house, then immediately afterwards you spend another hour reading about him on the web."

"It was for work. I'd been at the 'Death Means Death' briefing in London that morning and wanted to catch up on the detail."

"Do you normally work late?"

"Not often. On this occasion I needed to do something familiar, to relax..."

Jane interrupts. "Did something happen at Johnson's cottage that caused you to feel unrelaxed?"

I say nothing. To admit to sexual designs on Johnson's wife would be the best way to incriminate myself. I can imagine the police train of thought: affair — discovery — argument — fight — murder."

Registering my silence, Jane continues, "The briefing in London. Johnson wasn't there?"

"Press only. Their press officer gave it."

"You stated you'd never met Johnson in person. Not even at party rallies, for example?"

I laugh. "Until recently, Making Sense weren't worth wasting time on. I used to call them 'Making Simple' because of their magic wand solutions: bring back hanging, boot out immigrants, conscript the unemployed, ban the unions. They mouth off about politicians short-changing the public, whereas they are the biggest confidence tricksters of the lot, trading on slogans without the slightest inkling of the complexity of the issues or the likely consequences of their policies."

Jane ignores my tirade. She's looking at another piece of paperwork. I suppose her job requires strict impartiality, though I sense she has no taste for politics. She says, "We haven't located the gnome. According to the neighbours, Johnson never had a gnome in his garden. Mr

Buckley, I could stretch to your suggestion of aggravated burglary of a valuable ornament from inside the house but I draw the line at a garden gnome. Either something very peculiar is going on or you're simply not being truthful."

I reiterate I'm telling her what I saw. I ask why the ornaments matter.

She replies, "Only they could serve to confirm your statements."

Jane picks another report from the bed. "Let's turn to something we *have* been able to verify, something you say Johnson's wife told you, that he was due to fly off to Paris. We asked the wife and she confirmed the Paris trip."

At last: news of Alison. I ask, "Has Alison seen my statement? Surely she can tell you what happened to the ornaments?"

Jane indicates to Forster, "We'll take a look at the main exhibit now."

He unlocks the clasp on his briefcase and takes out a transparent polythene bag containing a gun. Jane motions for him to hand it to me. "Take a good look. Don't open the bag. Is this your gun?"

I say I recognise it as the gun given to me for the play scene with Mister Clown.

Jane's pleased with my reply. "I'm glad you didn't answer in the negative. Makes things simpler for us both — it has your fingerprints all over it. The thing is, it has only your fingerprints, nobody else's."

Making what must sound like yet another fantastical invention, I reply, "Mister Clown didn't touch my gun. He had his own gun. In any case, he had gloves on. Big outsized white clown gloves."

Jane says, "Just so you know, forensics have confirmed this was the gun used to shoot Johnson dead." She holds out her hand for me to return the bag.

Jane sorts through her paperwork. "In your statement you claim this man, 'Mister Clown', called over to the cottage to rehearse a scene from your student play, that the script required you to shoot him, at which point he ran off and you never saw him again."

"That's correct."

"What did you do with the gun afterwards?"

"I put it on top of the writing desk."

"Which is where we found it. Forget Mister Clown. Let's suppose, for whatever reason, you did in fact shoot Johnson. Then, something happened which caused you to panic. Leaving in a hurry, you forgot to take the gun. As a novice, you agonised over whether you should return to the scene of the crime. Fingerprints you weren't concerned about — you don't have a criminal record — but you worried the gun might be traced. By the time you'd made up your mind to return, the body had been discovered."

I ask, "It sounds like you're saying nobody actually heard the gun go off; the body was discovered later?"

Jane replies, "That *would* interest you, wouldn't it? Forensics tell me whoever planned the murder did so with care and forethought. The gun's fitted with a top-of-the-range silencer, obviously leaving nothing to chance. Johnson's chauffeur discovered the body. He arrived at the cottage at ten to collect Johnson for the Paris flight. The front door was ajar and there were no lights on. Thinking that meant Johnson was about to come outside, he went back to the car. After waiting a quarter of an hour, he worried they'd miss the flight and went inside to warn his boss. Seeing the body on the floor, his first thought was Johnson had collapsed from ill-health, then he saw the blood, and the bullet-hole through the head: an execution-style killing. When we got there, we saw the murder weapon left behind. We took a chance and set a trap. We'd been waiting less than ten minutes when you came back."

I say, "You've only the chauffeur's word for the sequence of events. How do you know *he* didn't do it?"

"We checked up on him, of course. He'd been driving Johnson to meetings, finally taking him to his office round about seven. Johnson said he'd make his own way home. He asked to be picked up later to go to the airport. We have the chauffeur on CCTV in town, going into shops, into a restaurant, leaving from there to collect Johnson at the time he said he did. His alibi's solid."

I reply, "Unless he shot Johnson as soon as he arrived at the cottage."

Jane wags her finger at me, "Mr. Buckley, you're trying to do my job again! We haven't entirely ruled out the chauffeur, although for reasons I'm not allowed to make public we think it highly unlikely the man would have risked it."

I ask, "When I walked in and the lights came on, you said my name. I assume Alison told you?"

Jane smiles. "Nobody told us your name. Johnson had it written in his appointments diary. We found it in the writing desk: 'David Buckley. Nine Thirty'."

I say, "That's impossible!"

She hands me a report from the bed. "See for yourself. We've had the page analysed. It's genuinely Johnson's writing. They identified the pen used as one from the writing desk."

I scan the report, which runs to two sides and is highly technical. I notice they date the ink, the diary entry apparently made some time in the last month.

I protest, "No murderer in their right mind would make an appointment in their own name!"

Jane looks at me significantly.

I add, "And why would Johnson agree to meet with me, of all people?"

Jane replies, "Only you can tell us that. In your statement you say you were told your play was being put on by the local amateur dramatic society. You claim also you were told the man playing Mister Clown had been running round town in costume, scaring people, in consequence of which he'd got himself a police caution for anti-social behaviour? Have I got that right?"

"That's what Alison told me. I've no direct knowledge of the events."

"Mr Buckley, our town, to its shame, doesn't have an amateur dramatic society. Nor does our police station have, nor does any police station in this county have a record of cautioning a man running around dressed as a clown."

Her studied incredulity is beginning to annoy me. "Look. Why don't you just ask Alison? She'll confirm everything."

Jane says nothing. She's busy making notes. A terrible thought occurs to me. Are the police withholding crucial information? Is Alison in fact the chief suspect? If so, rather than clearing my name, my appeal for her to back me up serves only to implicate me as willing accomplice. I decide on attack as being the best strategy. "You think his wife committed the murder?"

Jane stands and goes over to the window. It's getting dark outside. Telling Forster to switch on the lights, she pulls the drawstring to close the curtains. She's not satisfied with the way the curtains overlap and fiddles with the leading edges to straighten their appearance. Then she turns to face me.

"We're certain the wife didn't commit the murder directly. Whether she conspired with an accomplice, possibly you, to act on her behalf, we are trying to establish. She denies ever seeing you in her life. We showed her your photograph. We'd like you to identify her, also."

Jane nods to PC Forster. He takes a photograph from his jacket pocket and shows it to me: a full-length colour picture of a woman in her sixties, expensively dressed in a vulgar sort of way.

I say, "I don't know this woman. Should I know her?"

"Her name is Mary Johnson," Jane replies. "She's Jack Johnson's wife. We know she was in Paris at the time of the murder. Johnson was due to fly out that evening to be with her for the weekend."

I'm dumbfounded. "But if what you are telling me is true, then what was Alison doing in Johnson's house and why was she pretending to be his wife!"

Jane gathers together her papers. "We'll see you same time tomorrow. Yes. Alison. Is there an Alison, or is she another figment, along with the stuffed ferret, the garden gnome, the amateur dramatics, and Mr Clown?"

# Chapter 9

## Another Death

This morning I could contain my impatience no longer. I went straight to the police station and demanded to talk to DI Magee. Jane was out on the case, so two of her detective constables agreed to take my statement. The recording machine started, I gave them every detail I could remember about Alison Tindell. I told them I was sticking to my story, that, as far as I was concerned, Alison was in the cottage that evening; she had let me in, acted as if married to Johnson, acted as if mistress of the house, had encouraged me to leave before Johnson came home, had persuaded me to come back later. I asked how I could possibly have known about Johnson's trip to Paris without Alison telling me. The detectives agreed they had asked themselves that question. However, they'd no difficulty coming up with an explanation: Johnson could have told me himself before I shot him. Alternatively, the information might have been given me by one of his party officials, which would also serve to explain why the appointment in his diary so precisely adjoined his intended time of departure. I emphasised that, plausible as these explanations were, I knew they were wrong, that, in my opinion, the police would be seriously failing in their public duty if they didn't try to locate Alison.

One of the detectives asked whether I thought Alison capable of premeditated murder. I could only reply the circumstances would have to be extreme, like killing in self-defence. They thanked me for the information, saying the place to start would be registrars' offices, to find the marriage of an Alison Tindell to a solicitor, then trace her forwards from there.

It's almost five and Jane and Forster are due at the hotel. I hear them coming along the corridor. When I open the door of my room, I can tell immediately there has been a significant development. They advise me to sit down. Now I'm expecting the worst possible news — they've found another body.

Jane consults her notebook. "Enquiries were made at several registry offices. The information obtained was cross-referenced against other records. We have traced an Alison Tindell, a student nurse in Birmingham during the period David Buckley was an undergraduate. Ten months after she qualified, Alison Tindell married a solicitor and went to live with her husband in Norfolk."

I say, "That's her! Have you found out where she is now?"

Jane comes over to me and puts her hand gently on my shoulder. "David, I'm very sorry to have to tell you. Your college friend, Alison Tindell, died twenty years ago."

# Chapter 10

## Peters

I've been asked to attend at the police station for further questioning. Sitting alone in the interview room, waiting for Jane Magee, I'm trying to make sense of it all. They tell me Alison has been dead twenty years. But I spoke with Alison on the night of the murder. How could it not be her? She had Alison's laugh, her height, the slight skin blemish above her upper lip; she talked of our shared past life, all those private memories only Alison could know; she even had the script of my play, for heaven's sake, a play I had assumed lost and had not thought about for thirty years. Yet it cannot be, because they tell me Alison drowned, and, although the body, when eventually recovered, had become too decomposed for reliable visual identification, they were able to confirm her identity through dental records.

A sombre Jane enters, followed by Forster, carrying a large packing case which he deposits on the table. Jane says, "We believe we've located the ferret. We'd like you to confirm whether this is the object you saw at Johnson's cottage."

She nods to Forster. He puts on surgical gloves and begins to unpack a large quantity of straw from the crate. Finally, he lifts out the ferret ornament and places it on the table.

"Please don't touch it," says Jane. "If you need it rotated, PC Forster will do it for you."

I say I am certain this is the ornament I saw on the night. Jane asks whether I am willing to sign a statement to that effect. I agree, and my statement is duly taken.

I say, "Is that it? Are you at liberty to tell me where you found the ferret?"

Jane says they have more questions to ask first. She says they may be some time and would I like tea or coffee while I'm waiting. I ask for tea, and she leaves the room. Forster puts the ornament back in the box, stuffs the packing straw on top, flicks the remaining bits of straw off the table, then leaves also.

I expect my drink to be brought along by one of the police station staff. Instead, it arrives in the company of a tall man, in his fifties, blond-haired, handsome, distinguished, dressed in a grey suit with bow tie, which makes me think he looks like a cliché for a psychiatrist. He introduces himself as Brian Peters. Apparently, he *is* a psychiatrist.

Peters switches on the recording machine. So, this is going to be a formal interview. We're briefly interrupted by the entry of a young policewoman carrying a cup of tea. "Is this wanted in here?" she asks.

"No, my dear," replies Peters. "We're already accounted for. Must be some other felon."

His male chauvinist manner deserves a police boot in the groin but she smiles at him bashfully. I can see Peters is quite a charmer for the opposite sex.

I am not at all upset by what follows. Since I have given such a crazy account of events — crazy to me, let alone to anyone else — I would have expected them to delve into my past. Peters is an intelligent, pleasant man. At no point do I sense prejudice in his attitude. He has my medical records and we go through my case together, like two scientific colleagues discussing an interesting experiment.

Buoyed by our civilised discussion, I say, "At least they can't claim my tale of the ferret was crazy, now they've found it."

In reply, Peters says, "Mr Buckley, I'm afraid DI Magee will be offering you an apology."

I laugh. "For doubting my word! It's her job!"

"You interrupted me," replies Peters. "I was going to say an apology for requesting her southern colleagues to break into your Bromley flat. They obtained a search warrant. As you were not in residence, they had to smash the lock. They replaced it, of course — being the police, they don't like to give encouragement to burglars — I understand you can collect your new keys at the front desk."

"What did they expect to find in my flat?"

"Nothing obvious. You're an intelligent man. If you had planned Johnson's murder, you'd have been unlikely to keep incriminating evidence in your home. Forensics found nothing either. The police officers did, however, find something totally unexpected."

"What was that?"

"An ornament. The stuffed ferret."

# Chapter 11

## My False Friend

Peters turns off the recording device. "I think it better we talk in private. Nothing said between us can be used in court that's not on record. So, the machine being off makes it possible to say what might not otherwise be said."

I respond, "What else is there to say? You're convinced I'm mad. I'm also starting to think I must be mad."

"Not necessarily, Mr Buckley. Let's look at our options, shall we?"

Peters paces the room like he's lecturing a class of students. "I believe three explanations are open to us. Firstly, the possibility you are being set up. The police are not inclined to that explanation, principally because the set-up, as described by you, involves an 'Alison', your friend from college. Because the lady died twenty years ago, you are the only person who could have concocted the detail of such an elaborate hoax, but then why would you set yourself up?"

He pauses to pour himself a glass of water.

"The second possibility is, as a fully sane man, you committed pre-meditated murder and have devised a convenient story for protesting your innocence. I think we can discount that. A man who plots murder will focus all his energies on getting away with it. An elaborate contingency plan for capture is unlikely to be high on his priorities."

"The third possibility is you are in fact suffering from a recurrence of your old illness, manifesting as an obsessive hatred for Johnson. You simply called at his house, shot him dead, and everything else is a fantasy involuntarily concocted by your mind in its disturbed state at the time."

I ask, "You're the medical expert. If called to court, which option would you favour?"

"If called as an expert witness, the third option would be the only one on which I would be qualified to pass judgement. Of course, I need more time to examine your records. As things stand at the moment, there is nothing inconsistent with your medical history that would prevent you from successfully carrying out a murder while living out an episode of fantasy, completely distorting the reality of the premeditated act in your mind."

I reply, "I'm not sure what's worse, going to prison, or being locked up in an institution for the criminally insane."

Peters stands with his back to me, talking to the wall. "Ironic, isn't it? Johnson murdered on the very day of his capital punishment initiative. Suppose his party do well in the next election. Johnson's murder may in fact create a groundswell of support, a kind of sympathy vote. They'll get their capital punishment bill through parliament. His murderer would be the first person to whom the backdated law would apply."

He turns to face me. "As things stand, I'm very much afraid the choice for you is between insane asylum or your neck swinging from a rope on a gibbet."

I ask, "What would you advise me to do?"

"I think it certain they'll press charges. I gather the circumstantial evidence is compelling — a diary appointment in Johnson's own handwriting, a sighting of you outside the cottage, your fingerprints on the murder weapon, your return to the scene. If you plead guilty on the grounds of diminished responsibility, I promise I'll use my influence to guarantee you the lesser of two evils."

I groan, burying my head in my hands. I feel well and truly trapped.

Peters carries on talking. "You know, it was a great day for the pursuit of justice when they made sound recording of police interviews compulsory. No longer possible for false claims to be made about the suspect's admissions. From your point of view, however, my recording the interview just now in line with strict procedure has one serious disadvantage."

"What's that?" I ask, only half-listening, my head still buried in my hands.

Peters replies, "It makes *me* appear more trustworthy than I am."

The harsh voice of Mister Clown rings out: "Pay me! Bastard!"

I look up, astonished. Peters is grinning at me.

"It was you! *You* were the clown!"

"Accuse me if you want, Buckley. Just remember, demonstrating a persecution complex against your psychiatrist is the surest way to confirm your mental illness."

"If you planned the murder, why are you offering to help? Wouldn't it be safer for you if I did get the death penalty?"

Peters raises his glass of water in mock greeting. "Let's just say Alison doesn't want you to die. Cheers!"

# Chapter 12

## Evidence in Court

Directly after the Peters interview, they formally charged me with Johnson's murder. My re-engaged solicitor eventually got me bailed. The evidence is circumstantial and I am not considered a danger to the general public, now the object of my supposed obsession has been eliminated. I sense Peters' intervention in my favour. He is obviously doing his utmost to assure me of his support should I enter a plea of insanity.

The release conditions included surrendering my passport, continuing to live at the hotel in town, and signing the police station register early morning and early evening. They allowed me a single supervised trip home, to collect two suitcases of clothes and belongings. Whilst there, in my Bromley flat, I slipped into my pocket an inconsequential set of rusty old keys, and hid, amongst the many documents I needed for my work, some papers of a personal nature.

Useful also have been my excursions to the town centre here: trips to the tourist office for leaflets, to the bus station for timetables, and to the public library to consult books of reference. They have provided a way of getting information without leaving behind an electronic footprint. Equally, I have taken care when drawing money from cash machines: regular amounts, nothing to attract suspicion, though always more than I've needed, to build up a contingency fund.

On one such trip, I spotted Jane Magee through a shop window, with a girl, aged about nine or ten, being fitted for school uniform. I considered going in but thought better of infringing protocol, with us being on opposite sides of a murder case. The same afternoon, returning from the library, and taking the shortcut through the park, I came across Jane sitting in the children's play area, watching her daughter enthusiastically swish backwards and forwards on a swing. Funny, every time I saw Jane, she wore a skirt, even on a wintry day like that day. And she had on black woollen tights to keep out the cold. She called me over by my Christian name; the only other time she'd dropped the formality of "Mr Buckley" was at the hotel, when she so gently and sympathetically informed me of Alison's death.

I asked, "Aren't we breaching protocol, talking in public like this?"

Jane laughed. "With that preposterous woolly hat hiding most of your head, I don't think anyone's likely to recognise you.

The girl jumped off the swing and asked in a strong local accent, the image of her mother's, "Mom, can I climb that tree?"

"Only the low branches. Don't go too high."

Jane said, "David, you understand I have to do my job. Yours is the most high-profile murder case we've ever had to handle. We're under tremendous pressure from the chief constable. We've considered everything. We simply can't identify any other suspect with both motive and opportunity. It's down to a jury now to decide."

"Don't you feel worried, then, sitting here alone with a murderer?"

"I trust Brian Peters' judgement. Your illness caused you to act against type. Please, please, consider a plea based on temporary insanity. It will prepare the ground for you to get a cure and an early release."

I wasn't going to lose this opportunity. I asked, "How well do you know Brian Peters?"

Jane looked at me in surprise. "That's a strange question. We're work colleagues. I've known him since I took up my post here five years ago. He'd been acting as consultant to our team for fifteen years before that."  She shouted, "Alison! Come down! That's too high!"

Taking position under the tree, ready to catch the girl should she fall, I said, "You called her Alison?"

"My husband really wanted the name. He had a cousin called Alison he was very close to. She died young. He promised her mother if ever he had a daughter, she'd be called Alison too — a way of keeping his cousin's memory alive. I resisted the idea at first but the name quickly grew on me. I like it now. I think it suits her."

I looked at my watch, "Jane, I have to go. It's nearly five. I'm due to sign the register."  I called up into the branches, "Your mum's getting worried. She wants you to come down now." The girl dutifully scrambled down, ran over to her mother and hugged her. I could see there was a very close bond between the two.

At the trial I entered a plea of "not guilty", despite the overwhelming case against me: my declared enmity to Johnson, the testimony of the dog-walking neighbour placing me at the cottage, the railway station CCTV footage showing my arrival at five thirty and return at ten o'clock, which times easily cover the estimated hour of death, my fingerprints on the murder weapon, my name in Johnson's diary in his own hand, my alleged going back to retrieve gun. Added to all this, the detailed reports of my hallucinatory illness, my "Alison complex", plus the story of Mister Clown only serving to confirm my distorted mental state. Equally, the imagined presence of the two ornaments — I've always had a gnome outside my own front door, and the ferret was seemingly mine, found in my flat.

The prosecution opened with DI Jane Magee's evidence concerning the evening of the murder. She described how she had been working the night shift, tied up in meetings with colleagues at the police station since six o'clock. At twenty past ten an emergency report came in of a man shot at Jack Johnson's house. Magee arrived at the scene to find a patrol car and ambulance already in attendance. She immediately recognised the dead man as Johnson — she'd been introduced to him once at a social event for legal professionals, and of course she had seen him often on TV. A curious feature of the crime was the gun had been left behind. Acting on a hunch the killer might return to retrieve the weapon abandoned in haste, Jane ordered the street to be cleared of emergency vehicles and the cottage be returned to its state when Johnson's body was discovered, i.e. the living room in darkness and the front door slightly ajar. She hadn't expected to be so lucky but within ten minutes the defendant entered and she arrested him.

Telephone calls have featured prominently in the trial. One thing I can't criticise Jane for: her thoroughness investigating every aspect of my statement. Regarding the phone calls to the cottage, yes, there were two unanswered incoming calls around the time I stated — from political associates of Johnson, both men. However, phone records show no *connected* incoming call, the one I claim Alison answered. Nor do the records show any outgoing calls, casting doubt on my claim of hearing Alison call back Mister Clown.

The two men who'd tried to phone Johnson were cross-examined in the witness box. Both had rung his mobile after failing to get him on his home number. The first caller left a message on voicemail; the second got through. Johnson was obviously still alive at that time. The man said he sounded as he always did, albeit especially buoyant because of Making Sense's big political announcement earlier that day.

One curiosity the police have not explained: when they arrived at the cottage, they found the telephone off the hook. That it had been so for some time was confirmed by several of Johnson's associates, who'd tried to call him between eight and nine o'clock, always getting the engaged tone. One such caller was questioned at the trial. Like the previous witness, he too had spoken subsequently to Johnson on his mobile. In fact, he'd mentioned to him the problem with the home number but Johnson said his wife was away, the place was empty, so the number must have been dialled incorrectly. The man said not; he'd merely selected the number as usual from his contacts list. He suggested Johnson's landline might have a fault. Johnson said he'd check when he got home, if he got a chance before leaving for Paris.

Inevitably, the trial examined the evidence for the inciting event: the phone call I claim fetched me to the north-east. Calls to our newspaper switchboard are untraceable in terms of internal extension routed to, so precise identification of the call to my office desk was difficult, with the time being just after lunch, a time when calls tend to peak. Nevertheless, the police did identify a number that had called several times in the morning, corroborating the evidence given by our telephonist. However, since the female caller on an unregistered mobile phone had not stated her name, they only had my word for her identity. Neither did it help me that the calls were traced as made from not from the north-east but from the north-west of England, in fact from the city of Liverpool.

Even my account of Alison and I having coffee has turned to my disadvantage. The police failed to find the patterned tray on which I described Alison as having brought in the mugs and jug of milk, nor were my fingerprints found on any coffee mug in Johnson's house. It's obvious the Alison story is setting everyone against me — there was a gasp in court when the prosecution revealed she died twenty years ago. How can I now claim I came back not for the gun, but for Alison?

Peters gave a masterful performance in the witness box, the dashing bow-tie-wearing specialist, sympathetic yet authoritative, going into great detail about my condition, standing up magnificently to the probing of the defence counsel. I sense his detailed explanation of my illness has made quite an impression on the jury. It seems he will get his way after all.

But Peters is not to get his way.

They say clever criminals with a master plan often succumb to the temptation of seeking to improve that which is already perfect. Had Peters not shown his hand, my mental state would have deteriorated, such that he would have attained his objective of permanently incarcerating me. Instead, hoping to scare me into cooperation, he revealed his reason for holding over me the power of life or death, thereby fuelling my determination to fight back.

I am convinced Alison is alive. She has a connection with Peters. Peters wanted Johnson killed. Alison was willing to cooperate, even going so far as to implicate a friend. Alison did not die twenty years ago; she somehow faked her own death and disappeared off the face of the earth. That is what I am about to do: vanish without trace.

# Chapter 13

## Escape

The double-decker bus grinds uphill before winding down the valley towards the neighbouring industrial town. Before my trial began, I travelled this route many times, six mornings a week, after signing in at the police station at nine. On the first few occasions, I'd remain on the bus all the way to the town library, but not since. I'd get off early, to have breakfast in a transport café. Important to establish a routine. In any case, I needed a big breakfast for a lot less money than the hotel. The saved cash has been accumulating.

Today, I get off at the usual bus stop but avoid the café. I walk to a dirt track behind a run-down housing estate. On one side, the graffiti-strewn breeze-block boundary wall of their back gardens. Unseen savage dogs will bark as I pass by. On the other side, the bank of a fast-flowing river, deep enough to drown in.

What have I been researching at the library? Wig-making, for one thing. Did I tell you I don't suffer from male pattern baldness? In fact, I've always enjoyed long hair. Last night I cut off my hair and shaved my head, carefully preserving the hair clippings amongst my few possessions in a newly purchased backpack. I've taken to going around town in my over-sized woolly hat. Another routine. As a consequence, I didn't look any different this morning when I got on the bus, even though from today I'm totally bald underneath.

I've read all the library books on fell walking and have purchased suitable walking gear at a specialist shop, paying cash of course. I've been practising, taking the sign-posted routes out of town into the countryside, killing two birds with one stone — firstly to break in my new boots, secondly to get fit for what's to come. I intend to cross the high hills separating the eastern side of England from Cumbria and Lancashire. Not an expedition a novice should undertake lightly, so I have signed up for a walking tour, again paying cash. I will disappear among a party of travellers enjoying an early spring holiday, walking during the day, staying at inns along the way.

Saturday. Court adjourned until Tuesday. I left for the five-a.m. bus, taking with me a plastic heavy-duty dustbin bag with a large object inside. I check as I enter the track behind the housing estate. Dawn has not yet broken. I'm not expecting anybody to be about.

Dog number one barks from behind the wall. From the bin bag I take out my backpack, which I temporarily hang in front of me with the strap around my neck. I keep walking.

Dog number two barks. I take off my coat. Underneath I'm wearing a hiking jacket. Coat goes into bin bag, which I knot tightly at the top. In the coat's pockets are my mobile and wallet, also, my bank cards, for which I have no further use — I finished emptying my accounts late yesterday and it's going to be a very long time before the credit card company are reimbursed for cash borrowed up to the limit.

Nobody behind or in front. I launch the bin bag into the river, the surprisingly strong current carrying it away faster than my walking pace. Relieved of bag and coat, I'm thankful to reposition the backpack, which has been pulling heavily on my neck. I swing it round to support it on my back, with the straps over my shoulders in the normal way.

I keep walking. Dog number three barks. I take off my hat, baring my bald head, feeling the unfamiliar sensation of cold air directly against my skull.

I reach the end of the track. A bald-headed man, "John Edwards", wearing a red hiking jacket and carrying a backpack, emerges onto the pavement and joins a queue at a bus shelter. The man in front is reading a tabloid with a headline referring to yesterday's psychiatric evidence against David Buckley: *Long-haired Looney!* Even within their standards of playing to the mob, that's hitting rock bottom. Thank you, tabloid press. You've just done me a big favour.

# PART 2

# FREEDOM

# Chapter 14

## The Walking Tour

We assemble in the village square in the shadow of the first hill. I have chosen a "seniors" walking tour. Even so, it's clear I will find the going tough. These people, all in their early sixties, are experienced walkers. Our guide, a young local man called Freddie, is a mountain rescue volunteer, which is reassuring. Our party consists of three married couples, two male retired schoolteachers and two widows who used to come on walks like this with their husbands. One of the widows, Fran, has taken a fancy to me, which could be awkward. If I am engaged too much in conversation I might let slip compromising information.

An incident occurred yesterday demonstrating the fragility of this lifeline to freedom. Waiting to check in at the first hotel where we were to stay the night, chatting to my fellow walkers, I noticed Fran, standing by herself, a little left out of the camaraderie, so I went over to talk with her. I have to own up to being strongly attracted by her kindly face and sympathetic expression. And the colour of her hair, blonde like Alison's. Unwisely, I might have already been sending out signals of more than casual interest, because she readily agreed to my proposal we share a table for two in the restaurant. Nor did the setting reduce the intimacy of the occasion, a cosy little corner nook illuminated by candlelight from a cut-glass bowl throwing out soft patches of yellow light. While we talked, it occurred to me Fran might feel flattered by my intense interest. In reality, I had taken the conversational initiative, probing her on her life story as a tactic to avoid talking about my own.

Fran insisted on treating us to a bottle of Chardonnay, so, as the evening went on and we enjoyed a superb meal together, I became more and more relaxed. I forgot the need to remain alert. I heard someone calling my name and turned to look. A man was greeting a couple who had just entered, "David! David and Susan! What are the chances of meeting you here!"

"That used to happen with me and Gerry," said Fran. "You'd think here in hill country you'd only meet strangers."

I remarked it could equally happen working in London. Amidst the throng you'd suddenly bump into somebody you hadn't seen for years.

"Do you work in London, John?" asked Fran. "I thought you said you lived in Bristol."

Keeping up a cover story requires concentration. Not for a moment could I afford to let down my guard.

I thought hard over my story. Anything to do with journalism was out, for obvious reasons. Technical subjects also, in case I should encounter a fellow "expert" on the walk. I even considered pretending to be a police officer but it would be just my luck we'd get a retired bobby, the worst of outcomes. I settled on being a private detective taking early retirement, which profession had the advantage, if questioning became too intrusive, I could plead client confidentiality and change the subject.

How did I come to choose Bristol as my place of residence? I arrived early with the intention of obtaining a moment with Freddie, to quiz him on the background of my companions. He told me they were all tough northerners. "Older people from the south don't tend to book the walks here until the weather's warmer and kinder," he explained.

The big test came later, when we sat round the fireside in the lounge and the news came on TV: an item on the Johnson murder trial, and my picture (long haired) briefly flashed on screen. The others asked if, as "a detective", I thought Buckley guilty. My rudimentary shaven head disguise must be working. I replied I had never been asked to handle a case so strange; mine had all been much more mundane. We broke up shortly afterwards. In the corridor outside my room, Fran said goodnight by putting her arm round me and kissing me on the cheek. The sweet scent of her perfume, the brief touch of her golden hair against my face, reminded me of what I had been missing all my life. She's a lovely lady, with a lot of vitality. I'd say we're only a night or two away from sharing a bed. I will have to decline that pleasure. With the police and Peters on my tail, I can do without the added complication of an inquisitive lover.

Day One of the walk. The paths have been chosen for their mild gradient, to break us in gently. We pass along lanes through open woodland, then by fields of cattle. On the horizon the grey outline of the high hills. Freddy informs us we are following an ancient track, treading stones laid centuries ago to assist the passage of horse and cart. Difficult to believe this now forgotten route was once a major cross-country artery. I fancy myself in the shoes of an eighteenth-century highwayman being pursued by the law and arrive at the night's hotel happy to have evaded capture.

Day Two. We are ascending to higher ground. Impressive panoramas of the valleys below — when we can see them. Up here, low cloud comes down to greet us, with a thick damp mist shrouding all but the black wet stones ahead and a few yards of sodden moorland turf to left and right. Every now and then, a sheep appears at the side of the path. Unlike the mountain animals of the Mediterranean, with the constant clink of neck bells, these creatures manifest silently or with a sudden bleat. In the mist, even a sheep can carry menace — you can appreciate the local legend of "The Boggart", a man-eating monster lurking the moors.

Day Three. One of the schoolteachers is paying attention to Fran, and she is responding in kind. I am happy for her, and for me, that I can continue in relative solitude. We start with a climb tougher than any we have made so far. My pleasure in possessing the fitness to manage the challenge with ease turns to apprehension at the steep descent, constantly having to brace against slipping on the treacherous wet screeds of loose stone and gravel. Should I break a leg, I'm done for. The life of a man on the run is an inversion of all that is familiar, the comfort of a stay in hospital being for me a passport to permanent incarceration or worse. I'm lagging behind the others in my excessive care not to come to grief. This causes some amusement. I joke that, being the tallest, my high centre of gravity puts me at a disadvantage. When we eventually make it down to reassuring tarmac, my knees can't stop shaking from the strain.

Arriving at the hotel, we hear TV in the lounge reporting David Buckley has absconded. Good that my escape didn't make news until today. It lessens the chance any of my party will identify me, since it's clear the police aren't admitting I actually disappeared on Saturday. Even so, I don't want to be socialising tonight. I make an excuse of retiring early to try to recover the use of my knees.

Day Four. Huge change in the weather, in complete contrast to yesterday. Blue sky and full sunshine reward our long climb to the summit with aerial views across the hills and dales for miles in all directions. I'm enjoying the walk and the pleasant company, a man without a care in the world. Then, in the evening, events occur to show me the error of complacency. The whole party sit down to dinner together. Somebody asks, "Where's Freddie?" Fran replies, "He said he might be a bit delayed." The soup arrives and still no Freddie. I'm filled with a premonition of danger. I leave the table and go to my bedroom, where I find my fears fully justified. Freddie is rifling through my backpack. Startled by my sudden appearance, he drops it to the floor as I enter. "Sorry, John, I've obviously got the wrong room. Mike told me he had some foot balm I could borrow." After he's gone, I check to see what's been disturbed. I'm concerned he might have opened my bag of hair clippings.

Later, when I go down to reception, there's a policeman asking to speak with our tour guide. Has Freddie put two and two together? I'm woefully unprepared. I can't rush upstairs, grab my belongings and jump out of a window. Where could I go at this time of night, at this season, on the open hills?

False alarm. Freddie's wanted to assist with mountain rescue — some walkers are feared lost. I hope they are found soon, because the last thing I want is for TV news crews to be milling around.

Day Five. Last night's drama is over, the missing walkers located. The next few days proceed pleasantly, though the penultimate evening brings an unexpected hitch. Freddie announces we will have company tomorrow. The mountain path follows the route of the annual police charity hill run, northwest police force versus their colleagues from the northeast. There will be spectators, and refreshment stops for the teams. I remember reading in a detective novel how Sherlock Holmes trained in the art of recognising facial features without the distraction of wig or hairstyle. Should Jane Magee be on the route, what are the chances she would pick me out? Better than fifty-fifty, as my being the tallest makes it less easy to blend in with my group.

I need to think fast. The hotel has the usual selection of tourism leaflets. Can I make use of them to manufacture a plausible excuse for being absent? An unpromising selection. I can hardly pretend to be on speaking terms with Lord Fancy Pants who owns Fancy Pants Hall, nor can I think of an acceptable reason why I would want to spend a whole day at the local kiddies' animal farm. The other places are closed: too early in the season. A faded leaflet at the bottom of the pile gives the best hope: High Shaw Commune, a community of young people living an alternative to the modern world, without radio, without TV, without internet, growing most of their own food.

I pocket the leaflet and call from the village phone booth. A languid, laid-back voice answers, "Millie speaking."

I say I'd like to visit tomorrow.

She says, "OK. Come any time," and hangs up.

Back at the hotel, I make my goodbyes to the others, saying I'll be meeting up with an old friend and unable to join them for the last day.

What sort of reception might I receive in my temporary detour to the commune — trust or suspicion? Furthermore, I'm seriously dreading the loss of cover from being a member of a group. As a lone walker, crossing the remaining hills, I will be seriously exposed.

**Chapter 15**

**High Shaw Commune**

My alarm wakes me at dawn. A quick wash, my things packed, I vacate my room. I'm concerned to leave early, before any police race organisers might arrive. Downstairs, the lights are on in the dining room, with a kitchen girl already laying tables. She offers to make tea and toast, an offer I'm glad to have accepted, because, when I get outdoors, the air is absolutely bloody freezing.

I set off at double speed, not so much to evade the law, more to build up heat inside me. "High Shaw" is signposted as being two miles up a steep track. In the cold and semi-darkness, I feel as though on a polar expedition. Even the wildlife seems to have gone into hibernation; there's not a sound on the moor, not even the cry of a distant bird, only the rhythmic grating of my boots on gravel, though at least out here in this desolate spot I can be sure of safety from discovery. However, with the sun rising behind me, casting a glorious warm light across the breadth of the moor, my mood changes and I'm pleased to be approaching the top of the hill sooner than I'd expected. But I'm worried by the lack of evidence of habitation, a thin line of telegraph poles in the distance my only reassurance of civilisation.

The puzzle resolves at the summit. A deep depression in the terrain contains the black stone farmhouse of High Shaw, with its walled compound of outbuildings and glasshouses. Many trees are growing to one side, a rare feature on high ground, the surrounding slopes providing shelter from the wind, as well as serving to completely hide the commune from the outside world. A buxom young woman, I estimate in her late twenties, is tending to a restless herd of goats. She has long purple dyed hair down to the waistband of a long maroon skirt. Oblivious to the cold air, she's wearing only a white tee-shirt top. She introduces herself in her laid-back way as the Millie I spoke with on the phone. We go to the kitchen of the house, where she makes tea and produces hot bread from the oven. She tells me the commune started when squatters took over the abandoned farm buildings. The kitchen decor is a relic of decades past; I suspect a shoestring budget. Despite that, the building feels clean, well-organised, and cosy, with a huge wood-burning stove heating radiators in all the rooms.

I'm keen to find out who lives here, because I'm starting to think a stay in this amenable, isolated place would be no bad thing, with the country on the alert for my re-capture. Millie says there's only herself in the winter, although some young guys will be arriving soon, and by the summer solstice the place will be overflowing with visitors. She explains the commune is a working community; all visitors are required to work on food production. She herself acts as housekeeper and is in charge of the goat farm, also the greenhouses in the low season. I ask whether I might stay for a month, that I might be allowed to pay my keep by working in the greenhouses or on the land. I tell Millie I know zero about growing plants and I'm keen to learn. Millie says she will personally supervise my progress for a fee of fifty pounds, paid in advance. If that's beyond my means, she will accept payment in three condoms. I'm having a problem understanding how the one is equivalent in value to the other, when she explains, "I haven't had a fuck since Christmas and I'm getting desperate." I produce a fifty-pound note, saying I'm a bit old for her and am sure the pleasure would be exclusively mine. She warns me the commune have one fundamental rule: "All sex is voluntary, but communal. Pairing into couples is forbidden."

Over the next few days, Millie and I build up a rapport. I like Millie. Her laid-back manner belies a young woman full of energy and enthusiasm. The working day is long, with many tasks to attend to: seed sowing in the greenhouses, harvesting winter greens, digging plots for the new season, milking the goats. Not a place where idlers could be tolerated. The evenings are long also, it being the darker time of the year and the only source of illumination old oil lamps and candles. We have no TV, not even a battery-powered radio. We cosy up by the fire, me writing poems, Millie playing guitar. When inspiration dries up, I switch to sketching her on a drawing pad. Despite my rudimentary efforts, I find with each shot I get closer to achieving an accurate likeness.

Millie is somewhat of a businesswoman and succeeds in extracting more cash in exchange for a private bedroom. Three young guys arrive a fortnight later. They are given the communal bedroom next to mine. On the night of their arrival, I hear, the other side of the wall, loud uninhibited sex. I count Millie as having six orgasms before she's finished with them, a performance repeated on subsequent nights. What must go on with a full house in midsummer is difficult to imagine.

One morning, while in the bathroom, I hear a scream of terror. I rush to my room, where I find Millie, her hands held up to her face. A mound of my hair clippings lies on the floor at her feet. "I was changing the bed sheet," she says. "I knocked your bag off the shelf. *That* fell out. I thought it was a scalp!" She asks, "Why did you shave your head? Are you on the run? If it's a sex offence or you've used violence, you'll have to leave."

I see no point in concealing the truth. I tell her I've been framed for something I didn't do and have absconded with the intention of proving my innocence. I take advantage of her ignorance of the news to present my story in the best light, omitting my mental illness. My frank admissions appear to satisfy her and no more is said.

A month into my stay I start to feel curiosity for what's going on in the outside world and consider it safe to make an afternoon excursion back to the hotel. Sitting in the bar with a pint of local brew, I watch television and scan the papers. No mention of my escape, nor of any search to find me. The case is no longer newsworthy — time to risk moving on.

Millie shows her disappointment when I announce I'm leaving but offers to drive me to my destination, a temptation I gladly accept, solving as it does the problem of travelling a further thirty miles incognito. However, as soon as we get into her car, I realise my mistake: a real old banger, having every chance of breaking down en-route. We rattle down the track from High Shaw, eventually reaching the road, where I then find out Millie is not the most competent driver in traffic. Inevitably, we get flagged down by a patrol car.

Millie asks anxiously, "What will you do?" I grab a map from the glove compartment and pretend to be reading it. I tell Millie to act normal, that it's probably nothing. I judge it better not to suggest her erratic driving is the reason we have attracted the cop's attention. He asks to see Millie's licence. It transpires one of her brake-light covers is cracked. He tells her to get it replaced and lets us on our way.

Mid-afternoon we reach the Lancashire village of my destination. Up in the cold air of High Shaw the season lags by at least a month. Spring is only just starting there, with a few struggling daffodils coming into bloom. Down here, in the warm afternoon sunshine, we are greeted by the tulips and greening trees of early May. Millie drops me near the village and parts from me tearfully. She says she has something for me to remember her by and produces the drawing pad with my sketches. I leave her on a promise that, whatever happens, I will keep sketching till the end.

I walk down a lane I haven't been along since a kid. I come to a garden gate, so heavily overgrown with creepers I have to tear away at the stems to open it. I similarly have to rip through foliage blocking the path to the front door. From my backpack I take out the rusty iron keys secreted on the supervised visit to my Bromley flat. The second key tried fits the lock. I enter my late aunt's house. Sanctuary at last.

# Chapter 16

## Sanctuary

I need time to recuperate, time to think, and a place where I can live, free from fear of capture. A distant aunt bequeathed me this house a year ago. The title deeds I hid among my work files on the supervised trip home when I also pocketed the keys. Undoubtedly, the police will turn my Bromley flat upside down. They will find nothing associating me with a house in Lancashire.

The garden's grossly overgrown state suggests my aunt lived here in infirmity. I intend to leave the front untouched, to maintain the impression of a building uninhabited. The back will be used to grow root crops and other vegetables. No neighbours will observe my activity — the dwelling stands alone, with hedged fields either side.

I have no services here. I requested cessation after my aunt died. A generator could provide the electricity needed to run the mini-oven and hotplate in the kitchen and power a table lamp at night. Lack of water is the bigger aggravation. Drinking water can be purchased but I need water for waste. In the garden shed, I find a set of shears and cut a corridor through a tangle of overgrowth in the direction of the bottom of the garden. I have been hearing duck calls; now I hear splashing. A vague memory is coming back of a river when I visited my aunt as a child. Eventually I break through and find the garden backs onto a canal, the land running all the way to the water's edge, with the towpath over on the other side. A barge chugs towards me, the occupants waving as they pass. I wave back, secure in the knowledge my waste water problem is solved.

My immediate need is to buy food. However, I hesitate to show my face in the village. The locals will want to know where this new resident is living. Then I remember, where Millie turned off the busy dual carriageway, we passed at the junction a large trading estate, a better option for buying supplies anonymously. It even offers an agricultural machinery store, where I part with two hundred and fifty pounds of my precious cash for the cheapest portable electricity generator they have. Returned home, I am soon boiling kettle after kettle, cleaning the house.

If a man wishes to reduce the chaos in his mind, he must first reduce the chaos in his surroundings. I make a tour of the house to decide what can be cleared out, and what can be retained. On the ground floor, in the cold uninspiring living room, musty old sofa and chairs encircle the fireplace like clapped-out cowboys round a camp fire. At the back of the house, the kitchen facilities are limited to stone sink, wooden table, and disconnected gas oven. Upstairs, there are two bedrooms, the larger with double bed, the smaller too smelly for habitation, also a small bathroom. Despite the sparsity of furniture, my relatives have stuffed every nook, cranny, cupboard and shelf with bric-a-brac, which will need to be sorted, and I suspect mainly junked.

Several days later, the place is transformed, my enthusiasm for my new home extending to redecorating: the peeling wallpaper stripped, blemishes in the walls smoothed and every room individually repainted.

Admittedly, the colour mix is somewhat eccentric, determined by the few tins of un-solidified paint I could find in the shed. The bright pink and dark green scheme reminds me of a rented house we painted up as students, a house Alison used to visit often. However, this activity has been no indulgence — a positive mental state will be a vital ingredient in my preparation for the task ahead.

The mattress in the small bedroom turns out to be the olfactory culprit, so I drag it downstairs, out the back door, and chuck it on a general rubbish pile behind the shed. Entering the house again, I find a twenty-pound note dropped from my wallet. Then I see another on a stair tread and another on the landing. Seizing a long sharp knife from the kitchen I rush outside, stabbing the weapon furiously into the mattress, ripping it to shreds. I wouldn't want this frenzied attack witnessed by my trial jury, nor the scene of manic celebration when I locate the leaking pocket where my eccentric aunt had secured her life's savings. My jubilation is short-lived, however. The fully dismembered mattress yields only five hundred pounds, a welcome bonus though not enough to make a significant difference to my funds. As a top journalist, a bachelor, living alone, I spread the surplus from my salary across several savings accounts and investments. Had all my money been in a single place, with my current notoriety I could not have converted it to raw cash without raising alarm. Instead, I have withdrawn unnoticed, sufficient paper money across all my accounts to keep me going for eighteen months or so. After that, I will be forced to seek casual employment, piecework, from anyone who's willing to pay cash and ask no questions. Maybe it won't come to that; eighteen months is a long way ahead. Much may have happened by then to transform my circumstances.

The house done, priority is to dig and plant the back garden. Three days cutting away the excessive tree and shrub growth brings a bonus in the form of a stash of firewood. Having fully cleared the area, some two hundred feet from house to canal, I get out my aunt's photo album to determine the position of the old vegetable beds. The previously worked plots will be both easier to dig and the more productive. The photographs show the land neatly marked out into squares with twine stretched around wooden pegs. Those same pegs I find hanging up with a ball of twine in a canvas bag in the shed. In deference to my aunt and uncle, I use them to mark out the ground in the old way.

Next, the question of what crops to grow. At times like this one misses the Internet, the easy access to information. I'm forced to fall back on the old-fashioned method, trawling through my aunt and uncle's gardening books to make up a list of seed and plant varieties to give me a succession of crops summer to early autumn. In the front garden I cut free some fallen trellis panels and bring them round to the back, to erect in a row close to the waterway. They will support runner beans and serve an additional purpose, that I will be less easily visible from passing boats when working outdoors.

What is the aim of this expenditure of energy? Firstly, to conserve my finite supply of cash; the more food I can grow, the better. Secondly, for therapy, to continue the healing process I began at High Shaw working alongside

Millie. Finally, for security, to minimise my current exposure to the outside world. My intention is to lie low for the summer. It'll be safer venturing further afield when the Johnson affair has died down.

Unfortunately, it's impossible to avoid trips to the local garage for petrol for the electricity generator and to buy groceries from their shop. The staff know my face and give me a friendly greeting each time. I don't like being so recognisable. Neither am I a hundred percent confident the police couldn't trace me to this property. My aunt had named two executors in her will: myself, and an elderly solicitor, now retired. I did the probate on the Internet, keeping the old boy out of it by sending him a letter: I believe the technical term is "power reserved". Would he be sufficiently on the ball, seeing the news of my escape, to think of informing the police of my aunt's will? Or might the police examine probate records anyway, in case they turned up anything of interest? I'm a sitting duck, with no choice but to sit it out. There is no better alternative than this house. I'm lucky to have it — only pressure of work prevented me from putting it on the market. Before the business of Johnson's murder, the idea of living in Lancashire held zero appeal, even as a temporary retreat or summer holiday location. Now, I'm beginning to wonder what I ever saw in dreary London commuter-land.

Evenings, I endeavour to put my library wig-making research into practice. I am already anticipating occasions when I'll need to temporarily reincarnate the old David Buckley, occasions when nobody should become aware of my shaven-headed alter-ego. The wig will be constructed from my hair clippings, plus suitable elastic backing material salvaged from my aunt's clothing. Women of her generation tended to be good at home-sewing. I find a treasure-trove of needles and threads in a kitchen drawer and sit at the kitchen table with my tools and materials laid out expectantly before me. However, although I have copious notes on the subject from my trips to the library, I discover the difference between theory and practice and almost give up with the uselessness of my efforts. I even get as far as searching *Yellow Pages* for the name of a professional wig maker. I soon drop that idea. Unless there is such a thing as a wig maker to the criminal fraternity, I risk David Buckley being recognised and reported. Instead, I persevere, and gradually a passable wig takes shape — the advantage of cultivating an unkempt hairstyle— I'd never have gotten away with it had my fashion been neatly combed.

I listen every night to the portable radio I found in the kitchen. So far there has been no further talk of the Johnson case. Making Sense are increasingly predicted to hold the balance of power at the coming general election. Worrying as this may be, I have bigger problems. I'll not resolve my situation by living the life of a hermit. Like it or not, I have to go out into the world, to meet the people who knew Alison, in the hope of piecing together her life story and shedding light on her supposed death. But how to travel? The police know I can't drive. They know I must use bus or train to cover significant distance. On public transport, CCTV is everywhere and could easily be my downfall. In the greenhouse, I found a man's racing bike, which must have belonged to John Edwards, my uncle. However, I see little use for the bike, other than for short excursions.

An even bigger issue is accommodation. The walking tour booked us in as a group. Travelling alone I'd be asked to produce ID at check-in. Of course, I have no ID, with my passport being in the hands of the police, and my bank cards discarded as unfit for purpose, due to being in the name of David Buckley.

The problems seem insoluble until, a few weeks into my residence at the house, I discover "the boat".

# Chapter 17

## The Boat

I wake to a glorious summer morning. From my bedroom window I have a view of the canal stretching into the distance, the glint of the early morning sunshine on the surface marking the waterway's passage through the fields. On the banks facing my garden a herd of russet brown cows have invaded the towpath and come down to the water. One animal wades the reedy shallows, craning its neck for a bite of waterweed. A flock of geese lands noisily on my lawn; a small motorboat chugs slowly upstream. On days like this it's tempting to think I could live out the rest of my life here, alone, at peace, tending my plants, writing poetry. However, the idyll soon turns to terror as I see the motorboat slowing to a stop and a man stepping out onto my land. He's dressed in suit and tie, despite the heat of the morning sun. He stands at the bottom of my garden, alternately surveying the canal and the house. I'm convinced he must be a detective.

I have prepared for this moment ever since the incident on the walking tour when I thought the guide had betrayed me to the police. I take from the bedroom wardrobe my "escape kit", a travelling bag packed full of essentials: clothes, survival rations, money, and so on. I dress quickly, race downstairs and leave by the front door.

Another man is waiting outside. "Just a minute, sir! Are you the householder?"

I say that I am. He flashes an ID card, which says something about a canal trust. "Could you come down to the water? I see you're in a hurry to go out. We won't detain you for long."

We join his colleague. They draw my attention to a fifteen-foot-high clump of Russian Vine growing in the corner of my land, overhanging the canal by at least six feet. I'd chosen to leave the creeper untouched because, with its profuse bushy bright green foliage, it screened the house from view. However, with the onset of summer, the vine has been growing by volumes, becoming increasingly top heavy. The officials tell me it might collapse under its own weight, fall across the water and cause an obstruction, dangerous if stems got entangled in the propeller of a passing boat. They leave me on an agreement to clear the ground, saying they will call back to check the work has been carried out.

I hack away all morning with shears and carpenters saw, making a huge bonfire of cut-down vegetation. It's only when I return to the task in the afternoon and have removed sufficient creeper from the land to come close to the water, that I uncover what looks like the stern of a boat. My first impression is of an old hulk that's been scuttled and left to rust but, as I chop at the stems close to the waterline, the exposed portion of the hull looks solid, with no evidence of decay. Accordingly, I attend to the foliage overgrowing the top. I succeed in exposing the cabin doors and experience a flicker of recognition. I go up to the house to fetch an old photograph album. There it is, amongst their holiday snaps, a picture of my aunt and uncle standing at the stern of a full length, traditional British narrowboat.

Prising open the doors, I step down below, tentatively at first, fearing the weight of my body might expose a weakness, sending the boat rapidly to the canal bottom. Inside, the wooden fittings feel damp, but solid, with no indication of rot, despite the pervading musty smell, though I am unable to reach any conclusion with foliage and accumulated mud still obscuring the windows. Mindful of the danger, I certainly don't intend venturing into the pitch-black interior. I spend a further two hours hacking away, progressively revealing the length of the superstructure, until, released from the vine's embrace, sitting clear, the vessel is evidently fully afloat. Encouraged by this, I return to the house to find a scrubbing brush and heat buckets of soapy water.

Seasons of vine growth have encrusted the exterior with a thick brown gunge of congealed, decayed leaves. I start by cleaning the roof, in the process uncovering three skylights, which afford tantalising glimpses of the interior. Next, I turn to cleaning the sides. The cabin stretches the entire width of the boat, except for a few feet at the prow and stern, so to clean the side of the hull facing the canal I perch precariously on the cabin roof, reaching down with a brush fixed to a pole. The near side I can clean from the canal bank, though even with this advantage the solidified dirt doesn't yield easily. Over the course of the afternoon, I make many trips back and forth to the house for hot water. Finally, with the boat completely cleared of the grime of years, it feels safe to go back down inside.

Seen in the sunlight streaming through the now crystal-clear windows, the interior is in remarkably good condition. The cocooning vine, rather than accelerating deterioration, may in fact have helped preserve the boat by shielding it from the worst of the British weather, keeping it in a drier state than if it had been left abandoned to the open air. The steps at the stern take me down to a private cabin with a foldout double bed. From the outside, with its limited height above water, the barge gave the impression of lacking headroom. What I'm now discovering is the interior wooden floor has been fitted well below the waterline, deep down into the hull, so even a man of my height can walk about without having to crouch or duck to avoid ceiling obstacles. Only one thing: that means when you're in bed at night you must be fully submerged under the water, vulnerable below the canal surface. I find that thought somewhat disconcerting.

From the back bedroom, a narrow corridor, with portholes onto the canal, runs past a shower closet, some storage cupboards, and two bed cubicles. With the corridor claiming a third of the boat's narrow width, barely enough space remains in the cubicles for the beds, though at least they are oriented along the boat's front to back axis, so there's no restriction on length, no danger of your feet getting squashed up against your cubicle wall. The corridor terminates at a galley space having a sink and cast-iron stove. Beyond the galley, a generous open-plan lounge stretches the full width of the vessel, with large windows on either side. Double doors and steps at the end go up to bench seats at the prow, to sit at and watch the world float by.

In contrast to the state of my aunt and uncle's house, the cabin exhibits no clutter or disorder, everything seemingly tidied away for the winter, awaiting revival in a spring that never came. The panelled walls and wooden floorboards will need re-varnishing; the metalwork could do with a coat of rust-proof paint, and I will need to bring in bedding and cushions and hang curtains on the lounge windows. The priority task is to clean away the dust of years. I start by clearing the cobwebs, occupied by large black spiders which I trap in jam-jars and release on my vegetable plots to wage war on insect pests.

The beauty of this gift from the gods has already occurred to me. If the boat can be restored, if the engine can be got working, I can go from one end of the country to the other, without fear of detection, privacy of transport and privacy of accommodation rolled into one. Should my required destination not be adjacent to a canal, it might be reachable by my uncle's racing bike, which could easily be tied to the roof. Agreed, the speed of a canal boat is little more than walking pace but this one disadvantage is undeniably outweighed by the advantages.

The hot weather enables me to work on the exterior, rubbing, scraping and sanding in preparation for repainting. I have an ulterior motive for this activity. Every time I hear a vessel approaching along the canal, I scrutinise the hand at the tiller. A family or a couple I don't want; a single man will be my best choice. Eventually I spot a man in his sixties with a friendly face, who looks mechanical. I call out to him, "Do you know anything about engines?" He slows his boat and brings it sideways to park in front of mine, expertly hitching his mooring ropes round my apple trees. "Fergal Flanagan. Pleased to meet you. Let me get my toolbox."

During the morning, he takes apart the whole engine. It's clear several components will need replacement. Fergal asks could I give him a lift to the chandler's depot. When I reply I have no car, he says, "No problem. We'll take my boat," and I'm treated to a five-mile canal trip with a rapid education on all things narrowboat. What I'm most keen to know is how far I can travel. I purchase a network map at the chandlers and Fergal points out our location, on the Lancaster canal, just south of the Glasson branch. He informs me I am in possession of a "57-footer", and meets my blank expression by explaining that, with its standard width of six-foot ten inches, such a boat can tour the whole network. Longer or wider boats are prohibited from some waterways due to size restrictions at locks and bridges. In other words, I have a big boat that can go anywhere.

Back home, we hear the glorious sound of the engine starting up. Registering my impatience to take the boat for a spin, Fergal insists we first check the viability of the electrics, now that the running engine can recharge the batteries. The system is somewhat old-fashioned, providing only interior lighting, a searchlight at the bow for traversing tunnels, and a single electrical socket in the lounge area. The small fridge in the galley hums into life upon the restoration of power. It will be a useful asset on the long-distance journey I expect to undertake soon.

With the evening drawing in, Fergal suggests hanging around until tomorrow. He says he's in no particular hurry and we will need a full day to give the boat a proper run. The situation is awkward. I can hardly refuse to offer him a bed but I'm concerned my primitive living-conditions might incur suspicion, especially my lack of mains electricity and running water. Luckily, as a narrowboat enthusiast, Fergal insists on providing the accommodation, so I can appreciate what canal living is all about. He gives me a tour of his arrangements, showing how he has organised the storage to make maximum use of the limited cabin space. He explains it's a bit like living on a submarine. Without everything being rigidly organised and tidied, conditions would soon become intolerable. Now that I am planning for mine to become my semi-permanent travelling home, it's great to get advice from an expert.

We depart early next morning, my hand at the tiller. Basic steering is easy, though less easy manoeuvring into a lock. Canals are built as a series of level sections, each at a height level with the local terrain, and with each section connected to the next by a lock. Your boat enters the lock, the gates are closed behind you, water is let in to gradually raise you to the level of the next section, the gates open and you continue onwards. Same procedure in reverse when you are going in the opposite direction, "downhill", so to speak. The problem with locks is they are usually quite small, only two boats' width and only just longer than a single boat in length. It's not easy entering without either bumping against the sidewall or scraping against the boat you are sharing the lock with. Unlike a car you can't just put on the brakes to avoid disaster, and the weight of a steel-hulled barge gives it momentum such that it will keep moving even when you've cut the engine. A careful balancing act of speed and trajectory is required.

Worse, at Glasson Basin, where we need to change direction for the return journey, I'm obliged to make the canal equivalent of a three-point turn. Because of my illness, I've never experienced a driving lesson. I imagine there's the same deep embarrassment of the beginner struggling through a tricky manoeuvre with spectators looking on.

At the end of the run, Fergal declares the engine has passed all tests. He tells me he won't be cruising my way again until the following summer. I invite him to visit then. Funny, my confidence that by this time next year all my troubles will be over.

A quandry is the degree to which I should renovate the boat exterior. My first thought is to paint it a kind of dull industrial blue, to discourage attention being paid. On the other hand, if I restore the original decorative patterning and make the deck attractive with pots of flowering geraniums, it might neutralise any suggestion the boat could be the domicile of an undesirable. Even better, an abundance of feminine touches might unconsciously suggest occupancy by a couple rather than a lone man. I settle for the prettier option. It will add to the task but time is my luxury. I know I can't start off until autumn arrives. In late September, I will stock my boat with vegetables and apples from my garden and with any other provisions I can think of that will minimise the need to go on land for supplies. The end of the summer will offer a further advantage, namely there should be fewer boats moving on the water during the day or tied up at night at the canal side, enabling me to get along faster and with more privacy. Until then, I can only wait; tend my garden; renovate the boat.

The canal inspectors have passed by. Naturally, they're pleased to see an old boat being restored, though today they gave information I didn't want to hear: the boat needs to be licensed, which will involve a safety inspection and a certificate. I'll not ignore the regulations; a pursued man does not want to further attract the attention of the law. However, any kind of form filling is anathema, risking exposing my true identity. In the evening I have a brainwave. The boat must surely have been registered before in the name of my late uncle, John Edwards, my adopted name. I might be able to renew the certificate without having to provide proof of ownership. Searching through drawers full of old documents, I find the papers I need. I guess I can print out a renewal form online, so next day I get out my uncle's bike and set off for the Internet café in the nearby town.

My grandfather had a fondness for saying, "If you want to know the time, ask a policeman." That would be a joke nowadays; you'd be hard put to *see* a policeman. Just my luck, at the first set of traffic lights in town, a police constable calls me over. Have I been recognised? I decide not to show panic by comically fleeing for my life, pedalling off at full blast.

"You're not wearing a safety helmet, sir."

"Sorry, officer. Stupid of me. The first time I've ridden a bike in decades."

"Take the right and you'll find a cycle repair shop. They sell helmets."

I dismount and wheel my bike sheepishly round the corner, thankful for my close escape.

At the Internet café, I hit a problem— the license web site requires payment to be made online by credit or debit card; there's no option to pay by post with a money order. It's not just that I emptied my accounts and disposed of my cards on my escape. Even if I still possessed a bank card, it would be foolish to use it, creating an electronic footprint that would not only betray my current location but also my canal-related activities. I return home despondent. If I had known of this problem on Fergal's visit, I might have given him the cash and asked him to make payment on my behalf. Sadly, Fergal has gone and won't be back till next year. Then I think of Millie. I ring from a call box. I tell her of the narrowboat and how I intend to use it. She says she's envious; travelling around the country by canal is something she's always wanted to do. When I explain my licensing problem, I'm touched by her trust in me that she shows no hesitation in providing her bank details. In appreciation of her help, I promise to rename the boat in her honour. The next few days see me with paint pots and brushes, painstakingly modifying the exterior decoration to accommodate the new name, *Millie*, and a special logo, based on her likeness in my sketch book. The following week, the boat safety inspector arrives. He passes the boat as canal-worthy, which means I can get it insured and licensed.

The end of summer brings unwelcome news, focusing my mind on the task ahead. Making Sense are now in coalition with the government. They have been granted a

free vote on restoration of the death penalty. All the
pundits are predicting their victory.

# Chapter 18

## Floating Home

A boat of less than seven feet width may sound cramped but what mine lacks in width it makes up for in its fifty-seven feet of length. Every spare inch of space has been put to use for storage: sacks of root crops and apples harvested from my garden, racks of tinned food, bottled water, crispbreads, UHT milk and anything else that can survive a journey of several months without perishing. I'm adopting a sailing ship mentality, minimising my ports of call, keeping on the move in anonymity and safety, making landfall only when absolutely necessary. I estimate it could take up to two weeks to reach my first destination: the city of Birmingham. I am impatient to get there, anxious to avoid the risk and delay of having to visit shopping centres on the way.

The morning of my departure I transfer my remaining possessions to the boat, checking I have left no clues to my sojourn at the house. In the hope of erasing fingerprints, I dedicated time to a comprehensive clean-up, even wearing plastic gloves in bed, to avoid inadvertently contaminating already cleaned surfaces. Most importantly, I have removed all evidence of possessing a canal boat.

The engine started, I cast off. I look back at my sanctuary of the last four and a half months. Will I return in triumph, or might I never see it again?

I have no qualms about the first part of the journey, six hours of travel without a single lock to negotiate, the wide canal passing through countryside familiar from that surrounding my house, flat fields full of sheep or cows, lush growth of vegetation and wildflowers at the canal banks, open vistas alternating with stretches shaded by tall trees. At intervals, attractive stone-arched bridges take roads over but I pass through no towns or villages, only agricultural land with the occasional house and garden running down to the water, the few people I see, those going by on boats. For my first foray into the wider world, I'm enjoying an easy start.

If I have given an impression of travelling in total solitude, free to go wherever and whenever I please, this will soon not be the case. I am approaching the "Ribble Link", a series of locks that lower the canal to sea level to join the tidal River Ribble. Boats cannot traverse the link alone; they have to be guided through. I already booked my place some weeks ago. Ahead, I see a queue of vessels tied up for the night and I steer to bring mine to a halt just behind a narrowboat named "Pam". It's possible my arrival will be ignored. I suspect not. Narrowboat owners are a sociable lot. I have been down below less than a minute when I hear a knock on my cabin window. I decided, when I next came into contact with people, I would retain my "John Edwards, retired private detective" persona that I adopted for the walking tour, albeit tempered by my new identity as novice holiday boater. My impersonation skills are about to be put to the test once again.

I go up on deck and confront a short stout man, I guess in his mid-fifties, bald, red-faced, though whether the latter is from sun or beer, I am unsure. He introduces himself in a friendly, jovial manner as "Derick". With a marked Liverpool accent, he says, "Come and meet Pam!" At first, I think he means his boat but Pam turns out to be a far more interesting proposition.

We step down from their prow into their front cabin lounge, where a woman, age mid-forties, is reclining on a bench seat, watching TV. She stands as we enter. With her logo'd T-shirt, cowboy belt, tight jeans, heels and voluminous hairstyle, she could be on her way to a country music concert. Derick introduces her as his wife, Pam, and explains she is the "captain" of the boat whereas he is merely the "chief engineer". This is my first time encountering an annoying trait of some inland boating enthusiasts, the tendency to go nautical at the least opportunity, for example wearing a sailor hat, or using expressions like "Aye aye, skipper!" It's a canal boat, for heaven's sake, not a nuclear submarine on an emergency dive to avoid enemy aircraft fire. However, any annoyance I feel, I suppress, as Pam and I shake hands and smile at each other. She's surprisingly pretty set against her husband, taller than he, with light brown hair and matching eyes. I confess I am rather taken with Pam. It's obvious she's dying to be shown round my boat, so I give the two of them a tour, starting at the prow end and finishing in my cabin at the stern, Pam asking if this is where I sleep at night.

The following morning, our boats queue up for traversing the waterway in pairs. The locks require some tricky boat manoeuvres and Derick insists on coming on board to help. Seems a generous gesture, but then I think he's worried a clumsy movement on my part might cause a nasty scrape against his boat. I'm not sure I welcome such close company. Luckily, he's a non-stop talker, and, with occasional prompting, I manage to get his entire life-story over the space of nine locks without needing to reveal anything of my own. During Derick's eulogy, I exchange occasional smiles with the quietly scrumptious Pam, who confidently maintains their boat dead parallel to us through each lock. I feel from her a genuine friendliness which I don't feel from her husband, despite his outward display of bonhomie and good humour.

The first big test of my boating prowess comes at the River Ribble. Steering down the narrow confines of a canal is one thing — at least if anything goes wrong you are only feet from dry land — but a river estuary a hundred yards or more wide is of an entirely new scale. I'm terrified at the prospect of losing my bearings, getting stuck on a sandbank and being sucked down with a falling tide. I'm more than happy to accept Derick's offer to continue piloting my boat, with Pam taking theirs in front, guiding us along the channels.

No sooner are we out in the middle of the estuary than a thunderstorm gets up. Water and sky merge into one great grey mass, with only a distant pylon to remind us we're in England and not transported to some Bermuda-triangle of a sci-fi horror. Emphasising the unreality, marker buoys race towards us, and pass. If you've ever been on a sea ferry, you'll know the similar sensation when approaching port. It feels like your ship isn't moving at all, rather the harbour is extending its long arms outward to greet and enfold you.

If the Ribble wasn't bad enough, we're about to negotiate a wide ninety-degree turn onto the River

Douglas. When Derick informs me with glee, we could find ourselves wedged in the mud if we take the corner too tightly, I promptly hand him the tiller. Having made it round, for two hours we're pushing against the falling tide, our progress along the bleak upper reaches of the river painfully slow. Unlike the pond-smooth canal, whose surface is broken at worst in bad weather by mere ripples, here on the river we're facing into the constant splash of miniature but determined waves. I'm relieved when we reach Tarleton, and the water narrows to the homely safety of a regular canal.

Derick joins Pam on their boat and I follow them in convoy southwards. Half an hour later, he calls back to me that they intend to tie up. My better judgement tells me to use this as an excuse to overtake and go on but so obvious an avoidance would be an unwarranted insult. In any case, what harm can there be in maintaining my friendship with this amenable couple for one more night? Tomorrow, they will turn east at the junction for Liverpool, I will go west, and that will be that.

I bring my boat to a halt twenty yards or so behind theirs and disappear below to cook supper. I expect them to call round to socialise. However, several hours pass without a squeak from my boating friends. The evening has drawn in and I am sitting in my cabin listening to the news on my portable radio, when I hear my name being called.

I go up on deck to see Pam at her prow door. She calls out, "Why don't you come over?" I call back that I hadn't wanted to disturb them. She replies, "Nonsense! Come over now!"

The canal here runs through farmland, with no public towpath, so I see little point in the rigmarole of locking up. I step onto the canal bank and walk up the field towards their boat. The prow door has been left open. Down below, the lounge area is empty. Pam appears from the galley carrying two small glasses filled with a brown liquid, "The only alcohol we have on board. I hope sherry's OK for you."

She's changed from t-shirt and jeans to a white dress, and she's made herself up for a night out. If she looked good before, she's almost irresistible now.

"Derick's gone to 'The Farmers' to play darts. You don't mind keeping me company? Tell me all about yourself."

This is precisely the kind of situation I want to avoid. I need to be on maximum guard. Sitting here relaxing with this fabulously attractive woman, like being on a first date, I could easily let something slip out of a desire to impress.

Pam says, "Derick thinks you do labouring work, because of your suntan. I told him you're not the type; you're more like an artist. Did you paint the picture on your boat? Is Millie an old flame?"

Sticking rigidly to my story I tell Pam I'm a retired private detective, adding that I do a bit of art as a hobby and that Millie is a friend of mine, a person I'm very fond of, though she's not my girl-friend.

Pam continues, "Is she really that well-endowed, or is it how you like to think of her? I can't offer much in that department, I'm afraid. My legs are my best feature." She crosses one leg over the other and pulls up her dress an inch or two.

Forgive me for sounding old-fashioned but this is hardly an acceptable line of conversation for a married woman sitting alone with a single man. She's surely not trying to seduce me?

Derick enters from the back of the lounge. The expression on his face says everything.

Quick as a flash, Pam says, "No darts tonight? I was just on my way to join you, when John called round." A clever lie which also sends me a clear signal as to her true intentions.

Relaxing his expression, Derick replies, "Bloody place closed for renovations. Being converted to a fancy Bistro. Tragic. One of the best traditional pubs on the cut."

Pam says, "Now you're back, why don't you give John a guided tour?" To me, she adds, "You have to see the new engine. Derick's pride and joy."

I follow Derick down the boat. Interesting to compare internal layouts. Despite being of identical length and width to mine, inside they have partitioned it quite differently, the galley and the bedroom particularly spacious, taking up the area occupied on my boat by extra cabins. The engine tour becomes something of a marathon, with Derick's ability to rattle away without pause for air. When we eventually get back to the lounge, we find Pam, sitting on the sofa, sipping sherry, watching TV. Derick seems anxious to impress on me that I won't see them tomorrow, as they have to depart very early in the morning. Apparently, there are swing bridges blocking the Liverpool canal beyond Aintree, with restricted times for passage of boats, and they need to arrive for the opening at nine-thirty. I thank them for their kindness in helping an obvious boating novice and walk back to my boat, with the two of them standing at their prow doors waving goodbye. I think that's it, until I go to bed and find a handwritten note under my duvet. Pam must have stolen away and placed it there. No doubt she deliberately distracted her husband with her suggestion of him showing me his engine.

The note has a mobile phone number and says, "If you're ever in Liverpool, give me a ring. Pam xxx"

Sensing danger, my immediate reaction is to screw it up and throw it in my waste bin. Then I retrieve it. I've remembered a fact from my trial, that the phone calls to my office on the day of Johnson's murder apparently came from Liverpool. Having a friendly contact in that city is too valuable a resource to throw away. I will keep Pam's number, in case I need her help in the future.

On waking next morning, the water ahead of my boat lies empty. My friends have departed. Playing a game of catch-up, I cast off but I see nothing of them. Eventually, the canal divides, one arm proceeding west to Liverpool, the other east, the way I must take for Birmingham. I admit to a brief crisis of indecision. Birmingham is where I must go if I want to unravel the mystery of Alison starting from her student past but, if Alison did indeed phone me from Liverpool on that fateful day, might I not find her more easily by first searching this possible city of her present? If Pam could be persuaded, like Millie, to become my ally, she could go places and ask questions I could not. But Pam is an unknown quantity, even more so her husband. Ultimately, caution prevails. I turn my boat to the east.

I have to admit I'm still shaken by the unfamiliar and precarious experience of sailing a boat down the aggressive Ribble estuary. Accordingly, I take a long break midday for recovery. By the end of the afternoon, reaching the wharf-side warehouses and factory scenery of the northern industrial town of Wigan, I feel my boating confidence fully restored. I tie up, yards from a lively evening pub scene. A pack of pretty middle-aged women on a girls' night out sit at tables, cackling away together, a temptation to emerge from my barge, rugged and T-shirted, the experienced sailor who's seen the world (well, I've seen Lancashire at least). A temptation I judge better to resist. I remain stuck inside, like an awkward teenager, spying on the local talent from behind my curtains. The dark-haired one at the end's showing nice legs. Pity this isn't a simple holiday and not a flight for my life.

# Chapter 19

## Making Progress

I wake at seven-thirty and take a quick shower — 'quick' being the operative word, the plumbing on this old tub primitive, the water pumped direct from a cold tank down in the hold, with no means of heating and absolutely freezing! Breakfast of egg on toast sizzles on the cast-iron stove, which I have kept going all night by loading with slow burning fuel. Sufficiently warmed up by the consumption of additional slices of hot toast, I'm ready to cast off at eight on the dot. It frustrates me I can't get away earlier but the engine noise and the water displacement from the passing of my boat would disturb other boaters. As always, I intend to keep a low profile, avoiding behaviour that might draw undue attention.

From here on, I'm travelling through an increasingly built-up area, culminating in the vast conurbation of Manchester. I had incorrectly anticipated this part of the journey would be stressful but, if anything, the busy city emphasises the serene isolation of my progress, a steady unimpeded four miles per hour, contrasting with the constant stop-go congestion of the surrounding roads. And, despite being in the midst of the metropolis, I feel no concern for my visibility steering the boat. Who would think ill of a passing barge?

The time I am most exposed is when working a lock. Canal etiquette requires two boats travelling in proximity to go through locks together, that their crews share the operation of the gates and sluices. Substantial time is saved through cooperation with other boaters. Against this, you are expected to join the friendly banter and I always fear letting compromising information slip. In these busy stretches of the canal, boats tend to travel in convoy. Meeting the crews at successive locks provides plenty of occasion to get to know people, and for them to get to know *you*. What I most dread is the suggestion we might have lunch together by going off to a pub or cafe. Each step away from my boat feels like a step into increasing danger. Often, I've tied up for a while and judged when the waterway is sufficiently clear of other travellers that I can continue unaccompanied.

South of Manchester, the scenery in the picturesque counties of Cheshire and Shropshire reveals more variety than the previously flat countryside of north-west Lancashire. The canal alternately crosses raised-up embankments then passes through steep and narrow wooded cuttings, reflecting the canal builders' determination to plough the shortest route across the terrain regardless of changing elevation of hill and dale. Similar to the Lancaster canal, with its isolation from modern civilisation, only occasionally does the waterway touch on the edge of an urban area, where picturesque canal-side pubs flank the waterside, tempting you to stop, but I'm not yet ready to risk their busy popularity.

As day succeeds day on my long and lonely journey south to Birmingham, I've had plenty of time to ponder Johnson's death. Politically motivated murder seems the most feasible explanation. Incomprehensible, when I met Alison at the cottage, that she should not only have changed sides but gone so far to the right. Now I understand, as part of her pretence of being Johnson's wife, she could hardly admit to still being a left-wing militant. Could she have joined a group who'd planned Johnson's assassination? Was Peters a member? Difficult to imagine Peters as a political animal. More likely his self-interest was seriously compromised. Then I can imagine he'd not hesitate to kill, nor would he baulk at pinning the blame on somebody else. But why would Alison agree to incriminate her close friend from college? Was murder not their intention; some other scheme was afoot — Johnson was to be blackmailed, for example, or set up for political downfall? Something goes horribly wrong; Johnson ends up shot; the perpetrators disperse in panic. Alison tries desperately to find me, to warn me not to return to the cottage. She fails, and once the police have intervened, she can do no more. The end justifies the means. My life and my freedom are to be sacrificed to their cause.

# Chapter 20

# Birmingham

My barge is approaching the outskirts of Birmingham. I feel a curious mix of emotion, seeing landmarks nostalgically reminding me of the pleasure of my student life, while at the same time being aware of the very real danger to which I will soon be exposed. My route takes me into the heart of the city, where I branch off onto the Birmingham and Worcester canal. A few miles further, I near the end of my journey: the leafy suburb of Edgbaston. I have to start with the hospital here, where Alison trained and worked. She had a friend, a medical student called Maureen, a local girl who lived at home with her parents in a block of flats close by. I remember our visiting her many times, including the hump-backed canal bridge we'd walk across on the way. You might think fate had planned for Maureen to live close to a canal, until you understand that Birmingham, because of its premier role in the industrial revolution, has miles of canals — more than Venice, they are fond of saying.

Too long ago to remember the address but I see in my mind the walking route from the bridge to the block of flats. I only hope there has been no extensive redevelopment to confuse my sense of direction. And I have to recognise the precise tower block, floor number and front door. Even if I find the flat, what are the chances Maureen's parents are still alive? Admittedly, it's a long shot, but it's all I have. I need to find Maureen, in the hope she kept in touch with Alison and knows about her life after her marriage.

Up ahead, the bridge, but there's a problem — the canal is securely fenced in. I call out to a jogger on the towpath. She tells me the next bridge has a flight of steps to the road. I go further and hope I can find my way back. I'm already having serious doubts as to the reliability of my memory. The bridge I remembered as being humpbacked is in fact flat, and there's a railway line running under it parallel to the canal. I don't remember the railway at all!

I bring my boat to a stop close to a rusty old mooring ring. I can't find a second ring and should get out my mooring stakes. In my impatience, I tie the boat by the centre line alone. I go down below, to make preparations with my wig, with the intention of transforming John Edwards into David Buckley, though scrutinising my old self in the mirror I realise with alarm I have developed a physical feature that cannot easily be shaken off between one character and the other: a deep sun tan from my summer of gardening and work on the boat.

At six o'clock of a fine October evening, I lock my cabin door and step off my floating home. I climb steps from the towpath up the embankment and backtrack to a road familiar from my time at university: big expensive houses with well-tended gardens fenced in for privacy. Why do I suddenly have the pleasant sensation of a summer day? I remember now the pungent smell of creosote, passing a fence on this road on a hot August afternoon when a man was painting it with preservative. Amazing how such a memory can remain vivid in your consciousness until the day of your death, whereas everything else experienced the very same day has likely already passed into oblivion.

At the next turning, I reach the flats and find there's only one tower block, contrary to the impression of my memory, which had substituted a whole complex. In the hallway there's a lift but now it comes back to me why we never used it — Maureen lived only two floors up — we always used the stairs. In the corridor, I knock on a door at random. An old lady answers. I explain I am trying to locate a friend, a former medical student who lived with her parents. The woman has been here all her life and knows whom I'm referring to. She points to a door at the far end. I ring the bell, aware I am on a precipice. As John Edwards I can go anywhere, question anyone. As David Buckley I am at the mercy of the people who once knew me. Which of them could not know of the sensational murder trial and of my subsequent escape?

The flats have those spy hole gadgets for security. I have a strong feeling of being assessed from the other side. The lady who opens the door is recognisably Maureen, despite the passing of time. Her manner is friendly and welcoming, which bothers me somewhat. "David! What a wonderful surprise!" She laughs. "You've had a lucky escape. I was about to call the police. There's been trouble with a con man in this area. At first, I thought you were him!"

Maureen ushers me into her living room. A wide window gives a panoramic view of the landscaped driveway leading to the flats, and of the pleasant spread of nineteen–twenties detached houses and gardens beyond. Part of the canal is visible. I feel empowered by my visual command of the area.

I ask tentatively after Maureen's parents.

"I moved away," she says, "but I was always homesick. When my parents died and a job offer came up in the hospital, I decided to move back to Birmingham."

What she says next throws me completely. "Will you be here next week? Alison's coming to stay, with her husband. He's representing a client in a financial dispute. You know she married a solicitor? She'll be delighted to see you. We've often talked about you, wondering what happened after you disappeared to London... David? Are you OK?"

I reply it's nothing: that I've been under a lot of stress lately.

Maureen says I look like I need a good strong cup of coffee and goes into her kitchen. She comes straight back, saying she's run out and she'll just pop down to the old lady at the end of the corridor. "Won't be a minute!" she says breezily, as she grabs her flat keys and leaves.

I sit on her sofa in a daze. What's real and what isn't? My arms are brown. No doubt about that. I can assume, then, I have been outdoors all summer but can I assume my aunt's house is real? Did I only get this tan from travelling on water? Who gave me the boat? Did *they* send me here? Is the boat real? Might I get back to the towpath and find only a blank stretch of water? I check my hair. It comes loose. The wig's real. I didn't imagine that. What about High Shaw? I could go back; verify the places where I think I've been. I could phone Millie, talk with her, find out what *really* happened. But Millie might not exist. Then what? Or suppose all that part is real: the walking tour, the commune, the garden of my aunt, the uncovering of the boat; but what went before is not? Suppose I merely left work and took a train to the north of England, imagining I had been summoned by Alison, imagining she seduced me, imagining her framing me for murder, imagining Jane Magee, PC Forster, Peters, the criminal case, the TV news reports? Having successfully convinced myself of being a man on the run, I returned to the relative sanity of being a man putting into place elaborate but entirely unnecessary plans to outwit the police.

There's a way I can resolve this in an instant. Telephone my workplace. No. Better than that. Telephone Alison.

Maureen's been gone a long time. Perhaps she can't get away from the old lady. Her address book must be somewhere. Find it. Ring Alison before Maureen gets back. No need to ransack the place. Gently does as gently goes. Open this cupboard door. Only plates and cups. Close it quietly. She won't know where I've been. What about this cupboard? Full of mementos: postcards, photo albums, holiday souvenirs. *This* is an interesting postcard — I'll keep it. What am I looking for? Her address book. Try the old-fashioned writing desk.

A pile of newspapers untidily stuffed into a drawer brings me sharply back. I see the headlines, "Long Haired Looney" and "Johnson Murder Suspect Vanishes". A distant police siren confirms my worst fears. I rush to the front door. I can't get it open. Maureen's locked me in. I run from room to room, desperate for a way out. The kitchen looks out onto a fire escape but the window is double-glazed and resists my furious efforts to smash it. Then I remember what I have to do — punch a hole in a corner with a sharp object. I rifle the kitchen drawers and find a meat skewer. I puncture the glass and fling a chair at it, shattering the panes in one blow. At ground level I walk away from the back of the building and clamber through a hedge to an adjacent road. Only just in time do I remember to whip off my David Buckley wig and become John Edwards, before a wailing patrol car turns into the road and races past.

My knowledge of the area's back streets has faded with time. I get hopelessly lost. I'm forced to make a circuitous route, following the road signs to the university and approaching the canal bridge from the other side. Not a moment too soon do I get down to the water, only to encounter a new scare: my boat has disappeared.

After a fruitless walk of a mile along the towpath, I turn back. I must search in the opposite direction before darkness. My mind races with a confusion of possibilities. Am I alternating between fantasy and reality? The narrowboat: fantasy; that I travelled here by some other means: reality; the visit to Maureen: reality; that she locked me in: fantasy? And there's a scenario far worse than mental instability — the boat has been stolen. When I locked up, I stupidly left the engine keys on the cabin table. Since narrowboats can't travel much faster than walking pace, I might have overtaken it. However, in my panic at finding the boat gone, I irrationally searched in the direction *away* from which it faced, which means I have effectively given the thieves a two-mile head start. The situation's hopeless: my means of transport gone; my shelter gone; my food gone; all my money gone. I will return to Maureen, ask her to ring the cops, and hand myself in.

Back at the mooring spot, I find the boat the other side of the bridge, on the far side of the canal, hidden under overhanging trees. It must have slipped my impatient tying up and drifted. How to retrieve it? The canal is fenced on the far side. I could cross over via the bridge and try to scale the fence but with the local police on my tail that's obviously not a good idea.

I see a narrowboat coming and gesticulate wildly, calling out my problem to the bargee. He slows, and steers to wedge his prow the other side of my boat, nudging it bit by bit back to the canal bank. The ten-minute operation feels like ten hours. At any moment, my pursuers might have crossed the bridge and looked over, curious to investigate the unfolding scene below. Twice my heart leapt to my mouth as I heard approaching sirens but the first patrol car crossed at speed, too fast to take in the canal, and the second from its sound turned off onto another road just before reaching us.

My boat back in place, I rapidly secure it, go down below, close the curtains and wait. I'm getting out of Birmingham as soon as I have the cover of darkness.

I'm nervous of travelling at night, for obvious reason of reduced visibility. And I find there's no moon. I do have a searchlight, for use when progressing through tunnels, but I dare not use it in the open air, risking drawing attention to my nefarious activity. I traverse the blackness at absolute minimum speed, in fear of a collision to rival the *Titanic*. Each time I pass a line of moored boats, I cut the engine, hoping to glide past unnoticed in silence. On this stretch of the canal, there are no locks and I believe I have a straight run from the city. Almost too late do I see in the blackness of the night the *Shirley Lift Bridge* heading straight for me with the inevitability of a catastrophic crash. I throw my engine rapidly in reverse, pushing my tiller hard to the side to run aground against the canal bank, the boat coming to a stop with a jarring thud which nearly throws me off my feet.

In my panic to escape from Birmingham, I'd not sufficiently consulted my map and should have been forewarned about this low road bridge, which has to be raised by an electrical mechanism to allow boats to pass. I could wait here till daylight but I don't feel safe this close to the scene of my escape. I take the torch from my toolkit and read the instructions on the bridge control box. I will be able to operate the bridge with my special waterways key but my big concern is traffic passing along the road. The lights will change to red as the bridge is raised, then I will have to return to my boat, pilot it through, go back to the control box, lower the bridge and have the lights go green again, a procedure of many minutes delay. The bridge showing a red light so late at night might prompt an investigation to identify the culprit. I am resigned to sleeping until the early morning, when I hope the road will be clear. My alarm clock goes off at the appointed time and I manage to work the bridge and get through with not a car on the road. Only some hours later, when I encounter the first of two further lift bridges, near the flight of locks at Lapworth, do I feel sufficiently distant from the city to be able to tie up in relative safety.

I can only speculate on the situation I have left behind in Birmingham. Have I made some fatal error which will hasten my capture, or will the police remain, as I hope, baffled as to my true whereabouts and intentions?

# Chapter 21

# First Sighting

Jane Magee has called a meeting of the team for the Johnson murder case. Brian Peters is present also. Projected onto a screen are photographs of a tower block, a floor plan of the building and a map of the area.

"Buckley visited a Maureen Ross. She works in one of the city hospitals and has lived almost all her life in the same flat. She's an old friend of the deceased Alison Tindell, so it looks like Buckley is still following up on his obsession. Ms Ross acted with a great deal of courage, humouring Buckley, making him think he was safe. She made an excuse about needing to borrow coffee from a neighbour and managed to lock him in her flat. As you can see from the photographs, Buckley smashed a window adjacent to a fire escape. He got out just before the Birmingham force arrived. A neighbour saw him running across the grass at the back of the building and climbing through a hedge onto a road."

A detective constable asks, "In the report, it says Buckley was heavily sun-tanned. We have his passport, so he can't have been abroad. Could he have been supporting himself by working on a farm?"

Jane replies, "You mean posing as an illegal immigrant, so he can't be traced by paperwork? If you're right, he won't be easy to find."

Another detective suggests Buckley could have been working locally in the city, as a builder's labourer. Jane Magee looks over at Peters.

"Unlikely," says Peters. "If he were already living in Birmingham, the nature of his obsession is such he would not have waited the whole summer before visiting Ms Ross."

Jane points to Maureen Ross's flat on the map. "Our best option is to find out how he got here. We know he can't drive, so let's consider the alternatives. Public transport. Taxi. Hitchhiking. Did a friend give him a lift? If he walked in from the city outskirts, we might pick up his route on street cameras."

**Chapter 22**

**A Phone Call**

Peters' home telephone is ringing. He picks it up. "What happened?"

On the other end of the line, a woman with a Birmingham accent: "I used the shock tactic, just like you told me. He believed me when I said Alison and her husband were visiting next week. The police gave the game away with their stupid siren going full blast."

"You said nothing about you and Alison?"

"No. You told me not to. Does he know about Greg's murder?"

"I don't believe so."

"And Alison committing suicide because of it?"

"As far as I know, the only thing the police told him was her body had been conclusively identified through the dental records."

"Brian, how did you know he'd come to me?"

"You're his only link with the past. He'll try again. Not at your flat. In the street or where you work. My advice is keep a personal alarm ready in your handbag."

"I can't sleep with the worry. How's Alison taking it?"

"She'll be fine. *You* need to calm down. There's nothing to connect either of us with any of this."

# Chapter 23

# The Professor's Wife

In the peace and anonymity of my new surroundings, tied up alongside a quiet rural towpath, I've had a moment to reflect how fortune saved me from a fundamental error. I thought I had chosen my escape route from Maureen's flat with sufficient caution, avoiding main roads and shopping centres, anywhere that might be covered by CCTV. I kept to the residential back streets, an area I would have known well during my time as a student, though it seems no longer. I got hopelessly lost and ended up returning across the canal bridge from the far side. In retrospect, extremely fortunate that I did so. Suppose the police used a sniffer dog to track my incoming route to Maureen's? What if the dog tracked me as far as the canal bridge? Thanks to my mistake, my scent will be on the pavement as one continuous trail leading the dog across the bridge and away from the canal towpath. I decide I cannot take the risk again of tying up so close to my intended destination.

My bad experience at Maureen's nevertheless provided a lead. I found a postcard she'd sent her parents thirty years ago, saying she was greatly enjoying her holiday with Alison and her husband at their house in Kings Lynn. On my cabin table, I spread out my map. It shows Kings Lynn as being on the east coast of England, in the northernmost part of Norfolk, the interconnections of rivers and canals enabling me to journey there, albeit by a long and complicated route. If I travel south along the Grand Union canal and at Northampton join the River

Nene going north, this will connect me to a network of canals and rivers that eventually flow into the sea near the town. My first action on arrival will be to search newspaper archives for any mention of Alison. Also, for her husband, though I'm doubtful of the advisability of meeting him. If he's still living in the area, no doubt he's forewarned. Just like Maureen, he might take me into his confidence only to betray me.

These problems I put aside while I concentrate on negotiating the Lapworth lock flight, nearly thirty locks in close proximity, and so narrow only one boat can enter at a time, which means a lot of waiting around. Lovely area, though. Leafy. Arcadian. I'll bring Alison here to see it.

At lock number twenty-one there's a junction with the canal for the town of Stratford-Upon-Avon, the birthplace of Shakespeare, the town where Professor Thompson lived. I remember as students being taken by coach to a party held at his house. Did the professor stay in touch with Alison after their affair ended? He's worth a visit. The easy option would be to tie up, find a telephone, get his number from directory enquiries and give him a ring but, should he report the call, the police will trace it to the middle of nowhere with the only feature of note a flight of canal locks, and my cover will be blown. Just as with Maureen, I am clutching at straws to obtain information. I ignore the risk of face-to-face contact. I turn my boat towards Stratford.

The canal system is taking me where I need to go, one might think built for my benefit. Of course, it's the other way round. They built the medieval precursors of our important modern towns on rivers. Back then, water provided a transport medium far superior to road in speed, safety and efficiency. Come the Industrial Revolution, canals were dug between towns not already connected. In turn, the canals fostered further urban development along their length. Even the coming of the steam train did little to disturb this natural order. Railways cost less to build if they can be made to follow level ground, which is why it's not uncommon to see railway lines alongside canals and rivers. Fortunately, all this history is non-existent for most people. That I can so conveniently travel by water will be the last thing to occur to the police.

The professor lived in the kind of expensive period house you wouldn't be in a hurry to move out of, so I'm hoping he's still there, unless, of course, he's already dead. The phone directory lists many Thompsons, but no professor. At the Stratford-Upon-Avon library I check out each address on *Google Earth*. Only one looks remotely like the house I remember.

The next question is how to present myself: as David Buckley, as John Edwards, or as a new persona? The third option's the safest. Can I provide a bona fide, something to inspire confidence? I decide on a bold plan. I have my solicitor's card. I will use it to back up an impersonation of a solicitor. However, I can hardly turn up like I've just stepped off a barge. Once, when I was waiting at a solicitor's office, the man himself swept in impressively from the street, wearing a cape. No need to go as far as that but I do seek out the best men's outfitters in town to purchase a smart suit and expensive-looking shoes. I'm concerned about my tan, though; I'll need a story to cover it. The other part of my story will be that I'm trying to trace an Alison Tindell, who is the beneficiary of a will and that a former acquaintance of hers has told me she was a student of Professor Thompson.

I feel somewhat self-conscious, in my new persona of respectable solicitor. In town, I hail a taxi to my chosen address and ask to be dropped opposite the church at the end of the road, so that my mode of arrival should go unobserved. A tall hedge encloses the professor's front garden. This same hedge prevented me getting a clear view of the house on *Google Earth*, but now, walking down the driveway, there's no doubt about the place. A painful memory is returning — the house where I introduced Thompson to Alison. How things might have turned out, had I not suggested she join me on the coach for that party.

No answer when I ring the doorbell. A note, in a woman's hand, is pinned to the door: *I'm at the church hall.* I try the building next to the church. An elderly woman, arranging vases of flowers on tables, looks up as I enter. If this is the same woman who hosted the party with her husband all those years ago, she's unrecognisable now, and I hope that I too am similarly unrecognisable. I take the initiative, showing my card and launching into my prepared spiel: "Mrs Thompson? I'm sorry, my secretary was supposed to have called you. I'm just back from a month in the Mediterranean and it's all a bit chaotic at the office this week. We're trying to trace a student of your husband. She's named as the primary beneficiary in a will."

The lady invites me back to the house. She explains her husband died ten years ago but she'll be delighted to help if she can. However, at the mention of Alison's name her demeanour changes to obvious annoyance. "May I ask who told you that girl was a pupil of my husband? She was a nurse, not an undergraduate."

It's clear the wife found out the affair. I play the innocent, apologising profusely for the mistake, saying I will leave immediately although if she can give me the slightest information that might help me trace Alison Tindell, I would be extremely grateful for it. She asks me to wait while she goes upstairs to look for something. I stand close by her front door, in case I need a quick escape route. I may be about to be given valuable information but, wise from the experience with Maureen, I dislike long disappearances.

She returns with a letter. "This came for my husband when he was away at a conference. Unsigned. I hid it. My instinct told me it was from *her*. I can't go into detail but that girl caused us a lot of trouble. After my husband died, I passed the letter to a colleague in the maths department. You'll see it's in code, a game my husband used to play with his students to challenge their ingenuity. I wanted to know what the letter said. I suppose that's why I kept it and didn't destroy it on the spot. The colleague was unable to break the cipher. It's not important any more. Take it! The address may help you."

Back on board, I study the letter in detail. Postmarked twenty years ago; inside, a single sheet of paper; at the top of the page, the Kings Lynn address as on Maureen's holiday postcard. It has to be from Alison. The remaining contents in code: row after row of random numbers. Strange such a letter should be sent in preference to the simplicity and relative privacy of an email or text message. However, I do remember the professor being something of a Luddite, his novels laboriously churned out on an old typewriter. With the date of the post mark the year of Alison's supposed death, does this letter implicate the professor in some way?

# Chapter 24

## Obstacle Course

My impersonation of a solicitor left behind, I put my thinking on hold till I have accumulated more evidence. So far, the reward for twice running considerable personal risk has been miniscule. I have gained nothing more than confirmation of Alison's old address. I hope to fare better at Kings Lynn, where I will be turning to public records for help, in the hope of obtaining useful information anonymously.

Canals may take me where I want to go but I have to go round the houses to get there. I'm obliged to take my boat all the way back to Lapworth. Although a distance of only fifteen miles, with thirty or more locks to operate you're talking more than a day's travel. However, I've learned to accept the limitations of the canal system. Nothing can be gained through impatience. I revert to tourism mode, enjoying my serene passage along the waterways of Old England, the freedom to go where I want, when I want, serving to underline what I stand to lose should my mission end in failure.

Two days later I arrive at the junction for the Grand Union Canal, where I see on my map some special obstacles ahead along the route southwards. First, the busy Braunston junction, a popular meeting point for boating enthusiasts. To my alarm, as I approach, there's a rally taking place, the canal bank crowded with people. I hear a brass band playing, and the squeals of children enjoying themselves on a bouncy castle. Boats are tied up two abreast, creating only a narrow space to squeeze past.

Catastrophic, should I as a beginner misjudge my steering and scuff against the side of one of these proudly exhibited vessels, or, worse, go wide, ignominiously hitting the far bank. Accordingly, I close the throttle and pass by at a snail's pace. I expect to find people laughing at my timidity but am greeted by smiles and friendly waves of the hand, in apparent appreciation of my considerate boatmanship.

Next, the Braunston Tunnel — well over a mile in length. I know the procedure: don waterproof gear; turn on your bow searchlight; turn on all your interior lights; maintain a steady speed of three miles per hour. Entering in bright sunshine, I anticipate a long confinement. Interminable blackness lays ahead, the exit a tiny pinpoint of light, seemingly staying a pinpoint forever, however much my boat moves towards it. People who have had a near death experience say it's like being pulled through a tunnel. Is this what I will see after they have hung me? With the cold dank air, the constant drip of water from the roof, and the earthy smell of the brickwork, I feel like I've been buried alive. A ventilation shaft at the halfway point gives a brief flare of daylight, then we are back to the gloom: the one spark of life, the reassuring constant rumble of the diesel engine, its volume greatly magnified by the concave tunnel roof. At last, after a very long thirty minutes, the light ahead grows into the recognisable shape of tunnel mouth. As I emerge into dazzling sunshine, optimism replaces pessimism. From here on there will be fewer obstacles. Tomorrow I should reach the River Nene.

# Chapter 25

# The Woman in the Graveyard

I discover the inland River Nene to be wider than a canal but not so wide as to require special navigation like the threatening expanse of the Ribble estuary I experienced in Lancashire. My boating confidence grows as I cruise this pleasant spacious waterway. Arriving at Peterborough, I share a lock with a man who's been working canal boats for decades. He laughs when I tell him I'm aiming for Kings Lynn. "You can't moor beyond Denver Sluice. The fall of the tide's too great."

It seems my idea of the boat taking me anywhere is somewhat naïve. I'll be at least ten miles short.

The city of Peterborough sees the last lock. Now I'm cruising the fenland waterway system, mile after mile of a network of drainage channels for the wide flat fields of the surrounding agricultural land. I once read that the fens are the least densely populated area in the whole of England. The isolation suits my purposes, though maybe I'm in danger of getting too much isolation as I'm starting to experience cabin fever. After weeks of travel and living alone, I can no longer resist getting out amongst people, even though all my instinct is against it. I run unknown risks by appearing in public but, if I stay on board, I might go mad — literally — I feel on the verge of a recurrence of my illness.

I decide to tie up at the agricultural town of *March*, the last area of population before my final destination. Turns out it's market day, so I take advantage of the town's outdoor market to stock up on supplies, which I bring back home immediately. The first foray having passed without incident, I venture out on a more substantial trip, going nowhere in particular, aimlessly sightseeing. Quaint low-roofed brown and red brick cottages line the waterway, hinting at their heyday in the age of barge transportation. Further into town are flat-fronted brown-brick Victorian houses intermingled with prosaic modern buildings. The architecture does not particularly distinguish but I am enjoying the falling away of tension bottled up through weeks of confinement.

I call in at a café and choose a table at the back, away from the windows. The waitress hands me a menu. While I'm perusing it, vacillating whether to order a full meal, I hear the café door open and a woman saying "Hello, Alison! How are you?" I look up, and experience the biggest shock of my life — Alison is sitting at a window table. The woman joins her. Is this for real, some fantastic coincidence? She's sitting with her back to me, so I can't see the face but there's no doubt about the figure and the hair. Should I confront her directly? Too many people listening in; I'll follow her when she leaves.

Since I might have to exit rapidly, I forgo the idea of having a meal and order tea and cake instead. When the waitress returns with the tray and I offer the money, she tells me to pay when I've finished. I explain I might need to leave in a hurry but the silly obstinate girl refuses to take my cash. We get into an argument and now she's raising her voice. I don't want Alison looking round and seeing me. I hand the girl a ten-pound note, telling her to keep the change. The offer of a generous tip does the trick and I'm left in peace.

Above the murmur of café conversation, I can't hear what Alison and her friend are talking about but I do hear the friend ask, "Are you going to the concert?" Soon after, they leave together. I follow at a discreet distance. I've formed no plan for their taking a car or taxi. Will I have to suddenly rush up and accost them in the street? I'm relieved when the women keep on foot through the back streets and alleyways. It appears our destination is a church, for a lunchtime organ recital. I wait outside for a few minutes, to give them time to find their seats, then tentatively enter and choose an empty row at the back.

I can't say whether it's a good concert or not. All my attention is on Alison. On the last grating chords of the final piece, I get outdoors, to wait in the road for the audience to leave. Alison's friend comes out but Alison's not with her. I assume she's talking to the organist A man comes outside. Looks like the organist. Still no sign of Alison. I go back inside. The church is deserted. Has she evaded me yet again?

There's a side door leading out to the graveyard. Alison stands with her back to me by one of the graves. I speak softly, hoping not to unduly alarm her. "Alison, I'm so glad I've found you!"

She turns around with a sharp intake of breath. I realise my mistake. She may be an Alison but she's not *my* Alison. She gives me no chance to apologise; a piercing whistle splits the air; the woman has set off a personal alarm.

I shout at her, "I'm not going to touch you!" She runs for the street, obviously terrified, leaving me no choice but to run in the opposite direction. I enter an alleyway, which I sprint down till I come to a road. Now, I'm lost and have only a limited amount of time to attain the cover of my boat before the police are called and my description is circulated. I approach someone with the intention of asking for directions to the river but check myself just in time. Recalling my actions on the day of my escape in the north east, I take a plastic carrier bag from my coat pocket, hurriedly stuff my coat inside it and put on my woolly hat — better than openly walking through town as "tall, bald-headed man, wearing a coat", which is how the lady will describe me.

My aimless wandering earlier this morning now comes to my aid. I recognise a street I know to be close by my mooring and get back on board without the risk of passing through town. I cast off, bring my engine to full throttle and watch the town of March recede into the distance, a lesson in the dangers of obsession.

# Chapter 26

## Norfolk

As forewarned by the Peterborough bargeman, I finally arrive at the limit of passage for non-maritime vessels. Solid steel tide gates, towering up ahead, form a barrier, blocking the way through to the river estuary. I turn back, navigating an alternative channel until I identify a suitable mooring. A row of poplar trees will screen my boat from an adjoining ploughed field, on the far side of which runs a country lane. My canal map indicates this spot to be only a few miles from Downham Market. My uncle's racing bike, which has remained tied to the roof for the whole journey, can now prove its value. I set off for a reconnaissance of the town and am pleased to discover it's on the railway. I plan to cycle to Downham station daily, to join the early morning workers travelling to Kings Lynn. Although I would prefer not to use public transport, by maintaining the behaviour of a Monday to Friday commuter I hope to blend in. The train will also give me the advantage of taking my bike, for flexibility of movement at my destination.

On the first morning, a man engages me in conversation on the station platform. He asks if I work in Kings Lynn. I tell him I'm an *Open University* student doing local history research for a thesis. I use the story at the newspaper office, saying that I would like to search their records from about twenty to thirty years ago. They tell me the archives haven't been digitised yet; they're still on microfilm, so I anticipate much laborious scrutiny. I can at least reduce the workload by homing in on the period between my leaving college and Maureen sending her postcard home, which must contain the date of the wedding; similarly, the period between the postmarked date on the letter to the professor, and the end of that same year, which must contain the date of Alison's death.

It takes me all morning to locate a single article: *Popular Local Solicitor Marries*. I look fondly at the picture of Alison — my Alison — dressed in a white wedding gown. The guy looks pleasant enough; they certainly sing his praises as a generous supporter of local charities, no doubt a quality attractive to his new wife. After the usual wedding information, the article concludes mundanely by saying the couple will continue to live in the town. The one shock is the picture of Alison's mother. The face of the woman I spoke with in Johnson's cottage stares out at me. I've heard it said, usually uncharitably, that a woman ages to be just like her mother but the resemblance between Alison later in life and her mother in this photograph is extraordinary. Even the hairstyle is similar.

Having confirmed the precise circumstances of Alison's marriage, I move on to the archives for the year of her death. A headline, "Body On Beach Identified", pinpoints the required article. It confirms a lingering fear I have held ever since being informed of Alison's passing, a detail I dared not ask the police to clarify, that the cause of death was not accident or illness, but suicide.

Unsettled by this new information, which has amplified the pain of the past. I need a break. I have on me the letter Alison wrote to the professor and the holiday postcard Maureen sent home all those years ago. Both state the same Kings Lynn address. I decide to take a leisurely bike ride. No need to stop and stare; just cycle slowly past to get a feel for the place. I do so, and the feeling I get is that this Greg Warby, the solicitor whom she married, must be extremely well off if he can afford a sizeable detached house, with surrounding manicured garden, and give pots of money to charity on top.

There's a pub at the end of the road serving ploughman's lunches. I sit near the bar, on the chance of hearing something useful. If my life were an old black-and-white British crime movie, a female member of the lower orders would enter at this point and start talking about "that solicitor who lives down the road, the one whose wife committed suicide, poor soul", or the man himself would enter (cue danger music) and demand a stiff drink. In real life, I enjoy an uneventful lunch and return quietly to the afternoon grind of my research. I look for Greg Warby's listing in the local Yellow Pages. There's none. Nor can I find a G Warby in the home numbers. He may have stopped practise, or moved away.

Next morning brings the dubious reward of locating a sequence of articles on Alison's suicide: first, the news of her coat, bag and shoes found abandoned on the beach; second, a report some months later of the badly decomposed remains of a young woman washed ashore; finally, the confirmed identification through dental records. Apparently, there could be no room for doubt. Her dentist had been asked to finish the capping of a pair of adjacent premolars damaged in a late childhood accident. Only one had been completed. The probability any other person could exhibit the same pattern of damage and partial repair, as exhibited by the corpse, was considered so unlikely as to be discountable. However, the impossibility of Alison being both confirmed dead, and, as I believe, very much alive, is eclipsed by an even more startling piece of information. The newspaper article gives the presumed reason for Alison's suicide: depression, after the murder of her husband.

Her *real* husband murdered; her *pretend* husband murdered. There has to be a connection.

# Chapter 27

## The Husband

The following day, my researches work backwards from the suicide. No problem locating the front-page headlines of Warby's murder. Apparently, he died in mysterious circumstances. Warby relied on his secretary to lock up the office but on this particular occasion he'd sent her home early, saying he had an appointment and would lock up afterwards. The secretary returned next morning to find the building unlocked. A light on the switchboard indicated Warby to be on the phone but when the secretary went to his office to deliver the morning post, she found him slumped on his desk, phone in hand. It was assumed he'd been trying to call for help. The autopsy showed he'd been dead at least twelve hours, the cause of death a single knife wound inflicted in a struggle. No money had been taken, no documents stolen, no apparent motive could be established for the killing.

Trying to make sense of it, my thoughts go round in circles until I realise a key fact is missing: Where was Alison? There's another report I need to find — the inquest into Warby's death.

The question of Alison has a straightforward answer. She'd driven down to London to meet a friend, a woman named Samantha Massey, who worked as a mental health nurse. They saw a show in the West End, before dining late at a restaurant. Alison stayed the night at Samantha's flat. She only learned of her husband's death when she got home the following morning and two policewomen called at the door.

At the inquest, Alison was asked whether she knew of her husband being under threat. She stated she did not. Had her husband had shown signs of worry or agitation in the weeks leading up his death? Alison replied their marriage had been under strain. They'd both wanted to have a child but she had been unable to conceive. Recently, her husband had become increasingly moody, which she attributed to her inability to get pregnant.

The secretary took the witness stand next. "Was it usual for Mr Warby to work after hours at the office?" She replied he rarely took appointments at the end of the day; the last time she could remember him doing so was six months earlier. The same thing occurred. Warby told her he had an appointment, that he would lock up and she could go home early. Just as she was leaving, two men arrived: smartly dressed, but rough types. They gave her a bad feeling. Although Warby often represented criminals, these men weren't clients. When asked if Warby met with the men on the evening of his death, the secretary stated she went home before they arrived. She could only surmise he was meeting them because, as with the previous occasion, no names were written in the appointments book. Normally a name would be written against the meeting time.

Unusually, a firm of accountants was called to give evidence. They drew attention to Warby's successful track record investing the savings of wealthy senior citizens. He received commission, which netted him considerable profit, though the practice wasn't strictly legal. Apparently, a recent investment scheme showed calamitous losses, which Warby had tried to disguise by drawing down substantial sums from his personal wealth. The assumption was he preferred to take the financial hit himself than suffer the destruction of his reputation. However, since only Warby had lost money over the affair, the coroner was inclined to think the matter coincidental, that it could not have provided anyone with a motive for murder. No further witnesses were called, and the inquest wound up with the expected conclusion of unlawful killing by person or persons unknown.

I spend the rest of the afternoon searching for follow-up news. I find none. I know newspapers so well. They move on. The tragic story of Greg and Alison Warby was superceded by news of a missing person search for a local woman, named Susie Gibbens. The Warby murder, seemed destined to become one of those cold cases for which no solution might ever be found.

On the train back to Downham Market I have a sudden a recollection of the London woman, Samantha Massey, mentioned at the inquest. I remember her as being Alison's friend at nursing college, blonde, similar to Alison; in fact people often mistook them for sisters. I rather fancied her at one stage, until I found out she was a lesbian and unavailable.

# Chapter 28

# The Men on the Beach

Following on from my researches into the death of her husband I feel obliged to visit the scene of Alison's suicide. However, staring at the shoreline won't help. I need to talk to people. What persona to adopt? I try on my solicitor suit, then take it off again. Too smart; too formal; way over the top. Could I risk being a journalist doing a piece for a magazine? I'll need new clothes.

The morning after a trip to the outfitters, I catch a later train than normal. I don't want any of the commuting crowd witnessing my new look of "working journalist". At Kings Lynn, I take a bus to the seaside resort of Hunstanton. It was on the beach here that Alison's coat and bag were found, the coat neatly folded, the bag sitting on top, her shoes to one side; inside the bag, her purse, bank cards and fifty pounds in cash. The neatness with which the items had been stacked, and the presence of the valuables, convinced the police of a suicide by drowning. They received further confirmation when they discovered Alison's car parked by the promenade, her keys thrown onto the driver's seat as though she had no further use for them. She had simply given up on her life.

I find Hunstanton to be an attractive town, apparently purpose-built as a seaside resort by a Victorian speculator. There are hotels, shops, cafes, pubs, amusement arcades. However, I baulk at asking questions in such public places. Should my activities attract suspicion, the police are only a phone call away and I have no means of quick escape. Since the suicide occurred on the beach, I decide to start at the beach. Who are the people who know everything about the beach and the sea? Local boatmen.

A conglomeration of huts, boats and winches on the shingle has a sign up: *Brown's Boatyard.* A man of about my age, dressed in overalls, is pushing down on a spokeshave, creating a long smooth curve on a plank stretched across two trestles. I introduce myself, saying I'm a journalist writing a magazine article on the "Warby affair" of twenty years ago. He sits down on the hull of an upturned fishing boat and motions for me to do likewise. "Don't remember tha' . Twenty years back? Me da' was in charge then. I'm his eldest son, Billy Brown."

We shake hands.

I explain, "Warby was a solicitor in Kings Lynn. He was murdered. They never caught the killer. Warby's wife committed suicide. She drowned herself in the sea. The connection with Hunstanton is this is where she did it."

"What did she look like?" asks Billy. "No chance she was a blonde piece?"

"Blonde. Very attractive. About thirty years of age."

"Tragic," says Billy. "Good looking girl, like you say. Remember her from one of our customers. We keep boats for people here in our yard, weekenders mainly. When they want to take them out, we launch them down our slipway. Winch them up the beach when they come back. This young fella, moneyed, educated type, had a small boat with a cabin. Took it out a lot. Difficult to forget *him.* Always a woman on board, weekends the same woman, weekdays, other women."

Billy tells me in their business they have to be discreet when people use a boat "for that sort of thing". He never got into conversation with the women or the man but he reckoned the weekend woman to be the wife, the weekday women the fancy bits. I'm beginning to build quite a different picture of respectable solicitor, Warby.

I ask, "The woman who committed suicide, she was the weekend woman?"

"No. The blonde came later."

"You mean he had another weekend woman before her?"

"The weekend one never changed. The blonde was a weekday one. Kept her going regular a long time. Reckon there must have been the smell of some pretty good catches of fish out on that boat!" Billy roars with laughter.

I feel thoroughly confused. I try to find a pattern that fits the facts. One: Warby takes a woman out at weekends, cheating on her by taking out other women weekdays. Two: Warby meets and eventually marries Alison. They go out on the boat weekdays. Three: Warby cheats on Alison by continuing his liaisons with the weekend girlfriend. What happened to Alison those weekends? Yes, as a nurse, she may have been working shifts but the pattern of her going out so often on the boat during the week doesn't make a lot of sense. If the implied purpose of the boat trips was solely for sex, the couple could more easily have had sex at home.

I offer to buy Billy lunch at *The Mermaid*, the nearby pub which backs onto the beach. Privately, I'm hoping, when we next meet, his memory will have become clearer. With the passing of twenty years, it wouldn't be surprising if he'd got the facts out of order. I arrive early and take a table outside. I hear the crunch of heavy boots on shingle and see Billy coming towards me accompanied by another man, same age or a little younger, hard to tell as he has a kind of gnarled mariner face. He's introduced to me as Jimmy Brown (no relation), a local boatman who runs a business offering fishing trips. I ask the men what they're having. Billy says he'll get the orders, so I hand him a twenty-pound note and off he goes to the bar. In the absence of his friend, Jimmy eyes me cautiously, I assume because he's seen through me but it turns out the reason is otherwise. "I'll tell ya and see how'ya go on wi' it," he says in strong dialect. "That's been on my conscience. No names, though. No saying tha's a boatman told ya."

I hear an incredible story. He'd been out night fishing. The sea was unusually calm. He'd returned and was folding up his nets when he saw a young woman come down to the beach. Dawn was only just breaking, so he couldn't get a clear look at her. He thought she might be a blonde. She took off her coat to reveal a one-piece swimming suit underneath. Then she calmly waded out to waist height and launched herself into the water. Jimmy said the woman was obviously a first-class swimmer, so he wasn't worried; he'd seen worse swimmers getting into the water at all sorts of mad times and weather. But here's the thing — not far off shore, a small pleasure boat with a cabin had anchored with its lights on. He'd noticed it on the way back from fishing. Jimmy felt sure the woman was aiming for the boat. Later, when police came round asking questions, he professed ignorance, worried he'd get accused of rape or murder. And when the body subsequently washed ashore and the inquest gave a verdict of suicide, he saw no point in admitting he could have prevented the tragedy.

I ask, "The boat with the cabin. Did you recognise it?"

Jimmy replies, "No chance. Too dark."

Billy returns with the beers. I ask him, "What happened to the boat kept in your yard?"

"Last we had it the gent wanted a towline bracket added. Remember tha', cause he wanted it under the hull, not at the stern like usual. Said he needed it for special equipment. Told me he'd information on an old wreck tha' sunk wi' gold on it."

Jimmy and Billy both laugh at the idea.

"You didn't believe him?"

"Load o' nonsense. Someone telling stories. Never turn away good work. Nor spoil their fun. Probably used that yarn on the ladies. As soon as we fixed it for him, he took the boat away from our yard. Said he'd got hold of a boathouse on the river."

Warby's boat could be the lead I've been waiting for. Might Alison herself have anchored her husband's boat off the coast, before swimming ashore, fetching her things from her car, setting up the evidence of suicide, swimming back out to sea and sailing off to a new life? If the boat is still in her possession, I might trace it and find her.

I ask, "Can you remember the name of the boat, Billy?"

His answer sends a shiver down my spine. "Couldn't forget tha'. German sort o' name. *Freud.*"

# Chapter 29

## The Medic

Hearing the name of the boat is my lightbulb moment. My confused speculations about Warby's boating dalliances fall away, to be replaced by a very different set of possibilities. How likely is it a solicitor would name his boat after a famous psychiatrist? How much more likely a medical man would do so? Could the boat have belonged to Peters? Was Peters here as a young man starting his career? Confident, educated, womanising Peters, cheating on his weekend boating partner with a succession of weekday women for casual sex? Then he met Alison. Did Warby find them out? Was this the real reason for the marriage problems referred to at the inquest?

In this new light, even the puzzle of Warby's murder has a straightforward explanation. Alison and Peters conspire together, the wife giving herself the convenient alibi of a visit to a friend in London, the lover making the mysterious appointment with the husband. Having done the deed, they fear their liaison and guilt might be exposed, so they contrive a further plan: Alison will fake suicide and disappear; Peters will seek a new job in a new area of the country, to be joined by Alison under a new identity when it is safe for her to do so.

I hope to extract further information from the two boatmen over lunch. Jimmy does most of the talking, about Hunstanton and the problems of the modern fishing industry. Difficult to follow what he's saying with his strong dialect, though I don't think I'm missing anything of importance. Billy, on the other hand, is strangely silent.

I ask at the end of the meal, "Have you anything you were wanting to tell me, Billy?"

He hesitates for a moment. "I've been remembering. Me da' took on a carpenter. Douggie Horner. You knew him, didn't you, Jimmy?"

Jimmy nods his head in solemn acquiescence.

"Funny sort of bloke. Good worker, but I didn't like him. Always prying. One day, police called and arrested him on the spot. We heard he got gaol time for robbery. Anyway, I remember now, him telling me the girl couldn't have committed suicide because he'd seen her still going out with the guy on the river. He knew the shed on the river where the boat was kept. A bit too interested in it all, if you ask me. Wanted to know where they used to take the boat when they went on their sea trips."

"You never saw the boat again yourself?"

"I didn't. *Jimmy* did, didn't you Jimmy?"

"Running my summer fishing excursions," says Jimmy. "We'd pass it. Couldn't see who was steering. Usually had a passenger. Girl in a bikini. She'd come out of the cabin to wave to us. "

I ask Jimmy was the passenger blonde and attractive. His answer confounds my expectation. "Wouldn't say tha'. Plain sort of girl. Beautiful big tits, though."

"How long did you go on seeing the boat, Jimmy?"

"Holiday season. Couldn't have been more than three months. Think it stopped around the time the body was found on the beach."

I ask, "Where was the body washed up?"

Jimmy looks at me incredulously. "Washed up! That body never washed up! Why didn't they ask the boatmen?

The body would have come in a mile along. Not where they found it, where there's a rip current pulling out to sea!"

The return bus from Hunstanton to Kings Lynn passes a pub on the outskirts of town. I ring the bell to get off at the next stop and savour a special pint, celebrating the return of my sanity. Before arriving in Norfolk, before access to newspaper archives, before talking to witnesses, I'd had ample cause to doubt my mental state, especially at times of stress: the shock of meeting with Alison, my arrest and interrogation, the murder trial, the desperation of my escape, the incident at Maureen's, the stalking of the wrong woman in the March graveyard. Now everything has changed. I have hard, cold evidence pointing to a conspiracy, one having its roots in something that took place here nearly a quarter of a century ago. Still imagining things? I don't think so. I've established the malign presence of Peters right from the start. His affair with Alison led to tragic consequences for the husband. Then Alison faked suicide. In order to leave no room for doubt, they got hold of a drowned body, of Alison's precise build and dental work, dumping it clumsily at a point where any local boatman knows it couldn't possibly have washed up. Yes, I know — the idea of a made-to-order dead body is all wrong, unless, in some bizarre Frankenstein-like procedure, a crooked dentist was paid handsomely to fake up the dental work on the decomposing corpse. However, I won't compound an improbable explanation with an even more improbable one. Something's missing; something that will make everything crystal clear.

There's still much that's obscure, however. Why did Alison risk showing her face in public, continuing to go out on Peters' boat after faking her death? And who was the plain woman, the one Jimmy described as having big breasts, seen with Peters after Alison disappeared? And was it coincidence the boat trips came to an end around the time the body was found on the beach?

I need to find out more about Peters' past life. Based on his womanising pattern of behaviour, I can take a shrewd guess — as a newly qualified medic, he worked at the local hospital.

# Chapter 30

## Nurses

The day starts badly. The recent string of successes blinds me to the need for caution. I don the my solicitor garb, confident I can wing it and bluff my way to a useful interview at the hospital. However, on entering the main reception area my nerve fails me. CCTV everywhere; of course they're heavily security-conscious. I'm on the point of turning on my heels and getting out as quickly as I can, when the receptionist asks if she can help. I make up the only question I can think of on the spur of the moment. "Sorry to trouble you. I don't know the area. Is there any place serving lunches close to here?"

My question turns out to be fortuitous. She directs me to a pub about half a mile away, adding that it's a popular haunt for the medical staff. I take a walk, hoping to glean information. A group of nurses sit at an outside table. Too young for my purpose; I need a female who would have been their age when Peters was in his twenties. No such lady appears, and I go home empty-handed. The following day similarly ends in failure. On the third day, I'm sitting pondering ways in which I might get to meet nurses of a certain age, when I spot an attractive woman, late forties, sitting by herself. She exudes an air of authority. I'm willing to bet she's a ward sister, or a matron. I take the adjacent table and ask, "Do you work at the hospital?"

She eyes me dubiously. The combination of super-smart suit, over-heavy tan and clumsy chat-up line is probably marking me out to be some sort of lounge lizard.

"I'm trying to trace an old school friend of mine — Brian Peters."

The woman laughs.

I laugh too. "I see he kept up the reputation he enjoyed in the sixth form!"

The woman says, "Sorry to say this about your friend. It was better for everybody when he left for a new job."

"Do you know where he went?"

"Somewhere in the north east. Working for the health service as a forensic psychiatrist."

I take what I know is a massive risk: "The last time I heard from him, he wrote me a letter from Norfolk saying he'd met an amazing girl. Her name was Alison. Did you know her?"

The woman regards me indulgently. "Was that before or after he got married?"

I exclaim, "I didn't know he was married!"

The woman stands. "Excuse me, I have to get back to work. It really didn't make a difference either way. Girls would willingly sleep with him, *knowing* he had a wife. He was so bloody handsome, getting him to go to bed with you was like winning the gold medal."

From the bitterness in her voice, I can see I've been speaking with one of Peters' boat trippers. Although his dalliances with nurses appear to be public knowledge and I've given the lady every opportunity to comment on his affair with Alison, it's clear from her response she knows nothing about it. So, Alison was a secret affair. Why? Were the couple plotting murder from the start of their relationship? At least one fact is clear. Billy told me the woman who went out on the boat at weekends never changed. From what the nurse has told me, the weekend woman must have been Peters' wife.

Thinking through these possibilities, I see the lady returning. She says, "You know, I do still care for Brian. He's not in trouble, is he? If you find him, you might warn him. There was a man asking for him about a year ago, an unpleasant type. I denied knowing anything, but somebody else might have told him where Brian went."

Back in my cabin, I summarise on paper the scenario best fitting the information I have collected: Peters gets married; Peters continues to have casual sex with nurses from the hospital; Peters meets Alison; she becomes his regular mistress; Peters and Alison plot to murder her husband; Alison establishes an alibi; Peters knifes Warby. As long as their affair remains secret, they are safe, but they worry they will be found out, so Alison fakes suicide and disappears. With Alison gone, Peters starts a relationship with a woman of plain appearance. A body is found on the beach; the body is mistakenly confirmed as Alison; Peters moves to a new part of the country. An unknown man has been making enquiries as to his present location. His purpose may have been benign, though I am inclined to believe his business with Peters to be of the sinister kind.

Next morning, I return to the newspaper archives. Previously I'd worked backwards as far as the date of the murder, leaving unexamined the ten-year period of Warby's marriage to Alison, in which either of them might have featured in the local news. I need to carry out a further comprehensive scan.

Hours of laborious poring over newsprint reward me with an article dated six months before the murder. Apparently, Alison and her husband had established a charity, a refuge for women, victims of domestic violence. It had been running successfully for ten years. Accordingly, they'd launched an appeal to fund a second refuge. A suitable building had been identified, situated on the south coast of England, and they were already advertising for the post of full-time manageress. Naturally, the precise location of the centre, as of the original, could not be published, for fear of abusive partners stalking their victims; such places carry out their day-to-day activity in absolute secrecy and anonymity. However, the article did give the name: "Sunrise Refuge". I pay a visit to the town reference library, where they kindly take the trouble to descend to their basement to find me a register of local charities from twenty years ago. The entry for Sunrise Refuge reads, "Directors: Alison Warby (Managing), Greg Warby, Brian Peters (Consultant)." Voila!

Despite these discoveries, I'm no closer to knowing the reason for Johnson's murder, nor to knowing where Alison is now. It seems I will have to return to the north-east. Before doing so, I carry out a final scan of the archives. The search produces nothing, until an advertisement for a local dental practice catches my eye: the name of one of the partners, Maureen Ross. I had forgotten Alison's medical student friend studied dentistry. Didn't Maureen tell me she'd moved away from home before moving back to her parent's house in Birmingham? Probably, her holiday with Alison decided her to set up in practice here. What more natural than her friend should come to her for treatment. And when the police came for records, Maureen could fake them to match the anonymous body washed ashore. Why would she do that? Jimmy Brown told me of the plain woman who succeeded Alison on Peters' boat. Maureen was plain. She struggled to get a boyfriend. Poor, plain Maureen, her one attraction being well endowed. Who should come along but handsome, debonair, boat-owning Peters. She would do anything he asked of her. And, when their relationship ended, he frightened her into silence, saying she would be imprisoned and struck off the dental register if the fraud were found out.

I'm still bothered by that body, becoming available at just the right moment, so precisely matching Alison's physique, at just the right stage of decomposition, exhibiting a dental profile sufficiently unusual for conclusive identification. Even if all these highly improbable coincidences happened, how did they get access to the corpse to match the altered records? Did Peters, as a medic, have a key to the morgue? Or was the morgue managed by a female, another of his conquests?

# Chapter 31

## First Contact

I have one final task before journeying back north. Up till now I've faced the daunting task of proving my innocence while continuing to evade a manhunt. However, the information I've obtained gives me hope I might now put pressure on Peters such that cracks begin to show in his scheme.

When I sorted the contents of my aunt's house, throwing out all the junk, I came across a full-length raincoat belonging to my uncle. It occurred to me it would make the ideal cover for top clothing. It might sound comic, like *Carry On Spying*, but think about it: what's the point of donning my specially made David Buckley wig disguise, if my clothes can easily identify me?

Next day, as bald John Edwards, daily commuter, I enter one of the stalls in a Kings Lynn public convenience. I emerge as David Buckley, hairy shabby raincoat man. I go to a back-street shop to purchase an unregistered mobile phone. The proprietor assures me it's ready to use, fully charged and loaded with credit. I walk to the bus station, where I stand in full view of a CCTV camera. I ring the direct line number given me by Jane Magee at my first interview.

"Jane Magee speaking."

"David Buckley."

"David… How are you?"

"We've got one minute, no more. I can produce a witness who saw Alison Tindell fake suicide. Maureen Ross, her dentist friend, tampered with the evidence. You know who *she* is but I bet you don't know she was once Brian Peters' mistress. *He's* the man you want, not me."

"David, more fantasy won't help. Tell me where you are and we'll come and collect you."

"You can accuse me of fantasy but you can't deny the facts. Look up Peters' record. He lived in Kings Lynn, as did Alison and Maureen. He knew them both. Some people I spoke to can confirm it."

Jane says wearily, "OK, David. Tell me who your informants are and we'll check them out."

"Jane, you know a good journalist always keeps faith with his sources."

"Then what do you expect me to do?"

"Check the facts. Here's a clue: 'Sunrise Refuge'. I have to go now."

I cut the call.

I conceal myself behind some empty coaches. Safe from prying eyes, my wig and coat are whipped off and shoved into a nondescript carrier bag. John Edwards leaves for the railway, to catch a train back to Downham Market.

# Chapter 32

## Fatal Error

The phone call galvanises Magee to action. She's anticipated this moment. The necessary permissions to access phone data already in place. She calls her two detective constables into her office. "Trace the number. Get the location. After that, the usual procedure with CCTV."

They return within minutes. "We've got a present for you. Buckley's forgotten to switch off his mobile. We're tracking it and we know where he's headed."

# Chapter 33

## Found

The police *will* trace my phone call. In the meantime, while trying to identify me from CCTV footage, will they respond with blanket coverage of the transport hubs? Might they have already dispatched officers to the railway station? Now, I'm getting nervous. Looks like I have no option but to forego the convenience of the train. I will cycle the many miles back to Downham Market.

Ninety minutes later, safe in my sanctuary, I close my cabin curtains on the late October evening. Early tomorrow, I will slip quietly away, the police none the wiser.

I hear a boat coming down river. From the sound, a fast launch. A searchlight shines on my windows. Heavy feet land on the deck. Above the noise of their engine, revving to keep their boat pressed against mine, I hear two men speaking. And a woman. I know that voice! How on earth has she traced me here!

# PART 3

# NETS

## Chapter 34

## Victoria

Phil Castle's having a bad evening. First, that weird guy who came and sat next to him on the coach at Kings Lynn bus station. A sort of hairy tramp in a smelly raincoat. Just as the engine started up, the tramp mumbled something incoherent, got up and left. Then the traffic crawled along as they neared London. Phil gave up all hope of making his train connection. He'd have to wait an hour for the next. Now, they've arrived at the London Victoria terminus and police are on the coach telling everyone to sit down and wait. If this takes any longer, he'll miss the last train home and have to pay a fortune for a hotel.

A mobile phone is ringing. Sounds like the noise is coming from Phil's coat, but it's the wrong ring tone. In a flash, two police officers wrestle him to the floor and have him cuffed with his hands behind his back. "David Buckley! You're under arrest!"

After extensive questioning, Phil Castle is released, his identity conclusively established. The old trick of the mobile phone slipped into the pocket. Wasn't that done in a *Jason Bourne* movie? Buckley's invented a new variation to cover his escape from town. In a corridor at work, Jane Magee can be heard telling Peters all about it. Peters appears less surprised than he might be — he's already been made to realise he's dealing with a formidable opponent. However, Magee says nothing of Buckley's accusation against Peters. She has her reasons for that.

## Chapter 35

## My New Friend

"Millie! How did you manage to find me?"

Millie steps down into my cabin, followed by two young guys with Mediterranean complexions. "This is Richi, and his brother, Geraldo. Come up and meet their dad."

We go on deck. The father is the one driving the launch. Richi jumps back on board their boat and flings over a travelling bag.

"My stuff," explains Millie. "I've come to help."

The engine cuts out, their bow searchlight is extinguished and Geraldo sets about with ropes, securing their vessel to mine.

Down below, Millie expresses delight at the cosiness of my wood-burning stove, which is giving out a welcome glow this chilly autumn evening. The dad asks to see the engine, so I take Geraldo and himself to the stern to look inside the engine hatch. When we get back, we find Millie and Richi already making themselves at home, opening cupboards and drawers to find out where everything is, creating supper for us all. I'm already beginning to feel possessive and am none too happy over this display of closeness to Richi. I wonder if they've been, or even are currently, an item. Geraldo is the taller of the two brothers, bald and clean-shaven. The much shorter Richi has the bearded sailor look, which I can imagine Millie finding attractive.

I ask her how she located me so easily, which is somewhat worrying. She replies, "If you don't want people to find out where you are, then don't send a picture postcard from Downham Market. I rang my friends in Ely — their family owns a boat yard, so I knew they'd have no trouble finding you. I decided to come down before you'd had a chance to escape."

I say, "Your friends have unusual names."

"Their mother's Spanish, although they were both born in England."

The rest of the evening, we sit round my candle-lit cabin table, with a bottle of my aunt's ancient, extremely potent elderberry wine, chatting and swapping boating stories, so that it's well after midnight before we say goodbye to Millie's crew. The powerful searchlight turned on, the ropes unhitched, the launch revs up noisily, releasing its grip, turning and making off rapidly upstream. With characteristic efficiency, Millie helps reorganise my storage boxes to free up a cubicle for her use. I sense she is tired and wants to get to bed, so I show her the complexities of working the shower. I'm not sure what to make of this new development, though it surely has to be positive. I'll be happy to have Millie's easy companionship and a second pair of hands sharing the operation of the boat.

Fresh from showering, Millie calls in to my bedroom to say goodnight. Her ample breasts are practically falling out of her nightdress; I hardly know where to put my eyes. She's still wearing the garment at breakfast and laughs at my embarrassment. She tells me to have a good stare to get over it but my staring only serves to send her into hysterics. "Really! I knew you'd named your boat after me but I didn't expect to find my body immortalised in paint.

I'd no idea I'd made such an impression. My shape's wrong, though. I might give you a proper look later, so you can repaint me."

Assuming Millie is teasing on the last point, I change the subject. Time to confess the affair of Alison: my student obsession, my illness and recovery, my life as a newspaper columnist, the phone call used to entrap me, the role of Peters, my escape to High Shaw commune and all that's happened since. Now Millie knows the whole story, I suggest she could start to call me by my real name. She replies she's sentimentally attached to *John* and, in any case, if she got into the habit of using *David*, she might forget and use it in public. I remind her she's aiding and abetting a criminal and therefore risks a prison sentence if caught. She dismisses the suggestion with a contemptuous shrug of her shoulders.

I ask why she has chosen to temporarily abandon High Shaw. She explains that communes are not all that their idealists would like to make them out to be. In the absence of rules and regulations, stronger personalities inevitably push forward to dominate. She says she's tired of being treated like a spare part; she prefers the winter months when there are few visitors and she feels her contribution properly valued. Also, she'd begun to weary of the impersonal sexual exchanges. She missed our evenings spent together by the fires, just the two of us cosying up together.

Millie asks what I intend to do next. I say I feel I have no choice but to return to the north-east. I show her on the map how we must backtrack south down to the Grand Union canal, then branch north again, through Leicester and Nottingham, to the industrial towns of Yorkshire. We agree to share the daily tasks, both domestic and mechanical. Should I be away from the narrowboat for any period of time, she will need to be fully competent in all aspects of its operation. I show her first my checklist of chores. These include things like clearing the ashes from the stove, general cleaning, and keeping items tidied away in their appointed spaces to keep the cramped interior liveable. Millie says the potted geraniums decorating the prow badly need watering and asks for the key to the front cabin door. I tell her the key has its place, like everything else, and she'll find it hanging up in a pink plastic tube by the door. Seconds later I hear her shrieking with laughter. She comes back holding the tube with the key. "What's this!"

"I found it in my aunt's greenhouse. Isn't it for making holes in the earth for planting seedlings? What do you call them? Dibbers?"

"They're usually thin and pointed. I've never seen one so big and with such a nicely rounded end. It looks like a hollowed-out dildo. It's the right size too."

I suggest we go up on deck before Millie gets carried away with her enthusiasm.

Next, I demonstrate the correct way to secure a boat to the canal bank, using pairs of mooring stakes, with the ropes at a forty-five-degree angle for the strongest possible grip. I relate how I nearly lost my boat and my freedom in Birmingham as the result of my tying up to the centre ring alone. It turns out Millie knows about knots from the Girl Guides. She squashes up against me on the narrow bench seat at the prow, taking my hands in hers, giving me an extended tutorial on knot types. We have never been physically this close before. Is she enjoying the intimate contact as much as I am?

Next, we start up the engine and I give Millie a quick course in working the tiller. Navigating the complex canals and river network of this area of the east of England will provide her with plenty of practice manoeuvring the boat. The countryside through which we are travelling is former marshland, slowly drained and reclaimed from the sea over centuries. The surrounding fields of rich black earth are stubble now. Come summer they will once again support cereal crops but at this time of year the land and the waterways are deserted. There's just the two of us, the flat empty fields, and the vast sky.

Midday, we tie up at a mooring near a picturesque windmill. Millie questions my plan to investigate Johnson's murder without my enquiries coming to the attention of the authorities. I tell her I have already decided it's too risky to go after Peters directly, that I first need to find out more about Johnson. In particular, I need to become acquainted with his personal and business associates. The only way I can think of doing so, without attracting suspicion, is for "John Edwards" to ingratiate himself with the politics of Making Sense by becoming an enthusiastic party member and campaigner.

After lunch, I sit beside Millie while she steers the boat, her compelling long purple hair trailing all the way down to her skirt. I reach up to stroke it, running my hand gently down the length of her back, tracing the curve of her buttocks. She turns to me and smiles. She doesn't resist my touch. If I had any doubts before, now I know we're becoming more than good friends.

Mid-afternoon there's a problem with the water pump. I go down below with my toolbox, open the service hatch and fiddle about with the mechanism. Not my favourite occupation! Working in the confined spaces of the hold is never easy. A whole hour passes before I have located and fixed the fault. While taking a shower to remove the grime and sweat of my efforts, I feel us pulling to a halt and hear Millie's footsteps on the roof as she fetches the front and back ropes to tie up to the bank. When I've dressed, I assume Millie is on deck and go to open the prow doors. I'm locked in. The key and its holder are missing from their place.

I call out "Millie? Where are you? Have you got the key?"

There's no answer.

I walk the length of the boat. I look through the windows and portholes. No sign of Millie.

I find her in the stern cabin, sitting on the edge of my bed, in her nightdress. She says, "We're going to play hide-and-seek for grown-ups. I've hidden the key holder. I'll give you a clue. I've put it somewhere on your boat you haven't been yet."

\#

Alison's using Johnson's phone. I hear the beeps as she dials Mister Clown. "Hello! ... I'm coming back north on John Edwards's canal boat. No, I can't ask him... Not now... I'll ring you back"

I wake to find Millie, fully clothed, sitting beside me. Pushing me towards the shower, she says, "Hurry up. Supper's ready."

I ask, "Who were you talking to?"

"High Shaw."

"I thought you people didn't believe in mobile phones?"

"Only when we're at the commune. They'd ruin the atmosphere."

I turn on the shower, wincing at the sudden jet of cold water over my head. I call out, "What were you talking to them about?"

Millie calls back from the galley, "They wanted to know the date of my return. I said I'd ring them back after I'd talked to you ___ John, what are you doing!"

I'm standing beside her, naked, in a puddle of water. "Your mobile makes touch tone noises when it dials, right?"

"Don't all mobiles?"

"But Alison wasn't on a mobile. She was using Johnson's landline. And she was in another room. Too far away for me to hear her dialling."

"She could have had it on speakerphone."

"Why go on speakerphone just to dial a number? It wasn't on speakerphone when she talked to Mister Clown."

Millie flings a towel at me. "John! Get dry! The food's ready."

Over supper, I explain. "Their plan was to find a scapegoat. Risky. If the chosen scapegoat has insufficient motive, the police will suspect a stitch-up and they'll widen their field of investigation. A diversionary tactic's needed, like with murder number one, where Alison faked suicide to put closure on any prying into her love life. For murder number two, they chose as scapegoat a man who supposedly suffers from hallucinations. The perfect diversion, plus you don't need the person to have motive; you only need to show mental illness. The garden gnome, for instance. Peters must have been stalking me in London, studying my behaviour, as any psychiatrist would. He followed me back to my flat and noticed the gnome. What easier than put a gnome outside Johnson's, specifically drawing my attention to it, using it as a means to describe the house rather than simply giving me the address. After I leave, the ornament is disposed of before Johnson comes back home."

Millie says, "Like the ferret."

"Not quite. I don't have a ferret ornament. That was an entirely original idea, an additional bizarre touch to reinforce the bad impression made by my insistence on the presence of the non-existent gnome, an impression made worse when the ferret was subsequently found in my possession, though how it got inside my flat I've no idea."

Millie asks, "Why were you so excited about the dial tones?"

"I suddenly realised the trouble they'd taken to fabricate my insanity. They wanted me to report phone calls that could be proved never to have happened. They had to make them sufficiently convincing for me to talk as if they had been real. They overdid it. Either, they put the phone on speaker, like you suggested, or they used a recording to make it sound like Alison was dialling out. The conversation I heard was all pretend, of course."

"You told me a call came in from clown guy."

"The police proved that never happened either. What I heard was a phone ringing, then Alison talking. The rings were almost certainly another sound effect. I thought at the time the sound wasn't like when the phone had rung previously. Alison faked the conversation. She was a bloody good actress at college. However, despite their clever tricks, they made one elementary mistake. They forgot to take the phone off. They only did that after two of Johnson's friends rang up unexpectedly. Meanwhile, Alison had to think up an excuse not to answer. The bossy neighbour story was ingenious — I always did think she should have given herself more credit for her cleverness. Look how she and Peters planned the whole concoction: the mad story of a method actor running around town in a clown suit; using my own play to suggest a throwback to the troubled times of my youth; the supposed ad-hoc rehearsal of a scene the means to get my fingerprints on the gun; the snare of Alison's erotic dancing; the invitation to return to the cottage and the waiting trap."

Millie looks puzzled. "There's something I don't get. Their plan relied on the police catching you red-handed returning to the cottage. Someone had to call the police. Was that person in on the plot?"

"Jane Magee told me the body was discovered by the chauffeur. He was booked to take Johnson to the airport."

"But how did Peters and Alison know the chauffeur was due to pick him up?  And suppose Johnson changed his mind. Suppose he decided at the last minute to drive to the airport himself. Then there'd be nobody to discover the crime and alert the police in time for your return."

"I imagine they had a contingency plan. They'd left the front door open to make it look like I'd run off in a panic. If the chauffeur didn't turn up, they'd phone from a callbox, pretending to be a passer-by, worried the cottage might have been burgled."

Millie says, "The timing's all wrong. The police had to treat the call as priority and get there well before eleven o'clock, the time you came back."

"This was Johnson, remember. They banked on the police giving top priority. If the chauffeur hadn't discovered the body, their 'passer-by' would no doubt have mentioned it was Johnson's house."

Millie says, "You've seen these things on TV. When a body's found, there's areas cordoned off with yellow tape, police cars and ambulances blocking the street, flashing lights, sirens. How did Peters know that wouldn't frighten you off? It was only his luck the police decided to play it low-key and set a trap."

"He knew my overriding concern would be for Alison. Either way, whether I saw police there or not, nothing would stop me going back inside that cottage."

"But if you did ignore a police cordon and go back in, wouldn't that prove your innocence? A guilty man coming back for the gun and seeing he was too late to retrieve it would have run away."

"Not if I'm as mad as they claimed at the trial."

"I'm not convinced. I think Peters already knew how the police would act. He somehow fixed it up in advance."

"He's been working with them twenty years, apparently. He's a familiar face. He might have gone straight from being Mister Clown to calling in at the police station, so as to be on the spot. How do we know he didn't wangle it to go to the cottage with the emergency response team, so he could suggest the trap idea himself? As for being convinced, you didn't see the way the jury kept looking at me. I'm a doomed man."

Millie takes my hand. "Hey, I'm not going to leave while you need me. But you know I'm going back to High Shaw when it's all over. I know there's someone you want more than me. Do you really still want her after all she's done to you?"

"I have to find Alison and talk with her. I can't believe she betrayed me willingly."

Millie says, "It's obvious where she is. She and Peters are living together. They may even be man and wife."

I shake my head. "I thought of that. It won't do. I gave the police a full description of Alison. She has an unusual birthmark above her upper lip. Peters is well in with the police. I'm sure they would have met his partner at a staff social event. Wouldn't Jane Magee and her colleagues think it strange my description of Alison so precisely matched Peters' woman? No! Alison was used because Alison was easy to hide. Even if she's still Peters' lover, she's leading an entirely separate life."

Millie suggests we go up on deck. I remind her that we're locked in and ask has she finished using the key holder she borrowed. In reply she says, "The night you got arrested by the police, did you have your house keys on you?"

"They made me hand over my personal effects."

"So, if Brian Peters *was* at the police station, he could have borrowed your keys."

I laugh. "Millie, you're a genius!  That's it! They never intended to put the ferret in my flat, only make it disappear. Peters saw my keys, seized the opportunity and added the final masterstroke to his plan. He must have driven down south that evening. Or did Alison take it? To think she may have actually been inside my home!"

Up on deck, we examine my figurehead painting of Millie. I agree, now I've made an intimate study of the originals, that there's room for improvement. Millie suggests we return to the cabin to make sketches. She asks how she should pose. I suggest, to get the required pendulous angle of her breasts, she should kneel on the bed, leaning forwards, supporting herself with her hands against the cabin wall. I expect her to remove her top but in characteristic Millie fashion she slips everything off. I've been sketching only a minute when she says, "John, this position is turning me on. Come inside me like this. You can do the drawing later."

# Chapter 36

## Joining the Enemy

The last few weeks have to be the most fun I've had in my life. Like a honeymoon, but not like a honeymoon. You wouldn't describe Millie and I as being in love, just very close friends, a friendship that has eventually found expression in sex. My boat, formerly a refuge for a lonely fugitive, has become a holiday home for a couple. On several occasions while passing through the countryside of England we have risked leaving our floating sanctuary for an afternoon out at some local tourist spot. Once, we considered going for dinner at a pub. We soon set aside that idea. With the age difference between us, plus Millie's striking hair colour, not to mention her prominent natural advantages, a British pub is the last place you'd want to visit if you wished to remain unnoticed.

We've discussed my plans for becoming a member of Making Sense. Having, in my career, analysed the thought patterns of the extreme right, I reckon I could achieve a pretty good impersonation of a disgruntled nationalist but Millie thought my look needed more menace. In her opinion, I needed a tattoo. I strongly resisted the suggestion, not wishing to be scarred for life. She pleaded with me to do it for my own safety but I argued a prominent permanent marking would work against me if unlucky to be found out. Eventually we compromised by purchasing temporary transfers: daggers for either side of my neck and a union jack for the top of my head.

Making Sense centre their activities in the north east of England, trading on the dissatisfaction engendered by depressed economic fortunes and high unemployment. Their headquarters, in Johnson's home town, would be the best place to sign up, were it not for its proximity to the scene of the crime. On the other hand, their branch offices, although safer, would be far less likely to yield information. In the end, events out of our control solved the dilemma for us. One morning, Millie returned from a shopping trip, with a newspaper announcing the death of the Member of Parliament for the north-eastern town of Scunthorpe. A high stakes by-election is to be held, with the potential to damage the balance of power currently enjoyed by Making Sense. Where to ingratiate myself was now a no-brainer. I might even volunteer for their door-to-door campaigning.

From the moment we left the canal system and joined the River Trent, our journey northwards encountered a succession of difficulties. Observed from the safety of its banks, a wide river may look serenely picturesque but it's entirely another mater when you're floating precariously on top in a metal tub. One becomes aware of the enormous force of the water beneath. Nominally, we maintain a maximum four miles per hour but since we are moving downstream, the flow pushes us along at a pace. You might think the speed bonus an advantage. However, rivers do not have the convenient predictability of canals, where you know the water ahead will be safe. Rivers can have sunken islands, sandbanks and other obstacles. We didn't know any of this until we called in at a canal-side shop earlier in the journey. The proprietor frightened us into buying a complete set of charts for the Trent and advised us to study each navigational section with the greatest of care, to be absolutely clear of the respective locations of deep waters and shallows.

We nearly came to grief at Nottingham. You turn off the river there to a canalised section that takes you right through the city centre. The temporary calm lulled us into a false sense of security. Joining the river again, we made the mistake of approaching too close a rushing weir. For five minutes the current held us in limbo; we could move neither forwards nor backwards, until, at last, we felt the boat gradually edge away from the danger. Underlining we were now in serious boating territory, the adjacent river lock, ten times larger than a typical canal lock, even had traffic lights at the entrance. The lock keeper asked our destination. I'm nervous of any such enquiry and left Millie to handle it. She reassured me afterwards the man had no suspicious purpose; he just needed to warn the downstream lock keepers of our likely arrival time.

Early this morning we left the Nottingham area and have been travelling non-stop ever since. The stress of having to consult charts is amplified by the lack of any safe place to tie up at the riverbank. We will be in the river's grip until Newark, some twenty-four miles and many hours northwards. On canals, I dislike travelling in convoy, fearing too intimate a contact with other boaters might lead to my identity being discovered. Now I miss the reassurance of their close companionship. Occasionally, speedboats towing water-skiers buzz around, or expensive sea-going launches catch up and quickly overtake but mostly we are alone in the middle of the wide water. Were this the blazing heat of high summer, we might feel exhilarated by our situation but the yellow-grey gloom and chill of a late autumn sky adds menace to our predicament. By the end of the afternoon, with the early winter darkness setting in, we are relieved to turn off the river onto the Newark dyke. Here we tie up and go explore the town.

Newark's town square market, strung with coloured lights and full of stalls selling Christmas goods, reminds us of the coming season. Adjoining are many quaint old alleyways, which Millie and I explore arm-in-arm like any young couple out on a shopping trip. Nobody could guess the extraordinary story behind our being there. We sit in the warmth of a teashop, as normal a situation as you could imagine. Tomorrow, I could be on a train, commuting to London, as if nothing had ever happened.

Next morning, two hours heading northwards brings us to the enormous Cromwell Lock. From here on, the Trent is strongly tidal, and we are required to wait at the lock, because we need high water to carry us as far as Keadby. Time it wrong and we might run aground, potentially a life-threatening situation. The lock keeper descends from his observation post to greet us. Probably, his colleagues have warned him of a pair of amateurs coming downstream. He checks we have an anchor on board, that we are wearing life jackets and that we have a working mobile phone. He warns us not to disobey the safe routes shown on our charts and to maintain maximum speed to avoid getting stranded in mud when the tide begins to fall.

Back on the river, we hear a rumbling sound, so loud we take it to be the drone of an aircraft engine. Then it appears round a bend: an enormous gravel barge. You don't argue with a vessel like that. We steer to keep well out of its way. Several more such leviathans pass before we arrive at Keadby, where we prepare for the challenge of turning off the river at a lock that forms the junction to the Stainforth canal.

Keadby junction is not one of your cosy recreational boating marinas but a fully-fledged industrial site. Our vessel is dwarfed by the intimidating high-sided lock and by a huge sea-going grain tanker tied up at the adjacent wharf. The current drags us sideways, causing an enormous thump as our bows collide with the walls of the lock entrance. I'm standing at the tiller, with Millie shouting instructions to me from the prow of the boat. We pass perilously close to the tanker. I suggest to Millie we swap places, because I'm more experienced at judging water currents and she is the better at steering. This time we get in at the first try and make it through to the still canal waters beyond.

Leaving Millie to sort out the mooring, I take the train from Keadby to nearby Scunthorpe and the headquarters of Making Sense. Preparations for their campaign are well under way with boxes of leaflets being delivered and volunteers signing up to help. I spot a room marked "Press" and stupidly can't resist the temptation to look in. Two guys, talking in a corner, look over at me as I open the door. One of them I recognise from the "Death Means Death" briefing in London, a journalist with whom I spent some time in conversation. He shows no sign of recognition. My rough barge-clothes, deep sun tan and bald head, not to mention my aggressive tattoos, must have totally transformed my appearance since the last time we met.

At the reception desk I think I'm doing great with my impersonation of a right-winger, until they ask for my address. I give that of an old school friend, forgetting he lived in the south of England. When they remark I'm a long way from home, I tell them I'm seeking farm labourer work and my accommodation addresses are likely to be temporary. They don't ask for ID. I guess under pressure of the election campaign they have no time to fuss over details. They tell me a march is planned for Saturday, terminating at the town centre. I know these demonstrations, supposedly based on the legitimate right to free speech, usually turn out to be expressions of xenophobia of the ugliest kind but, if I'm to have any chance of coming into contact with the people who knew Johnson, I cannot fail to attend. David Buckley, proud left-winger, will have to swallow his principles to become John Edwards, prototype fascist.

# Chapter 37

## The Supporter

"BRI – TAIN – FOR – THE – BRIT – ISH!"
"BRI – TAIN – FOR – THE – BRIT – ISH!"

We're chanting, advancing in ranks to meet a police cordon. On the other side, a hostile crowd, students shouting abuse. Once, that would have been me over there. It should still be me.

I met my fellow demonstrators at campaign headquarters, all men, a curiously mild, inconsequential, pot-bellied, middle-aged lot. Taking the bull by the horns, I raised the subject of Johnson's murder. "They haven't caught that Buckley guy yet, the one who did it?"

One of the men replied, "MI5 did it. Blamed it on a loser. Thought killing Jack Johnson would stop us winning. Wrong about that, weren't they!" The men laughed.

How like these people to be into conspiracy theories! Always someone conspiring against them. Lefties, immigrants, Muslims, MI5, you name it. In the 1930s they would have been saying Jews and Communists. I asked if any of them had known Johnson personally. They hadn't but they indicated a young guy with a shaven head and large shiny black plastic earrings, who went by the name of "Tozzy". Apparently, he'd "done jobs" for Johnson.

The call came for us to form into ordered lines. I pushed forward to make sure of being next to Tozzy in the front row. In between chants I tried to strike up a conversation. Difficult, due to his repeated tendency to shout out "Fucking wanker cunts!" at the slightest provocation.

Obviously, not the right time! I hoped, when we'd got the march over, I'd get the chance to buy him a drink.

We've come to a standstill at the police line-up. On the other side, an assorted mix of peaceful activists plus troublemakers spoiling for a fight. A large brick hurtles over the police helmets in the direction of Tozzy's head. With almost paternal concern for my precious charge, I throw out my hands to stop it, demonstrating all the instinct and precision of a premier league goalkeeper. The pain is worth the look of admiration and friendship on Tozzy's face. Unfortunately, he instantly picks up the brick and clumsily hurls it back, hitting a police officer in the face, drawing copious amounts of blood from the man's nose. Four policemen separate from their line and march towards us, batons drawn. It's clear I'm to be included in their intended arrest. Tozzy shouts at me, "Run!" and we take off down a side street. We find out too late we're in a cul-de-sac.

Tozzy says, "Fuck! We're cornered."

I say, "Tozzy, I'm on the run from prison."

He looks at me for a second, then says, "I'll get you out of it, mate. I owe you one." He knocks furiously on the front door of a house. "Come on! You fucking wanker cunt!" A young woman holding a baby opens the door. She screams as Tozzy thrusts past her, with me following close behind. With more brain than I would have given him credit for, he whips the key out of the back door of the house and locks it from the outside, giving us precious seconds needed to gain the advantage on our pursuers. Exiting by the backyard gate we sprint through a maze of alleyways until we're sure the police have lost our track.

Tozzy suggests we hide out at his place, which turns out to be the small childhood bedroom in the council house where he still lives with his parents. On the bedside table, an untidy stack of equipment: binoculars, compact video camera, audio recording device and other items of surveillance technology. He tells me he fancies becoming a private eye. He says he "enjoys following people." He'd done a few small jobs for Johnson; he'd done them well, so Johnson offered what he called "the big one". Johnson said it would be worth a lot of money if done right. He even hired Tozzy a fancy car and got him kitted out in a smart suit, ordering him to stop wearing earrings for the duration.

Johnson wanted a doctor followed; he didn't tell Tozzy the name, only the address. He was to wait by the doctor's house, follow his car, find out where the man went and who he met. Tozzy said the man spent most of his working day at the police station, probation centres or the criminal court. "No way you'll see me walking into those places. I've done enough time in them already."

I'm convinced Tozzy's talking about Peters. At last, a link between Peters and Johnson. I ask, "Was the doctor tall? Would you say he was handsome?"

The last question doesn't go down too well. "Are you saying I'm fucking gay or something!"

I rephrase the question. "I meant, do you think women would find him attractive?"

"Yeah, I expect so," replies Tozzy, "and, yeah, he was tall."

Tozzy says he kept on the doctor's tail for a few days, then went back to Johnson with nothing to report. He expected to get fired. Instead, Johnson thanked him for sticking to it, gave him a big wad of banknotes, and ordered him to keep on the job. Clearly, whatever Johnson wanted out of investigating Peters was well worth paying big money for.

Now Tozzy's story gets *really* interesting. The doctor met with a woman, a blonde in her fifties. Tozzy can't remember the exact name of the place, the 'something-something studio'. They'd be there for about an hour, then the blonde would leave. After the first meeting, Tozzy followed the doctor but he only went home, so at the second meeting Tozzy followed the blonde. "That was a real day out. She went to a bus stop. Waited behind her in the queue; sat next to her on the bus. She asked for a ticket to the railway. I asked for one too. At the station she went to the platform for Liverpool, so I had to fucking buy a ticket. When we got there, I kept behind her. She didn't see me. Went into a theatre."

I ask, "Did you follow her inside?"

"Didn't need to. Only got her picture and name up in fucking lights on a fucking great poster on the wall!"

"You told Johnson her name?"

"Yeah. Wasn't interested. Said he wanted to know about another woman. Gave me a camera. Told me to keep it in the car. Wanted photos of the doc with her."

"Who was the other woman?"

"Never found out. Last job I did for him. Next thing, gets himself fucking killed. I've got all this stuff and nothing to do with it."

#

Millie's face registers enormous relief at having me safely back. She tells me the radio reported the march turning into a riot, with many arrests made by the police. She asks, "Did you find out about Johnson?"

"I found a link to Peters. Johnson was having Peters followed. Something to do with a woman Peters was meeting in secret."

Millie looks at me curiously. "John? You've found out where she is, haven't you?"

I reply, "It should have been obvious really. Once Alison had changed her identity, she couldn't go back to nursing, because of her qualifications being in her old name, but she could demonstrate a skill at interview that didn't need a diploma. What's the one profession where people routinely work under a false name? She's been working as an actress, in plain sight. She may even have been in films or on TV. I know the city where she lives, I know where she's working, and I know her new name."

# Chapter 38

## The Photograph

The police will be searching for two men involved in the serious assault of a colleague at a political demonstration. No doubt they will conduct enquiries at Making Sense's headquarters. How stupid of me to use the address of an old school friend when I signed up. I only hope his family have moved on and the house has new occupiers. If not, might a connection be made between an anti-social marcher and an address known to David Buckley?

The worry predisposes me to a dark mood. Millie and I have a discussion about Alison that turns to a heated argument. Perhaps motivated by feminine rivalry, perhaps by concern for my safety, it's clear she doesn't trust Alison one inch. She begs me to exercise caution, that I might walk into a trap. Millie says it's obvious my obsession is preventing me seeing that the Alison of today is no longer the Alison I knew. In the end, I'm persuaded and agree it will be safer for Millie to make the first contact. The disagreement resolved, we head west, Millie piloting the boat, me keeping out of sight below deck. Only when we encounter our first lock, a full three hours later, do I dare show my face on top.

Next morning, Millie goes off in search of a web cafe to research the career of actress Teresa Lewis (Alison's adopted stage name). When Millie arrived with her smartphone, she brought with her a shortcut for my researches. However, if I had wanted the Internet, I could have obtained it at any time by purchasing an unregistered mobile. Caution told me to resist the temptation. The police don't know where I'm living, where I'm travelling, what I now look like but one thing they do know: as a journalist, I am by habit highly computer-literate. Do they have sophisticated ways of tracing Internet searches and correlating them with mobile phone position? Too big a risk. I prefer to confine my data access to short concentrated bursts, from varied locations distant from the canal. And the bonus of having Millie to do the research for me is I avoid showing my face. Thinking back, my daily visits to the newspaper office at Kings Lynn might have drastically compromised my security had their records been transferred to electronic format, the tedium of having to wade through page after page of microfilm at least compensated by the total anonymity the medium provided. Nobody could have the least clue what I was looking for.

Millie returns around midday. The information she brings back paints a very different picture from the glamorous career of outrageous deception and universal public acclaim I had imagined for Alison in her new guise as a professional actress going under the name Teresa Lewis. Following an early success, a successful West End role, as *Stella* in *A Streetcar Named Desire*, she has worked as a showgirl and lingerie model. In recent years her stage appearances have been increasingly sporadic. Over the Christmas season she is to star as The Wicked Witch in pantomime at Liverpool. All this information, Millie gleaned from the bio page on Teresa Lewis's web site. Something else she has gleaned is a printout of a photograph. "Is this her? Wish I had legs like hers!"

I take the printout with trembling hands. The hairstyle is changed, which makes the face quite unlike at Johnson's cottage but there's no doubt about the eyes and the smile. Exactly as I remember from Johnson's place.

We decide to use the journalist dodge that proved successful with the fishermen in Hunstanton, except this time it will be Millie who'll be the journalist. She'll phone the Liverpool pantomime theatre to make an appointment to interview Teresa Lewis. For extra realism she will give her name as of a real columnist for a local paper. She'll say she's bringing a photographer with her. On the day, the photographer (me) will arrive early, requesting to take photographs before the supposed interview starts. That way I hope to be taken to Alison's dressing room without her suspecting an ambush. It's possible she'll raise hell, press a panic button, call security, but I doubt it. She's in this too deeply. I will have the upper hand and therefore assume I can expect her quiet cooperation.

I take another look at the photograph, "Millie, this can't be her! There's no blemish above her lip!"

Millie smiles. "John, don't be naïve! Obviously, she's well made up and the picture's been retouched. Look at the smoothness of the skin."

# Chapter 39

# Dragnet

We're approaching the beginning of the arduous journey we must make across the Pennine mountain-range to the city of Liverpool, where I hope to at last meet again with Alison. The canal route is one of the highest in England and with the coming of winter I'm concerned to get across the higher elevations. Should there be a spell of severe cold weather, we'll be iced in, unable to go anywhere.

To maximise our progress, Millie and I have agreed to forego stopping for lunch. One or the other of us will have a hand at the tiller from eight in the morning until dusk. This morning I take the first shift. The canal has joined a river in full flood. The sensation of the strong flow against the boat is almost visceral. It will greatly retard our speed relative to the land. I call down to Millie to look at the map. She tells me we're a good three miles from the next lock, following which we'll be turning off the river onto a canal in the direction of Leeds. An hour later, when I hand over the tiller, we've still not reached the lock. I'm down below when I hear Millie call out "Lock ahead!" then, "John! Hide! It's swarming with police!"

I've no idea what's going on, nor time to think; hiding on a narrowboat is almost an impossibility. My only hope is a bench seat with a hinged lid disguising storage space underneath full of fruit boxes. I yank the boxes out, hastily stacking them in a pile, dive in and close the lid on top of me. From the darkness inside, I can hear nothing but the diesel engine's rumble. A change in its pitch and a change in the motion of the boat tell me Millie is slowing to enter the lock. I never thought to instruct her how to work a lock single-handed. She'll have to improvise. I'm relieved when I hear the muffled rush of water and feel the slow rise of the boat. So far, so good. After a few minutes, the rising stops. Complete silence. Suddenly, the thud of footsteps on deck. People are coming down into the cabin.

Someone's sitting down on the bench seat. I hear Millie's voice: "Here's the map." A second person sits on the seat. "What's this blue line?" The voice is unmistakeable — Jane Magee.

Millie replies, "Blue is river. Red is canal."

"And this arrow?" asks Jane.

"The lock where we are now."

"So, the water's going this way?"

"The other way. The arrow points uphill. We've been against the flow all morning."

"We?"

"Me and my boat."

"You live here alone?"

"A few weeks more. We'll be tied up for the winter soon."

"Your name's Millie?"

"Yes. You saw my picture?"

"Did *you* do it?"

"My boyfriend."

"Trust a man to paint a woman like that but it's a brilliant likeness! Tell your friend from me when you next see him. Thank you. You've been very helpful."

Five minutes later I hear the engine rev up and feel a forwards movement. I don't know whether Jane's still on board and have no alternative but to remain in my place of confinement until Millie can release me. The boat finally slows to a stop and I hear Millie up above fixing the prow and stern ropes.

She comes down below and frees me from my prison. "That was a close one!"

"You know who that was? Jane Magee!"

"I thought so."

"What was going on?"

"Police everywhere, on the lock, on the canal bank. Like they were hunting for something. They had an overcoat stretched out on the ground with a guy taking photographs. The Magee woman was in charge. I worked the lock, ignoring them. Then, she came up to me and asked did I have a map. I intended to bring it out to her but she followed me down the steps. I saw a pile of your clothes lying on the side cabin bed and had to whip the curtain across before she could see. I nearly died when I saw the fruit boxes out on the floor. I grabbed the map and plonked myself down on the seat to stop her getting curious."

I tell Millie of the disposing of my overcoat in a sealed bag, intending the water should sweep it a long way downstream. The location must have been upstream from here. Presumably, the bag snagged on an obstacle near the lock, remaining stuck in the water for months before discovery. How ironic my ruse to trick the police nearly ended in my downfall. I need to take greater care with my schemes. The next mistake could prove fatal.

# Chapter 40

## Another Phone Call

Peters' mobile is ringing. He picks it up. "Hello! How are you? How's the new flat?"

On the other end of the line, a woman with a well-spoken voice. "Wonderful! You told me to ring if anything happened. Val Melia, the drama critic, just phoned. She said they're doing a big feature on Christmas panto. She wants to interview me at the theatre about my wicked witch role. She's said she's bringing a photographer."

"Congratulations! Good for your career!"

"Yes, but I met Val Melia in person once at a first night party. He's a man, not a woman."

Peters is silent for a moment. "When's this for?"

"She said it would be in few weeks' time. I told her to ring back because we hadn't been given the rehearsal schedule yet. David Buckley's behind this, isn't he?"

"I'm rather afraid he is. The man is a more formidable opponent than we'd judged. Make the appointment. I'll warn the police. When Buckley arrives, you can say you can't talk at that moment because you've got an unscheduled rehearsal. Tell him to come back later. They'll arrest him as he leaves the building."

"I'm terrified!"

"Why? Can you imagine Buckley causing you harm?"

"I'm terrified of the police."

"They've no evidence connecting you to Alison. They're still of the opinion Buckley's delusional. The fact he's now hooked onto some random actress will only strengthen their opinion."

## Chapter 41

## Following Peters

Jane Magee is used to working undercover. A woman, particularly a certain type of woman, can get close to a certain type of man, taking him off guard. More than once, Jane has posed as a high-class escort, not as far as having sex but as far as necessary to obtain useful information. So good is her mimicry that many a criminal has stood in the dock, blissfully unaware the business-like detective inspector giving evidence against him is the very same woman he once chatted up in a bar.

What does Jane Magee know about Peters? She knows he has dealings with an actress called Teresa Lewis. She knows he's having an affair with a second woman. She knows nothing of Buckley's researches but she's ahead of him. She knows the second woman had a connection with Johnson. She knows Peters and the second woman meet for sex at a seedy hotel. She knows they avoid higher-class establishments due to the risk of running into friends or colleagues.

Today, Jane will once again enter the lion's den. She checks in at a hotel, ready to get into character. The proprietor is aware she's a detective. They have an agreement. He won't interfere with her business, so long as she turns a blind eye to his. In her room, Jane takes a shower. She understands to successfully change character you have to live the character. First the perfume, then the seductive underwear —she chooses a basque — stockings, of course, and obscenely high heels. Makeup, dress, lipstick. She's ready.

She waits in a car opposite Peters' hotel. She doesn't have long to wait. Peters pulls up. He goes inside. Jane allows five minutes for him to find the room where he's to meet the woman. Now it's time for the kill.

# Chapter 42

## The Wicked Witch

A canal journey across the Pennine mountains in December is nobody's idea of fun. The weather has been atrocious. Standing at the tiller, with the prevailing wind from the west, we've constantly faced into driving rain. Particularly punishing has been the freezing cold metalwork of the operating mechanism at lock gates. And to add to our misery this canal also has many pedestrian swing bridges crossing it, which we have to individually wind open with a metal handle. We were forced to admit defeat and delay our progress while Millie went off to buy leather gloves. When she returned, she proposed we reduce the length of our shifts, swapping over at the tiller hourly. Her suggestion has made the journey more tolerable, and now the wind has abated. Nonetheless, my mood slips rapidly towards depression. We are nearing Gargrave, the most northerly point of the canal and therefore the nearest point by water to High Shaw commune. Millie is about to leave me.

We tie up at Gargrave lock. Any other occasion, I'd be enjoying our expedition to the village, a pretty place, all mellow Yorkshire stone. Not now. All I can think of is the moment when Millie will be gone. We talked it over last night before we made love for the last time. Millie said we could never live as a couple at High Shaw, because pairing up is against the rules but she wanted me to know she'd abandon all that to live with me at my house in Lancashire. However, she was unwilling to enter into a relationship with a man who wanted another. I would have to choose between her and Alison.

I couldn't disagree. I could only say to part voluntarily had to be better than to be parted by force. Until the question of my long-term future was resolved, to enter into a serious relationship would be grossly unfair to any woman. And since both my emotions and my fate were tied up with the same woman — Alison — I had to see the matter through to the end.

This morning, Millie helped me with one final task. She made the phone call that will seal my fate, one way or the other: she spoke with Teresa Lewis and they agreed a date for the interview. Now we're sitting in a pub opposite the village post office, waiting for Millie's friends to arrive. She has with her the kit bag full of stuff with which she arrived at Downham Market on that first day of the happiest period of my life. A car comes slowly down the street and pulls up by the pub. Millie hands me her boat keys. I tell her to hang on to them, as a pledge she will come back to me. We kiss for the last time; she picks up her bag and I watch through the window as she gets into the car and it drives off. The walk back is a lonely one. Entering our cabin, I find Millie's nightdress on the bed. It smells of her perfume.

The absence of Millie underlines how much easier it is to have two people working the boat. A flat-out effort is needed to traverse the increasing number of locks on the steep gradient descending the far side of the Pennines. At Wigan I join the canal I travelled on to Birmingham, except this time I'm going north. I pass the pub where I tied up next to the girls' night out, then the branch northwards to

Tarleton, where I parted from Derick and Pam. I remember Derick telling me about the swing road-bridges crossing the canal before Liverpool and their limited operation times. Anxious not to get trapped the wrong side of these obstacles, I make the decision to tie up before them, close to Aintree racecourse. I will use my bike to travel the seven miles from here to Teresa Lewis's theatre. I'm reminded also of Pam's attempted seduction, and the note with her mobile phone number she left on my bed all those weeks ago. I will take it with me tomorrow, in case of emergency.

The long-awaited day of my interview with Alison arrives dry but bitterly cold. In the pale light of a December morning, I untie the racing bike and set off. The appointment isn't until evening but I have only one shot to get it right and it would be unforgivable to blow the opportunity. I need time to case out the theatre, its stage door entrance, and my quickest route from there to connect with the roads taking me back to safety. I call first at the newsagents near my mooring, to purchase a large-scale street map. On this, I mark with a pen a convoluted route, following a zig-zag of insignificant back streets. Should anything go wrong and the police be on my tail, I could be easily intercepted on the main roads. I enjoy the effort of cycling this deliberately extended route, exhilarated by the extreme cold endurance test and the thought of my meeting with Alison being only hours away.

My city reconnaissance tasks I complete sooner than expected and now I'm getting nervous. I feel exposed and vulnerable walking the busy streets. I crave anonymity. If

Pam and Derick live nearby, then a visit to their house could provide welcome seclusion. I find a call box and ring. Pam answers the call. She asks if I know the "Museum of Liverpool". She and some girl friends are spending the afternoon there. She asks a favour: that I pretend to bump into her by accident. She doesn't want it getting back to Derick that we met by arrangement.

In the museum I spot Pam and her friends. I edge closer, to give her the opportunity of recognition. She calls out, "John! What are you doing here?" She introduces me to the others, and I spend an enjoyable afternoon touring the museum in their company, at the end of which we agree to go to a pub for drinks. Another hour and I will make the excuse I have a train to catch. The timing should be perfect for me to return to the theatre, or rather it would have been perfect, had catastrophe not struck at that moment.

I didn't notice Derick enter the bar. I only heard him shout, "It's *you*! I knew it!" before being roughly grabbed by my collar and thrown to the floor, hitting against a table and turning it over with a dramatic smashing of glasses and plates. A scene of chaos ensued: women screaming, two heavies struggling to keep Derick under control and the barman shouting for someone to call the police.

Thirty minutes later, I'm in a terrible place — a police station! Statements are being taken from witnesses and now they want to see my ID. I fib that my wallet is lost, that it must have fallen onto the pub floor in the fight. They ask whether I wish to make an official complaint, since the witnesses have confirmed me as being the innocent party. I say not, and since Derick has already agreed to pay for the damage, the police seem happy the matter is resolved. They tell me to leave before they release him. The desk sergeant advises me with a wink to "keep well away from the pretty wife".

Already late for my appointment, I realise with panic I really *have* lost something in the pub, not my wallet but the plastic bag containing my David Buckley wig. Should my mission be caught on CCTV, they need to see the David Buckley they are expecting to see, not the bald John Edwards disguise which has served me so well, even to the extent of protecting me from recognition at the police station this very evening. I dash back to the scene of the altercation. The debris has already been cleared away but I find my bag untouched, underneath a table.

By the time I arrive at the theatre, darkness has fallen. A lit-up poster, stretching the full height of the building, lists the TV personalities starring in the show, with Teresa Lewis credited way down the list. Approaching the façade, I hear a screech of brakes followed by a gigantic crash. At the side of the building, a lorry has skidded on black ice and smashed into two parked cars. A crowd is gathering, though it looks like nobody has been hurt.

I find the theatre stage door unattended — the doorman has joined the crowd at the crash scene. I could take advantage of his absence to enter unobserved but this might create difficulties having to explain my presence on leaving, so I decide to wait for him to appear. After all, my appointment is legitimate; they are expecting me; I have no need to act suspiciously. On the other hand, delay increases the risk of something going wrong, particularly if other actors arrive, destroying my chance of speaking with Alison alone. Ultimately, fear prevails and I wait no longer.

The dressing rooms have the stars' names on the doors. I knock on the door for Teresa Lewis. There's no reply. I try the handle, expecting the door to be locked. It opens. The dressing table mirror lights are on, a woman's handbag on the floor, discarded clothes on a chair. So, she's here, somewhere in the theatre.

The far end of the corridor leads directly to the stage. Dead centre, I see a woman illuminated by a single spotlight. She wears the costume of the wicked witch.

"Alison?"

She starts when she hears her name. "David! We're about to rehearse. We finish at ten-thirty. Come back at eleven."

I move towards her, to touch her, to hold her.

A voice cackles out, "Ha ha ha ha ha! What have we here?" A second witch emerges from the other side of the stage. I move into the shadows. Not good to be seen as David Buckley.

Walking off stage, I take the wrong corridor. No matter. A side door to the road has been left ajar. Better than making my presence known to the doorman.

"Come back at eleven." When did I last hear those words? An agony of a wait on that evening; an agony of a wait now. I pass a late-night web café. I'll do what I did then: go to the Internet for information.

Teresa Lewis's web site is easily located. There's a lot there. Notices from past shows: mostly stage work; no television. Pictures of her dancing in musicals. A page about lingerie modelling. I'll look at that in a moment. I'm looking at the bio page. I want to know how she faked it. A lot of detail about her childhood. No mention of drama college, though. That *would* be too difficult to fake.

Next, her first big break: Stella in *A Streetcar Named Desire*. No! That can't be right! Surely the date is a typo. The year after I left college. Alison was still Alison then.

There's a link to the newspaper reviews. I click on it. The blasted Internet chooses this moment to hang. "Come on! Come on!" People are staring at me. Better keep my voice down.

The page loads. Several rave reviews. I scroll down, checking each for the date. There's no mistake. Teresa Lewis is Teresa Lewis. She's not Alison. I've been duped. I think of Millie's words when I remarked on the lack of the lip blemish on Teresa Lewis's photo: "Obviously, she's been well made up." The lip blemish was an add-on, skilfully done in makeup, to clinch any doubts I might have had on meeting the woman. In daylight I might not have been fooled but she'd taken care to have Johnson's living room dimly lit. I remember when I turned up the lights to read my play script, that she turned them down again, and how she turned them off altogether before we came close to say goodbye.

Should I return to the theatre? What's the point in continuing the charade? "Come back at eleven?". Another trap? I retrieve my bike and return to my boat. The conclusion is inescapable: if Peters needed to take the risk of hiring an actress to pretend to be Alison, then the real Alison no longer exists. A fisherman saw her calmly swimming out to sea towards Peters' boat. A faked suicide? Billy Brown's employee claimed he saw her on the boat subsequently. What happened next? Did she commit suicide later for real? Was there an accident? Was she deliberately killed? Whatever, we can dispense with fantastical stories of faked dental work or faked dental records. The body found on the beach matched Alison's because it *was* Alison's body.

I'm more able to accept the death of my friend than I would have expected. Perhaps I'm numb, in shock. Perhaps it's the relief of knowing for certain Alison did not betray me. Perhaps I'm in a mental daze because previously clear facts no longer fit. How come Teresa Lewis knew all those stories from my student time with Alison? Had Alison told them to Peters? Even if she had, that he could recall them in precise detail is highly unlikely. Was that the reason for his affair with Maureen in Kings Lynn, that he could pump her for information about the deceased Alison? What reason could he have had for doing so, twenty years before he contrives his elaborate plan for the murder of Jack Johnson?

Next morning, I wake before dawn. During the night, the temperature has plunged dramatically. I check the deck outside. My feet slip on ice. I'll need to spread salt. Best for the moment to buy a few packets of table salt from Mr Patel's corner shop. He's only just opening up when I get there. He brings out a sandwich board for the local newspaper. The headline: *Liverpool Actress Strangled In Theatre.*

# Chapter 43

# Frozen In

I take the newspaper to a transport café and order a cooked breakfast. I need to get some heat inside me while I study this latest development. They found Teresa Lewis collapsed on the stage of the theatre last night. She'd been strangled. It's assumed the killer gained access through an open side door, because the doorkeeper stated nobody had entered by the stage door between the time Teresa arrived and her body being discovered.

I am in no doubt of the killer's identity. Peters feared his actress accomplice would crack under pressure. He guessed my interview hoax and with great cunning contrived to turn Teresa Lewis's murder to his advantage by placing me at the scene of the crime. Had the doorkeeper not been distracted by the road accident, had I not chosen the wrong exit and left by a side door, I would have been identified as the man who had made an appointment to see the actress that evening. Can I be sure I left no trace in the theatre? What about fingerprints on the door handle of Teresa Lewis's dressing room? Because of the cold weather, I'd worn gloves. Did the other actor, the second wicked witch, see me in the shadows at the side of the stage? The newspaper report states Teresa was the only one to have arrived early. So, the second witch was Peters. That would explain the unattended side door. Teresa had opened it herself, for Peters to gain access unobserved. They must have planned it together. The same scheme as with Johnson. Send David Buckley away, inviting him to return later, straight into a police trap. I'm guessing on the first occasion Teresa Lewis was completely innocent of any knowledge she was an accomplice in setting up Johnson's death. Tragically, on the second, she had no idea she was setting up her own.

Three skillfully planned murders: Warby, Johnson, Teresa Lewis. What chance now of bringing Peters to justice? The one person whom I'd thought could shed light on this — Alison — does not exist. I could contact Jane Magee; tell her what happened in the theatre but that would only achieve what Peters had intended, placing me at the scene of the crime. I will go back to Gargrave, tie up for the winter, and from there walk the hills to the sanctuary of High Shaw. With Millie's assistance I may yet find an answer.

Dawn has broken by the time I get back to the canal. The surface has totally frozen over during the night. I'll sit out the weather until the canals are clear for navigation. I find a call box and telephone Millie, telling her of all that's happened and of my intention to come back to High Shaw. She tells me not to move; she will come to me soon, so we can take the boat back to Gargrave together.

# Chapter 44

## Missed Opportunity

Jane Magee regrets the day she watched and waited for Peters at the seedy hotel. Had she acted with more foresight, with less hesitation, she might have prevented Teresa Lewis's murder. Magee has to find Buckley. He's the only person who can bring closure to this affair. Where is he? Why hasn't he made contact? If Buckley suspects Teresa Lewis was the lure to frame him for a second murder, then he would not telephone from the Liverpool area. He'd want to get well away. It's been a fortnight now, a bitterly cold fortnight with sub-zero temperatures, but the transport network is up and running, the roads are moving. Buckley could have got himself anywhere in the country. Has the man no curiosity for the progress of her investigation into Peters?

PC Forster knocks on Magee's office door and enters with a bundle of reports. "Sorry I'm late. Bit of a family upset leaving the house. Our pet goldfish we keep in the garden pond has died. The kids found it this morning frozen solid in a block of ice."

# Chapter 45

**Showtime**

Temperatures have been rising rapidly. The ice sheet covering the canal has melted away. Millie should be here any day now.

I've been to the corner shop. As I unlock my cabin door, a familiar voice behind me says, "Hello, David."

I turn to see Jane Magee and PC Forster.

I say, "Come inside. It's chilly out here."

I lead them through to the lounge area of the boat and rekindle the fire in the stove.

"A lot more comfortable down below, isn't it?"

"Very cosy," replies Jane. "I've been here before, of course, but then you know that, don't you?"

"How did you find me?"

"You can thank PC Forster for that. Something he said drew my attention to the reason you hadn't left Liverpool. We didn't know which boat, so we had officers scout the canals. When I saw the name 'Millie' on the list, I remembered on my last visit the young lady pulling a curtain across a cabin space but not before I'd spotted a bundle of a man's clothes on the bed. When she lied to me about being on the boat alone, I assumed she was covering for a partner who'd been in trouble with the law. I let it be. We had bigger things on our mind at the time. When the name 'Millie' came up again, I thought the man might have been you. A plain-clothes officer walked past you yesterday. The baldness threw him momentarily but he said close up no doubt about the face. Where is the young lady, by the way?"

"She's gone home for the winter."

"You know she's facing a prison sentence for aiding and abetting?"

"What do I have to do to keep her out of it?"

Jane signals for Forster to handcuff me. "We'll talk about it. We have a lot to talk about."

I hold up my hand for Forster to wait. "Do you mind if I retrieve my wig? I'd like to be David Buckley again."

# PART 4

# LIVES

# Chapter 46

## Greg Warby

"My advice, Miss Lees, is to leave the money where it is. I see no advantage in transferring to a new scheme when you are getting such a high return. If something better comes up, of course I'll let you know."

Greg Warby smiles pleasantly at the old lady as he helps her from her seat and shows her to the door. His finely honed old-school manners have impressed many an elderly client. He's done well for them and they for him. Above all, they have felt him to be an honest man with whom they could trust their money. Fortunate, then, he'd been able to cover-up the recent disaster.

The truth is Greg Warby's neither fully honest nor fully trustworthy. Firstly, he's on commission from the investment companies. Not strictly legal, because the advice a solicitor gives is supposed to be impartial. Secondly, he's taken risks, which up till now have paid off, apart from that one foolish gamble. Spotting an opportunity to double his returns, he secretly moved all his clients' money into a speculative scheme, and lost the lot. Needing to rapidly recoup his losses or face the certainty of a prison sentence, he committed a further act of recklessness: he stole from a criminal gang and now it's payback time.

Certainly, the strain is affecting Warby's marriage. It pains him that to protect his wife from worry he's had to shift the blame on her, excusing his uncustomary lapses of temper as being caused by her inability to get pregnant. A pity. Until this recent situation, Greg and Alison Warby had enjoyed ten years of harmonious wedlock. Surprising really. If you'd seen the two of them at that first party, you'd have thought an unlikely pair. Dressed in her hippy clothes, Alison looked like a fish out of water, set against the local dignitaries and their overdressed wives. Warby attended in his best suit. He'd organised the reception himself, impressed by an article Alison had written for the local paper about her experience as a nurse treating victims of domestic abuse. He sent her a letter, offering to provide legal advice for free, should she be interested in setting up a victim support charity. Now he was meeting for the first time the woman he'd up till now only talked with on the phone. Her speech at the reception had been impressive, as had been his in securing donations. How natural they should celebrate by dining together at a restaurant. And how natural, after they discovered over dinner how much they had in common, that they should round off the evening with sex. Warby knew he'd found somebody special. He'd tired of all those respectable girls seeking the security of marrying into a family of solicitors. Alison didn't care for any of that. She liked him for his concern for the disadvantaged, and because he was good in bed.

Despite their intimacy, Alison never once saw Warby's bad side. However, there *were* people who saw it. Dodgy-ness recognises dodgy-ness, so when Warby was asked to represent the members of a criminal gang accused of a violent gold bullion robbery, they sensed at once here was a man with whom they could "cut a deal". Their proposal came at the best, or rather the worst time for Warby, at his most vulnerable due to his recent disastrous investment.

The gang slipped him a key to a lockup garage, and the phone number of a fence who could be trusted to pay cash for the gold. Fearing for his safety, Warby made a preliminary reconnaissance trip to the lock-up. He was relieved to find it openly situated in a residential street, and not, as he'd imagined, at the end of a dark alleyway. He'd taken along his kitchen scales to weigh the gold — a beginner's mistake since a typical gold bar, despite its small size, weighs at least two stone. Returning later with heavier-duty equipment, Warby verified the total weight corresponded to the gargantuan size of the haul reported in the newspapers. His concern now was that the fence might not be trustworthy. He put the question to him directly on the telephone. The man said, "I know who your clients are. You don't mess with people like that!"

They arranged the transaction with the gold exchanged for suitcases stuffed full of used bank notes — just like in a crime movie, Warby thought. However, the percentage he earned on the deal, although substantial, nowhere near could fix his money woes. Knowing the gang would be handed down long prison terms, Warby decided he could bide his time. With the men behind bars he could make hay with their stolen money any way he pleased. No need to worry about paying them back. He'd have fifteen to twenty years to recoup the "borrowed" cash. He might even make the criminals a profit.

Neither Warby nor the police knew of two gang members still at large. The men called at his office late one afternoon. Warby explained that for safety he'd laundered the money in a portfolio of fixed-term investments and they'd have to wait six months for it to become available.

One of the men, Douggie Horner, who'd driven the getaway van for the robbery, seemed satisfied. The other man, Mick Creeson, a skinny jittery character, pulled a knife, saying he hoped for Warby's sake this wasn't a double-cross. Horner had to calm him down with a story of how he'd once done a bank robbery where they similarly laundered the loot, the joke being they invested in shares of the bank they'd just robbed. Warby didn't tell the men a third of the money was missing, swallowed up fixing his recent catastrophic losses. Nor did he tell them the investment story was a ruse to buy time; he'd merely hidden the suitcases of cash in the attic of his home.

Six months have passed. The time of the appointment has arrived. Warby still has the cash, though only two thirds of the amount the criminals are expecting. He desperately needs an excuse for the missing third. To show any hint of weakness would be fatal; he must take charge, show strength. He'll say he's not in a position to give the criminals all the money; he'll continue his lie about having invested it, explaining that cashing in such large sums risked attracting attention and that he'll be giving the men as much as he dared draw down in one go, with the remainder coming to them in smaller, regular instalments. The cash that, unbeknown to the criminals, he has retained in his attic, he will use to finance the initial instalment payments, to prove his good faith. Meanwhile, he'll be making plans for he and Alison to abscond, by emigrating, or moving somewhere else in the country. Or a more practical option might be to betray Horner and Creeson to the police via an anonymous tip-off. With the whole gang serving time, Warby would make up the money through canny investment.

Warby feels enormous relief when Horner and Creeson accept the proposed arrangement but, when he asks them to wait at his office while he goes to fetch their money, matters go rapidly downhill. Creeson pulls a knife, suspecting Warby is about to spring a trap by calling in the law. At the sight of the knife, Warby panics, and in the ensuing struggle receives a fatal stab wound. The criminals flee empty-handed.

On the edge of losing consciousness, Warby desperately tries to phone for an ambulance, He manages to dial two digits of "999". The third digit is missing. Warby is dead.

# Chapter 47

## Alison Warby

The morning Alison Warby committed suicide, she checked the weather forecast on her mobile phone. Events had conspired against her. First, the shock of her husband's murder, then discovering he'd been mixed up with a criminal gang, those two men who'd accosted her in the street after the inquest, demanding she pay back an impossible sum of money. Alison should have gone to the police. Instead, she turned to Brian Peters.

The Sunrise project had been running eight years before Alison met Peters. Employed initially to consult on the psychological needs of the residents, he rapidly ingratiated himself as unpaid volunteer director. To disguise his real motive, he always communicated with the Warbys via Greg, to avoid any suspicion of being sweet on his wife. A chance encounter with Alison in town led to her accepting an offer to go out on the boat, and all that inevitably followed. Alison had missed the joy of casual sex, sex for the sheer fun of it. She hadn't conceived in her marriage, probably due to a medical condition. Now the reason would be that she secretly went on the pill. The arrangement suited them both: financially secure in their marriages to their respective spouses, with the bonus of illicit sex as the spice on top. Warby's murder put a sudden, brutal stop to all that.

Peters kept away from Alison until after the inquest. A wise decision. The two men who had been following her, waiting to threaten her, might have taken an unhealthy interest in his presence. He and Alison searched for the money together. They discovered the suitcases, resting across beams in her attic. They lugged them downstairs, closed the curtains, spread out the money on the living room carpet, counted and recounted it. They couldn't believe the size of the haul. Even so, the total fell substantially short of the demanded amount. Alison's immediate instinct was to go to the police to obtain justice for Greg. Peters frightened her off the idea, saying she risked becoming a revenge target, summarily disposed of, just as her husband had been. Unsure what to do, Alison phoned her friend, Samantha Massey. Samantha offered the use of her London flat as a place to hide from the gang. She also suggested Alison appeal for help to her old lover, Laurence Thompson. Many times, Alison tried to phone Thompson. Always the wife picked up the phone. In desperation, she posted off a letter, the contents disguised with one of the professor's secret code tricks. The letter went unanswered. With the criminals soon to call back for their money, Alison took the only way out.

# Chapter 48

## Teresa, the showgirl

To say Teresa Lewis's career was going nowhere would be putting it kindly. More accurate would be to say her career had gone. In her twenties, her résumé had stated she could act, sing and dance — what they call a "triple threat". Now, aged fifty, she wasn't a threat to anyone. All she could look back on, a single West End triumph, playing Stella in *A Streetcar Named Desire*. What else had she achieved? Dancing in musicals. And when the business deemed her too old, set against the younger dancers, opportunity dried up completely. Worse, on top of the lack of work, the lack of anywhere decent to live. Endless, seedy, rented flats. She dreamed of a place of her own, a place to grow old gracefully, a place she could decorate with mementos from *Streetcar*.

At least the web site brought in money. She started it as a conceit, like the walls of the flat of her dreams, a place to show off the few pictures and reviews from her one past glory. The photo-shoot changed everything. A fashion-house needed a model for a new line of lingerie for the mature woman. Against all her expectations, Teresa landed the contract. For a laugh, she put up one of the pictures on her web site. A flood of emails resulted, from men of course. One correspondent asked for a whole set. He said he'd willingly pay whatever price she asked. That gave Teresa the idea. Every month she'd buy sexy underwear. A friend would take the photos. They'd be announced on the web site and men would pay to download them. The lingerie didn't come cheap but the number of guys willing to pay a fiver a month more than compensated, comfortably supplementing her income, though falling far short of securing a mortgage on that dream flat.

Teresa felt confident of building her customer base. With her thick blonde hair, five-foot-six-inch height, full bust and shapely legs, frankly the underwear never looked better. Of course, you had to put up with the creeps, the men who made obscene suggestions. Like this latest one, who said he could give her an acting job. She'd heard that before. You go to a hotel room for "the interview" and end up propositioned, or worse. She ignored the private message placed through her web site. Less easy to ignore his second message. The man suggested they meet at any restaurant in London she cared to name. He didn't expect her to do it for free. He'd book the interview through her agent at the going rate for her time. Or, if she preferred, he could give her cash, tax-free, in a brown envelope. Teresa chose the brown envelope.

The occasion began disastrously, with a fire at a tube station disrupting the transport network. Teresa arrived an hour late, certain her opportunity would have gone. She found the man still waiting. He opened by saying that due to her lateness the agreed fee was now invalid. Just as Teresa had suspected, a cheat after all, but the man continued he would pay an extra hour for her perseverance. Teresa should have sensed it was all too easy, but she didn't. The respectability of the man, expensively though tastefully dressed, his confident, relaxed manner, his educated accent, told her she would be OK.

They took a table for lunch. When asked what they'd like to drink, the man ordered mineral water for them both, another point in his favour, not getting Teresa intoxicated. The conversation began on the subject of her CV. The man showed particular interest in her *Streetcar* performance. He asked how she had prepared for the role, in order, as the notices had put it, to "so convincingly get into character". He suggested she must be good at mimicking accents, that it couldn't have been easy for a London girl to play a woman from America's Deep South. Teresa found herself indulging in her past glory, talking more than she should. The man showed no boredom. On the contrary, his searching, detailed questions proved he was paying full attention.

Next, they talked about her modelling work. The man said she had the perfect figure and legs for what he had in mind. Teresa's heart sank. He's going to ask to see me naked, she thought, but he changed the subject again. From a briefcase he produced a CD and a script. He said he'd like Teresa to listen to the CD at home. He apologised for the sound quality, taken from an old family reel-to-reel tape recorder. She would hear two female voices on the recording, one a young woman in her twenties, the other her mother, in her forties. He wanted Teresa to play the role of the younger woman but thirty years on. The mother's voice should help assess how the younger voice would age. She needed this right, because, in the script, her character was in conversation with a male friend, someone she hadn't seen for thirty years, reminiscing about shared events in their lives.

The man said he noticed on her CV Teresa had been a dancer. He apologised that the script obliged her to do some erotic dancing and hoped she wouldn't think she was being asked to do anything too obscene. When Teresa asked at what theatre the show was to be put on, the man said he'd explain all that when he was sure she was right for the part. He said he'd contact her again with the details of time and place for the audition.

Teresa found nothing in the material to give cause for concern, though she doubted the dialogue would be sufficiently engaging for an audience. The guy playing "David" would have to be a top-quality actor to keep his reactions interesting against essentially a monologue on her part. When the call came, she was pleased to find the audition held at a well-known acting studio instead of the proverbial hotel room, though disconcerted to find only the man waiting for her, not the usual crowd from the production team who would normally assess you for a role.

The audition went well. The man expressed approval of her performance, especially her mimic of the young woman's sexy laugh. He asked would she mind him making a recording on his mobile phone so he could play it to a colleague. The repeat performance done, the man questioned Teresa about her skill in makeup. He produced a photograph of a young woman's mouth with a slight skin blemish above the upper lip. Could she do this so that close up, in low room light, it would look real? The strange request, made even more bizarre by the cold, medical nature of the photograph, should have been another red flag but Teresa continued to be sucked in by the novelty of having her talents genuinely appreciated.

The man said he'd like to meet her the following week at the restaurant they had met previously. He specified her clothes, an out of fashion hair style and to come made up with the lip blemish. Still suspecting the man to be a creep after all, Teresa asked if he had any special requirements for her underwear. The man laughed. He had already seen her in her underwear on the web site but, save for a brief erotic dance, it wasn't that kind of role.

Teresa arrived for the interview all fired-up to know the details of the production. Once again in her life, she experienced deep disappointment. The man told her he represented a national newspaper planning a sting operation to publicly humiliate a political rival. The performance venue was to be a cottage in the north east of England. As Teresa had already seen in the script, she played the character of a politician's wife. The man said he himself would be playing the role of Mister Clown. He admitted to being a ham actor but said that didn't matter as the character was supposed to be bad at acting. The only problem was that, as the "David" of the script was the victim of the sting, they had no way of knowing how he'd react, so Teresa would have to be ready to improvise to cover the unexpected.

The money offered was enormous, enough for a deposit on a mortgage on her dream flat. Teresa reluctantly declined, saying what she was being asked to do was against her conscience, against the ethics of her profession. The man showed his disappointment but accepted her refusal with good grace, saying he would call her in a few days, in case she changed her mind. Bad timing for Teresa that she should see an advertisement in *The Stage* for a Liverpool theatre company seeking an older actress for a permanent position. At the audition they gave her the job on the spot. She would need decent accommodation in her newly adopted city. On the high of success, she threw caution to the wind. When the man called her back, she accepted his offer of the money.

Teresa worked hard. The Alison role required her to memorise a great number of anecdotes in order to maintain a convincing ad-lib conversation with "David" for three hours. Simultaneously, the upcoming winter pantomime season in Liverpool involved learning lines for several roles. She would catch the early morning cross-Pennine train, to rehearse as Alison in the north-east of England, dashing back to the railway to get back to Liverpool in time for afternoon panto rehearsals.

The man had given Teresa an unregistered mobile phone. She was to use it to call Buckley at his newspaper on a specified date and secure his agreement to visit the cottage that evening. When the day arrived, it seemed the whole venture would have to be abandoned, due to the victim being out of his office, but at two o'clock her call was put through. Confident Buckley had fallen for her Alison impersonation, Teresa secretly congratulated herself on a clever ad-lib which she added for realism, when she gave her character's married name "by mistake", then hurriedly corrected it to the maiden name. With the sting now live, she left Liverpool later than she had intended. A further delay, due to a breakdown of the train, threw the project into doubt a second time, and she arrived at Johnson's cottage with less than an hour to spare.

The man had brought with him a large wooden crate containing props, including a ferret ornament, a gun in a plastic bag, and a coffee tray with two mugs. He removed the TV from the corner table and replaced it with the ferret, explaining the animal contained a video spy camera which would capture everything. The two of them discussed the lighting. Teresa expressed concern that in bright light the made-up blemish on her lip might be too obvious a fake. She moved round the room, studying her face in a hand mirror, while the man adjusted the wall lighting dimmer switches until they had agreed the optimum level of illumination.

Next, Teresa went upstairs to the bedroom to change into her Alison clothes. When she came back downstairs, she found the ground floor in darkness. A silhouette at the front door gave her a massive fright. The man was placing the gnome ornament outside. They adjourned to the study for a final rehearsal of Mister Clown, before Teresa returned to the living room to await the arrival of Buckley. Entering the room in darkness she felt a sharp jab of pain as she collided with and noisily knocked over a heavy wooden stool. Without thinking, she called out "Shit and Blast!" A few seconds later, someone rang the doorbell. Teresa froze, unsure what to do. Buckley wasn't expected for another thirty minutes. The bell rang again. Teresa tiptoed to the window. Buckley had arrived early. Like the first night of a play, where everything that can go wrong does go wrong, Teresa fumbled to find the light switches.

Lucky for her, Buckley seemed oblivious to her unfamiliarity with what was supposed to be her own home, and, from then on, as she settled into her performance, everything went to plan. Even the two unexpected incoming phone calls, she took in her stride, flawlessly improvising a credible excuse not to answer though, after the second such call, she decided it would be safer to take the phone off the hook.

The climax of the show for Teresa had to be the lap dance. She loved dancing, loved revealing her body. She knew Buckley would be savouring her every move. Pity the exhibition had to be so rudely interrupted by Mister Clown.

Now there remained only the invitation for Buckley to return for sex. Teresa took the precaution of opening the door and switching off the room lights before coming close to hug him. She remembered the man's advice not to overdo the seduction. "Make your appeal sexy in a subtle way," he said. "If you haven't hooked him with the scantily clothed dance, nothing you say will bring him back; and if you *have* hooked him, he might get suspicious if you overact your desire."

As soon as Buckley had departed, Teresa changed out of her costume, while the man, still dressed as a clown, packed away the props. He told her that when David returned in the expectation of making love to Alison, he'd find a camera crew lying in wait to confront him with a humiliating playback of the evening's events, the culmination of the newspaper sting.

Teresa left by the back door. At the railway, she found to her annoyance the train to Liverpool had been cancelled due to the broken-down engine car that delayed her arrival. The next to leave wouldn't be until half ten, so she went to the station buffet to escape the cold of the platform. At ten o'clock, she was horrified to see Buckley coming in the buffet door. He'd focussed his attention on an Internet terminal, so she slipped past him unnoticed. Although Teresa had rearranged her hairstyle, removed the lip blemish makeup, and changed from skirt and top to trouser suit and winter coat, she felt sure Buckley would have recognised her, had he seen her.

Next morning, Teresa received an early call. The man told her the sting had gone catastrophically wrong. Buckley had murdered Johnson. The newspaper were keeping silent, should they incriminate themselves, and they warned Teresa to do the same, or she might find herself prosecuted for conspiracy. The man advised her to stay out of the affair and enjoy the rest of her life. Teresa took his advice. Life can be cruel. She would have little left to enjoy.

## Chapter 49

## Brian Peters

One thing you could say in Brian Peters' favour. No way was he a snob. The educated accent and debonair manner disguised a working-class upbringing on a council estate in Dagenham, his father a factory hand, his mother a cleaner. An only child, Peters respected his parents for their graft and sacrifice putting him through college. At Oxford, and later at medical school, he felt intense irritation any time a student from a privileged background demonstrated a patronising attitude to "the poor", an irritation he felt towards his wife's family, prominent London financiers, but then he had married her for her money, so he only had himself to blame.

Peters' marriage was one of convenience on both sides. He got the trappings of wealth; she got the trophy husband. Her daily commute to London to the offices of the family firm cleared the way for him to seduce nurses on his boat. Even better when Alison came along and he got to enjoy the kind of sex no other woman could supply. Now all that was on a knife edge. One of his jilted nurses, the little cow, had snitched to his wife. Whatever the final terms of the divorce, he anticipated being reduced to a state of poverty, and under no circumstance would Peters accept a return to being poor.

Greg Warby's death changed the rules of the game. Nervous of his affair with Alison coming out, Peters worried he might be accused of murder. The subsequent revelation of the criminal gang made the situation worse, not better. With a substantial part of the stolen money unaccounted for, Peters' life would come under threat as much as Alison's. Disappearance seemed the only viable option — separately and by different means. The fortune found in the attic would provide for him to continue to live in the style to which he had long been accustomed: smart clothes, posh restaurants, expensive cars, the best hotels — assuming Alison would agree to share it, and why shouldn't she, once they had married after a safe interval of time had elapsed?

Harder for Alison, the idea of abandoning her beautiful spacious home. However, convinced by Peters of the threat to them both, she set about organising her own demise. On his side, he scoured the employment opportunity columns of medical periodicals. After his divorce, he aimed to disappear into a new life far from Kings Lynn.

In preparation for the suicide, Peters relocated his boat from Brown's boatyard to a private mooring on the river. On the day, he set off before dawn, sailing along the coast to anchor a few hundred yards off Hunstanton. A night fishing boat briefly chugged past, but the sea and the beach were otherwise deserted, the water exceptionally calm. He could hear only the gentle lapping of light waves against the boat. Then, the lapping appeared to be increasing in intensity. Gazing towards the beach, he could just make out the breaking of the water as a dark shape approached.

At that moment, the devil took hold of him. "Why this elaborate charade? Why not kill the woman and keep the money for yourself? With Alison alive, you face the constant threat of encounter with the criminals. But, with

Alison dead, her body washed ashore, a presumed suicide, you, as her unknown partner, will be safe and rich — doubly rich, in fact. Yes, the sex is great but you'll have no problem finding another Alison with all that new-found wealth to underwrite your seductions."

The boat oscillated in the water as Alison, panting sumptuously from her exertions, pulled herself up on deck. He'd seen her like this many times before, though for a different reason. He thought it a pity to have to kill her. He asked, "Did it all go to plan?"

Alison entered the cabin to dry herself with a towel. "I parked on the promenade. Not a soul around. I left my handbag and clothes on the beach between the pub and the boatyard. Somebody should find them."

Peters followed her into the cabin. Closing the door behind him, he said, "Welcome to your death!"

**Chapter 50**

**Tozzy's Lucky Day**

Tozzy's mother shouts up the stairs of their council house home, "Tommy!"

Tozzy shouts back, "What?"

"You've got a visitor! Not the law this time."

"Send him up!"

"It's a young lady. Tidy your room!"

Tozzy makes a feeble effort to get his room respectable, sweeping the tangle of surveillance equipment from his bedside table into a carrier bag. He's never had a female visitor before. Must be a new probation officer or that plain skinny bit of legal aid he'd been landed with after his arrest for assault at the Making Sense march.

The woman who enters his bedroom is best described from Tozzy's point of view as full-frontal cleavage.

"Tozzy, my name's Millie. You helped my boyfriend escape the police … at the march."

"Oh, yeah," says Tozzy. "He's all right, is he?"

"Not really. He's back in the cells. We need you to help us. I'll pay you for it."

"How much?"

"That depends on how long it takes. You'll have to come and live at my place till the job's done. Can I sit down while I explain?"

Millie sits on the bed. Tozzy's aiming his gaze down her top. She specially chose it this morning for its lack of cover. She knows he's already in big trouble over the Scunthorpe incident and it will take all her charms to persuade him to do what she needs him to do.

# PART 5

# PURSUIT

# Chapter 51

## Stolen

The desperate loneliness of my renewed incarceration would have been unbearable, were it not for the kindness of PC Forster. My recapture being early Saturday, he said he didn't expect anything to happen over the weekend and asked would I like some reading material, such as newspapers or magazines? I replied that if any of the charity shops in town sold paperbacks, could he get me a novel or two by Laurence Thompson? Forster asked what kind of books Thompson wrote. He laughed out loud when I replied, "Detective stories." Later, he returned in triumph with a box of ten. I felt acute embarrassment at not having the money to pay him but he said to forget it.

I took out the books and arranged them in order of publication date. Difficult to decide which to read first. Thompson enjoyed moderate success with his early novels. Not until the fifth did he find the winning formula: crime thrillers built around his headstrong central detective character, Jane Weatherall. I'll have to ask my Jane whether she's read any and what she thinks of the antics of her namesake. I decided to start with the most recent of the collection, *Vanished*, published the year of Alison's death. The storyline engrossed me from the outset and I was grateful to be absorbed in its world. However, come next morning, I'd lost interest in further reading. I lay back in my bunk, my mind wandering randomly over all that happened during my months of freedom.

I remembered my visit to Thompson's home, being given Alison's letter, and a long evening down in my cabin, studying the numbers in an attempt to break the code. Thompson's wife told me a colleague in the maths department had been unable to break it, so what chance I? For that matter, what chance Thompson could invent such a code? It could not have been mathematical; all his games would have been literary in nature.

There's a Sherlock Holmes story where the famous detective and Dr Watson try to decipher a numerically coded message. They decide the numbers refer to words in a book having its pages organised into columns. Watson suggests *The Bible*; Holmes says not; there are too many differing editions; the book has to be standardised. They settle on a popular Victorian almanac, which turns out to be the correct solution.

Could I apply similar reasoning? Unlikely Alison continued her affair with the professor, owing to the distance separating their respective homes. Therefore, they may not have met for many years. If the code in the letter referred to a book, how would they know whether the other possessed the book in question? It had to be not only an obvious choice but one which they could both separately get hold of, a recent edition at the time. Perhaps the professor's latest novel, the one published closest to the time of Alison's suicide, the one I had just read, in fact?

I could remember the first three numbers in Alison's letter: (21,116)  (35,117) (150,106), probably because I stared at them so long, trying to figure them out. Obviously, the number before the comma was the page number, the number after the comma the word to be counted to on the page. I picked up the novel to test my theory. Page 21, 116th word: "Omelette". Not a good start. Page 35, 117th word: "Club". Final word: "Help" "Omelette Club Help". Disappointing. Wrong idea. Or wrong book.

One thing I did remember from studying the numbers previously: they all began with a 1, 2 or 3. That partly made sense; detective novels average at three hundred or so pages, so I wouldn't expect to see numbers like 500,001, meaning the first word on page 500, because there wouldn't be a page 500. On the other hand, why no numbers like 63,008, meaning the eighth word on page sixty-three, or 40,012, meaning the twelfth word on page forty? Was it just coincidence the code apparently excluded pages forty to ninety-nine?

Had I not been obliged to sweat out the whole day, with nothing other to do than read yet more novels, I might have given up on the puzzle. As it was, I kept going. The exclusion of pages forty to ninety-nine had to be some kind of trick, an obfuscation designed to disguise the otherwise obvious pairing of page number with word number. Suppose the exclusion were *any* of the first one hundred pages? How would the first two numbers that I remembered (21,116 and 35,117) fit in?

Then, I saw it. The comma was the code's dirty tricks department, intended to throw the reader off the scent. This was a literary code. The person who devised it was no mathematical genius. They did, however, understand punctuation. By moving the comma one digit to the right, the first number becomes 211,16. We get page 211, which is an allowed page number. The 16th word: "Urgent".

Move the comma similarly on the next number. We get page 351, 17th word: "Need". The third number was already for a page number above one hundred, so I could assume correct the previously found word, "Help". The opening of the message then became "Urgent need help." I'd cracked the code. I resolved to request my defence team to retrieve the letter from my possessions, in the hope it would reveal information supporting my case.

#

Monday morning. They've taken me up from the cells to the familiar interview room. They tell me my arrest briefly made front-page news, though no doubt it'll be forgotten about until the resumption of the trial. It's a sobering thought that after my inevitable extinction I can expect to be forgotten about completely, outside of my work colleagues and those few whose lives I have recently touched: Millie and Jane especially.

Jane enters the room accompanied by a young policeman. The recording machine started, she states the time and date, then requests her colleague wait outside. As soon as he has closed the door, she pauses the recording.

"David, I have to warn you not to say anything against Brian Peters, neither in recorded interviews, nor to your solicitor, nor to any visitors you might have. You're booked for three sessions with Brian, to assess your mental health. I couldn't get him off the case without attracting his suspicion. However, I've insisted 'for his own safety' that two officers will be present in the interview room at all times. Their presence will deny him the chance of talking with you off the record. Make no accusations

234

against him. Most importantly, give no indication you've made the discoveries you have passed on to me. We must keep hidden what you and I know of his activities in Norfolk, which, incidentally, I can now confirm."

"Does this mean you believe my story?"

"I'm saying the situation with Brian Peters is at a delicate stage. Any carelessness might provoke a catastrophe."

I'm tempted to point out a catastrophe has already occurred, namely Teresa Lewis. However, no way can I admit to knowledge that would implicate me in a second murder.

Jane releases the pause button on the recording device. She asks, "Why Liverpool?"

"The weather forecast. I came down to sea level, hoping to avoid being frozen in. Moored on the outskirts of the city, the canal froze overnight and trapped me."

"Where were you headed?"

"Shouldn't I be speaking with my solicitor?"

"Of course. We'll postpone the interview." Jane switches off the recording machine.

I stand, ready to be taken back to the cells. There's a knock at the door. Forster enters. He hands Jane a document and mumbles something in a low voice. I catch the word "stolen".

Jane says, "Sit down a moment, will you. Mr Buckley, while I read this fax from my colleagues in Liverpool. It looks like your boat has disappeared."

I feign surprise but of course I know this has to be Millie's doing. I assume she came with her set of keys. Lucky I insisted she held on to them when we parted at

Gargrave. What will she do with the boat? I hope she will clear out any evidence incriminating herself. She may also try to disguise any connection to my aunt's cottage, a futile aim, because they only need examine the official canal boat registry to identify the boat's owner as being one John Edwards, residing in Lancashire. At least, I can take comfort Millie will rescue my money and my private documents from the special waterproof compartment I built deep down in the depths of the hold.

Jane breaks into my thoughts. "Mr Buckley, I would have bet on the young lady being the cause of this but a man was seen starting up the engine. However, the witness wasn't a hundred percent sure of the identity of the boat in question, so let's hope, for your sake and ours, he was mistaken and this isn't the work of a thief or vandals."

Back in my cell, I feel little concern. What use is the boat to me now? I'm happy for Millie if its disappearance into the hands of a third party will ensure her identity remains undiscovered. Then, I remember. Alison's coded letter is on board: my one hope of salvation.

## Chapter 52

## Turning The Tables

The first psychoanalysis sessions with Peters have been strained to say the least, both of us knowing the other to be in possession of many compromising secrets. Two police constables dutifully kept guard in the room for the duration, as Jane had promised, thus preventing any conversation off-the-record. Peters asked several leading questions about my summer activities but I wasn't to be drawn. His manner was edgy, impatient, far from the confident relaxed medical specialist of our first meeting. It's clear I have him seriously rattled.

How much does Peters know? He will know of my visit to Alison's friend, Maureen, but almost certainly he has no knowledge of the stolen postcard leading me to Kings Lynn. Had Maureen discovered its absence and reported the loss to Peters, I would have been intercepted in that town, and all my plans would have come to nothing. Furthermore, I'm confident he has no idea I have built up an intimate picture of his love life, nor of the methodology of the fake suicide, nor that I have strong grounds for suspecting him of Warby's murder. As for Teresa Lewis, Peters didn't know his liaisons were under Tozzy's resourceful surveillance. How I homed in on her so precisely must be for him a complete mystery and, of course, a serious threat to the integrity of his scheme, one which caused him to take desperate measures to silence his accomplice. Yes, he's rattled. What will it take to break him?

My third session has been delayed, rescheduled for this afternoon. No surprise arriving at the interview room to find only Peters, a female police constable on guard outside. Obviously, he has re-engineered the situation; I guess Jane Magee is out of the building, unaware of this change in the arrangements. No surprise either that Peters leaves the recording device switched off.

"Sit down, Mr Buckley. I'd like, if I may, to take a fresh approach. Shall we talk about Alison?"

I sit facing Peters. "Alison's dead!"

"That's what the police say. I won't insult your intelligence by pretending the Alison you thought you saw at Johnson's cottage was the real Alison but let's suppose Alison is in fact alive."

"The evidence suggests not."

"Suppose the evidence is flawed?"

"Then it should be easy for you to prove she's alive."

Peters laughs. "For me? Did I say I knew where she was, knew whether she's still alive?"

"So, we're playing a cruel psychological game, like the game played at Johnson's cottage?"

Peters stands and paces the room in lecturer mode. "Let's look at it this way. Let's imagine what *might* have happened. Assumption number one: Alison was in serious trouble. She resolved to fake suicide as a means of escape. The fake is skilfully executed. She gets away with it. Then what? Assumption number two: Alison needs a new identity to begin a new life. Changing your identity isn't easy. You need documents; you need expertise. Assumption number three: Suppose Alison has a friend, a professional person whose job gives him unique access to records, access to a knowledge base of state-of-the-art forgery techniques. This friend supplies the ID. Alison becomes, let's say, 'Samantha'. Samantha gets work; she gets training and promotion in her new career. Eventually she might re-marry, have children even."

I say, "And when Alison is used as the unwitting partner to a murder plot, she can't come forward to expose the conspiracy without also exposing her own crime."

Peters slaps his hand on the table. "Precisely! Now we're thinking on the right lines!"

I ask, "How does this help? You implied just now you don't know where Alison is."

"The person who helped her change her identity knows her new name, knows where she went to live, knows what her first job was. With that information, it surely can't be difficult to trace her."

Where is this leading? What's in it for Peters, and, more importantly, what's in it for me? I ask, "And when she's found? Then what? I'm in no position to go to her, or for her to come to me."

Peters picks up his briefcase. He draws out a bound document. "Some light reading. An American medical paper. You should find it interesting." He fastens the briefcase and leaves the room.

I read Peters' document, a re-print from a journal, describing the rehabilitation of prisoners convicted of crimes committed while they were deemed to be insane. No specific mention is made of murder but the implication is clear. Peters wishes me to change my plea, on the promise of an eventual release and meeting with Alison. He's probably bluffing about needing to find out where she is now; he may already know where she is. Or did Alison herself suggest the plea bargain? Should I stick to "not guilty", new facts could be brought out at the trial prejudicial to herself, as well as to Peters.

All this on the assumption of Alison being alive; of having successfully faked suicide. With Maureen's assistance, yes, Alison's dental records could have been altered to match the corpse washed ashore, and I don't doubt Peters could have wormed his way into the morgue to examine the body. What seems way too convenient is, first that a body should appear at just the right time, second that it should precisely match Alison's physique, third that it should be so decomposed as to oblige identification through dental records, fourth that it should just happen to exhibit dental work ideal for providing conclusive identification. How much simpler to explain the washing ashore of the body if it *was* Alison's body.

On the other hand, suppose Alison *is* alive. If she conspired with Johnson's killers, there's no way I can expect to meet her. Alternatively, if she was an unwitting accomplice to Johnson's murder, then it still leaves unexplained how Peters got possession of my stage-play script and trained his actress so convincingly in all those many student anecdotes, material Alison could have only provided voluntarily.

On balance, Alison is either dead, or unwilling to reveal her true identity. So there's little point putting faith in Peters. Fortunately, I don't have to make that call. He doesn't know it, but I have Jane Magee on my side. I have every faith in her thoroughness to know she will leave no stone unturned in her investigation of his early

240

professional life in Norfolk and of his subsequent dealings with Jack Johnson. My only worry is that weeks have gone by and she's given no indication she's close to bringing charges. In fact, I've not seen Jane Magee since that brief interview shortly after my arrest. The clock is ticking. Tomorrow I am to be taken to court for a preliminary hearing, recommitting me for trial.

# Chapter 53

## Millie's Story

Millie lies next to me on the bed. I listen to the beeps as she dials High Shaw on her mobile. "Hello…We're back on the boat... No, not yet... I'll ring when I know."

Feels like I'm dreaming, but I'm not. I'm on the run — for a second time.

A police van took me to court three days ago for a hearing prior to the recommencement of my trial. The van returned empty-handed.

The story is best told from Millie's point of view, starting from the time of my capture. As promised, she arrived in Liverpool to help take the boat back north. Coincidentally, she had chosen the day of my arrest to travel down from High Shaw commune. Arriving late in the afternoon, just as darkness set in, she found the boat locked up.  After reviving the stove and checking the food stocks, she sat at our cabin table, reading the entries in my logbook. She smiled when she saw the last entry, made early that morning, reporting the melting of the ice and noting my looking forward to having Millie back. Still not suspecting anything amiss, she went off to the local shop to buy supplies. There she saw the late edition newspaper headlines announcing my recapture.

What to do next might have fazed anyone else, but not Millie. She determined to spirit away the boat immediately, to deny the police its confiscation. However, with a maximum velocity of four miles per hour, whichever way she went, the police would have only a limited length of waterway to search before they found her. The boat would need its external appearance changed, and fast, to be no longer recognisable. If she could book it in at a boatyard for a paint job, that would give the additional advantage of taking it off the canal network and out of view of searchers. She phoned Richi and Geraldo in Ely to ask if they knew of a yard close to Liverpool. They suggested a place thirty miles to the east and promised to fix things up for her for Monday morning.

Thirty miles might not sound far but it's equivalent to an eight-hour journey by canal. Millie knew she'd have to travel through darkness, with the aim of berthing at the boatyard before police discovered the absence. She went up on deck, cast off and turned the ignition key, the growl of the engine shattering the quietness of the night. Millie told me she shook like a leaf through fear of discovery. Fortunately, grossly underestimating my accomplice, the police had put no priority on watching the boat, and Millie started her journey unhindered.

A cloudless sky lit by a full moon gave her full visibility of the water ahead but a bitterly cold wind had set in, decidedly colder than the time we crossed the Pennines together. Her journey was taking her back, lock by lock, towards those same hills, to higher, colder elevations. In several stretches, the canal had not yet thawed. The prow pierced the thin sheet of covering ice like an icebreaker, with a terrible rending and crunching sound. At two in the morning, halfway into the journey, Millie encountered a seemingly insuperable obstacle, a lock water paddle frozen solid, preventing transit through to the next water level. Despite the force she applied to the windlass, the mechanism wouldn't budge. Exhausted and chilled, she went down to our cabin and lay on the bed in tears. But Millie is not one to be easily beaten. She searched the toolbox, hoping for a wrench or some other gadget to lever open the stuck mechanism. Instead, she found a blowtorch, with which she managed to heat the metalwork sufficient to unfreeze it. She told me the blowtorch had one final, regrettable task to perform. Having reached the boatyard in safety and tied up in their pond, she prepared to remove the compromising name and logo from the hull. She took a photo on her mobile phone for remembrance, applied the torch and burnt both her name and her likeness back to bare metal.

Millie had agreed with Richi and Geraldo they would drive up to meet her on the Sunday. She booked a room for them overnight at the local inn. There, in the evening, she explained the whole business: that I was a fugitive, that Peters and Alison had framed me for murder, that I had made discoveries which could prove my innocence, that I had been recaptured and that she had stolen the narrowboat to keep it out of police hands. She did not expect the boys to betray her but she did have concerns they might refuse to help. In fact, the opposite occurred. They suggested Millie use the registration details of a 57-footer owned by their boatyard, to disguise all association with its past. Mine would be repainted as "Wanderer", the name of the narrowboat it would now be impersonating. The boys offered to stay to supervise the repainting. Once ready, they could pilot it to a prescribed rendezvous. Millie said she would like it taken to Keadby, the nearest location by canal to Scunthorpe, her aim being to track down Tozzy. With his criminal past, she hoped he might know some way in which I could be sprung from custody, a faint hope, but the only hope she had.

A few weeks later, Millie brought Tozzy to the boat, which had arrived without incident at the Keadby mooring. A bed cubicle had been cleared to accommodate him, with Richi sleeping in the other cubicle, Geraldo making a bed in the lounge and Millie back in our cabin at the stern. The first evening, a conversation ensued on the subject of my rescue. Millie had read in the papers of my upcoming pre-trial hearing and asked Tozzy if he knew the courthouse and whether it was a high-security affair.

"Nah. The building's old," replied Tozzy. "All they do is lock you in a room till it's your turn."

Richi asked, "What sort of door is it? Could you force the lock?"

"No chance!" said Tozzy. "There's always two coppers outside, waiting to take you to the courtroom."

Geraldo, the practical one of the two brothers, handed Tozzy a piece of paper and a biro. "Draw a plan; where the room is; the corridor layout; where the stairs are."

Tozzy roughed out a sketch, the speed of execution suggesting he'd had more than one encounter with the place. Jim asked him to draw in the room's windows. Tozzy replied that it didn't have any— only a skylight. Richi asked if the skylight was alarmed. Tozzy said it didn't need to be, because, if you smashed the glass, the gap would be too narrow. He'd thought of getting out that way himself and decided it was hopeless. "And the door's solid wood. You couldn't punch your way through."

Geraldo said, "Pity about the skylight, then. You could be up and away and nobody would be any the wiser."

Tozzy said, "You could get through the skylight if you had outside help."

"Didn't you say it was too narrow?" asked Millie.

"The glass is, but there's a loophole," replied Tozzy. "If the frame was pushed out, then someone thin, like me or your boyfriend, could squeeze through, I reckon."

Richi said, "The problem is the window frame will be set solid. You couldn't be up on the roof hammering away. It would take an age. And you'd still have the problem of the loosened frame falling into the room with a great crash."

Geraldo asked Millie for a pair of scissors and one of the galley's cardboard storage boxes. He said he needed a stapler as well. He proceeded to cut out a rectangle from the base of the box. "This rectangle represents our window frame," he said. "See how it fits in the hole I've cut out, same as the way the window frame fits into a hole in the roof. Now, we don't know what holds the real frame in place. There might be an overlap; cement might be used; it doesn't matter. All we know is we want to loosen the frame so it can be lifted out quickly but not have it so loose that it's in danger of crashing down into the room, as Richi was saying."

Next, Geraldo cut out two long strips of cardboard from the box and stapled them along the edges of the previously cut out rectangle. "What I'm suggesting is we get up on the roof and screw to each side of the window frame two long wooden battens, similar to the way I've stapled on these cardboard strips. Then we can loosen the frame well in advance, knowing our battens will overlap the roof tiles and prevent it falling inwards. Also, the battens will make it easy for two of us to lift the frame straight out on the day of the escape."

Millie asked, "How much time would you need?"

"At least three hours to loosen the frame. We'd have to go up on the roof in the dead of night."

"What happens if it rains after you've loosened it? Won't water drip through into the room?"

"We'll use silicone sealant to fill the gaps. And we can fit an overlapping clear plastic sheet, which will deflect most of the water if there's a downpour."

Richi said, "Sounds brilliant to me. How high is the ceiling, Tozzy?"

Tozzy replied, "About twice my height. Could be more."

"Then we'll need a rope ladder and we'll need some grab-irons on the roof, to take John's weight."

Millie said, "I worry we'll be unlucky and they'll come into the room for him just as he's climbing up the ladder, or there won't be sufficient time to get away before they unlock the door and find the room empty. The other thing I'm worried about is how we get him away? If we use a car, we might be caught by the number plate appearing on CCTV; on foot is too slow, public transport too risky."

Nobody speaks. "I suggest you sleep on it, Millie," said Geraldo. "I'm sure you'll think of something."

Unbeknown to myself, in the week of the court hearing, Geraldo and Richi were only streets away, staying at a travel lodge, while they attended "Beginners French" at a language school in town. Millie had booked them on the course as cover for less wholesome activities. Late one night, they left their room, taking with them two long pieces of wood and a large tool-bag containing a rope ladder and an assortment of DIY items, including hammer, chisels and battery-powered drill. In an alleyway at the side of the courthouse, they shinned up a drainpipe onto a ledge. From there, they scaled a number of balconies and parapets until they had found the way to the skylight. Easy drilling and screwing the support battens to the window frame but it required three careful hours of tile removal and patient chiselling to loosen the frame sufficiently that it could be lifted out. Richi volunteered to test the ladder. He experienced no difficulty squeezing through the hole they had made, nor climbing down into the room. When he turned on the lights, he saw a quantity of dislodged ceiling plaster all over the floor. He stuffed the lumps of debris into his pockets and brushed away the scattering of fine dust before hauling himself back up the ladder. The two men carefully replaced the skylight with its supporting battens, applied sealant to fill in the gaps, and rolled out and tacked onto the battens a sheet of transparent plastic to further guard against rain. Returning to their hotel they woke Millie with a phone call to report success.

Millie figured getting out of town without being identified would be tricky. The police would examine CCTV footage in the hope of capturing David Buckley on foot or by the registration numbers of the cars driving through town. It seemed far safer for David Buckley not to leave town at all. The dissimilarity in height between Geraldo and his brother and the fact of the taller Geraldo being my height, plus my residual summer gardening tan being a similar shade to Geraldo's half-Spanish skin tone, gave her an idea. On the morning of the court hearing, Geraldo and Richi would leave the hotel together for their final French class. Geraldo would give Richi his overcoat and hat and proceed to the course alone, explaining that his brother was "unwell". As soon as I had been rescued, Richi would give me Geraldo's hat and coat to wear and we two "brothers" would return to the hotel to lie low for a few days before simply checking out and driving off in Richi's car. Geraldo, on the other hand, having concluded the French class, would catch a train, to await our return to the boat at Keadby.

Millie and Tozzy would arrive by bus and take separate routes through town to rendezvous with Richi close to the courthouse. Richi had previously scouted the area to identify a rendezvous point not covered by CCTV. Millie planned that any video footage should only show them individually moving through town; it should not give any clue of a team of people involved in the escape. Millie herself, suspecting that she had already been identified as my accomplice by Jane Magee, wore a wig and dressed in such a way as to flatten down her ample bosom.

For Richi and Tozzy's climb of the courthouse roof, Millie reckoned blatant exposure to be the better plan. She gave them each an orange visibility vest to wear, to look like legitimate construction workers on a repair job. They duly scaled the building and positioned themselves behind the parapet, ready to lift out the skylight.

Millie hoped the court hearing would proceed ponderously but she could make no assumption as to how long I would be locked in the waiting room. It would be essential to put the escape plan into action as soon as I arrived. She waited at the courthouse side entrance for the police van to pull up and watched as they hurriedly escorted me inside, running the gauntlet of newspaper photographers. She then made a call on her mobile.

Tozzy had obtained the help of his best mate and his mate's girlfriend. On Millie's call, the couple proceeded to the end of the corridor of my confinement. There they saw two police officers standing guard outside the room door, just as Tozzy had predicted. Tozzy's mate rang Richi's mobile to give the OK for lifting out the skylight. At the same time, he and his girlfriend launched into an argument that rapidly turned to a vicious fight, with a lot of screaming and scratching on the part of the girl. I heard the commotion in the corridor and hardly had time to take in what was happening when I heard a noise above and looked up to see the skylight vanish into thin air. A rope ladder dropped down through the void and I heard Tozzy's voice calling down to me, "Come on mate! Get the fuck out of it!"

Climbing up the ladder, I could hear the policemen shouting at the fighting couple, trying to restore order. As soon as I had squeezed through onto the roof, Richi gave me a visibility vest to disguise myself as a workman. He pulled up the ladder and replaced the skylight, "It'll help us if they can't figure out from below how you escaped," he explained.

We climbed down to the rendezvous, where we found Millie waiting with Geraldo's coat and hat. Richi and I returned to the brothers' hotel room, while Millie and

Tozzy split up, Millie shopping in town before taking a train back to Keadby, Tozzy going to a pub where he'd arranged to meet his friends.

At the courthouse, the altercation between Tozzy's mate and his girlfriend had delayed the start of the hearing. Order restored, the couple dispatched with a caution, the judge sent down for David Buckley. The two police guards returned red-faced to report his escape. It was assumed Buckley had taken advantage of the corridor disturbance to pick the lock of the door, as the skylight was known to be too small for anyone to squeeze through, and in any case, from inside it could be seen the glass had not been smashed.

Arriving at the narrowboat, I didn't recognise it, so changed by the repainting. Millie got straight down to business. Addressing the others, she said, "You three go off to the pub, so John and I can fuck like crazy. Don't come back for at least two hours, and don't get drunk either."

The newspapers have been full of allusions to Houdini, Dick Turpin, and other notorious escape artists. Rather than being permanently forgotten by the world, my name will go down in history. In the circumstances, Millie and I have had to accept being confined below deck. Tozzy stays up top with Richi and Geraldo, his purpose to act as a lookout and also to make himself visible. The waterways will come under scrutiny in the search to find Millie and her fugitive boyfriend but a passing barge with a crew of three men and no woman on deck is unlikely to be stopped and searched. We keep ourselves occupied below with cooking and cleaning. It would have been a good time to work on deciphering Alison's letter to Professor Thompson but the novel providing the key to the cipher is back in my gaol cell. Instead, we've enjoyed some political discussion. I've begun to realise, because of getting to know Millie on a deeper level, that she's quite a political animal, like Alison used to be, though not quite so radical. She shows me a newspaper article where some idiot in Johnson's party is claiming people's voting patterns are changing because they're "tired of relying on experts".

I say, "Yes. I read it when in custody. Typical of the confidence trick these unscrupulous political gangsters play on the public. If their computer breaks down, where do they take it? To the dry-cleaners? Of course not, they take it to a computer repair shop — to the experts. If they get a stain on a garment, do they hand it in at a computer shop? It goes to the dry cleaners — to the experts. According to their wonderful logic, when people get on an aeroplane to go off on their Spanish holidays, they should dismiss the captain and take a vote for which passenger should fly the plane. No doubt the arsehole with the loudest mouth will be considered the most qualified for the job. On that basis, I'd say the politician who came out with that crass piece of idiocy would be supremely qualified for the role, if not *over*-qualified. What they really mean is people are tired of experts who tell them things they don't want to know. Their brains have become so addled with the endless stream of celebrity-obsessed crap on TV, they're prey to anybody who'll come up with an alternative to reality, so as long as it has the emotional feel-good factor. Take global warming. How else do you explain the degree of opposition to the idea — people who openly admit they understand nothing of the science, at the same time denigrating all scientists as being stupid? It's emotionalism, pure and simple."

Millie says, "But you can hardly blame people changing their voting patterns when the only future government offers them is a choice between minimal wages and unemployment."

I reply, "I don't blame *the people*; I blame *government,* for deserting the working class and playing up to the multi-nationals. Decades ago, people believed the march of technology would raise up ordinary people's lives. Now they're being condemned to a kind of no-man's land. Not only is it morally wrong, it creates an extremely dangerous situation for the future of society as a whole."

Tozzy comes downstairs. The boys have sent him to make a pot of tea. Our discussion comes to an abrupt end. We don't want Tozzy overhearing anything that might upset his political sensibilities.

Millie changes the subject. "John, Alison's not dead. I *know* she's not dead. You said it yourself. How come Teresa Lewis could recite all those anecdotes from your college days? Even if Alison or her friend Maureen told those stories to Peters years ago, why would he have committed them to memory? It seems obvious to me. The only person who could have remembered her life in such fine detail was the person who experienced it first-hand."

I reply, "Then why didn't they use Alison at Johnson's cottage. Why take the risk with Teresa Lewis?"

Millie says, "I tried to think of it from a woman's perspective. She was fond of you once. She may have been too upset at the prospect of betraying you."

"You're saying she wasn't in a fit state to take part?"

"Possibly, but then I had a better idea. Suppose Alison's living with somebody and her absence from home that night was too difficult to arrange? Suppose, in fact, she's living in another part of the country. She couldn't just tell her partner she was going out to see a friend, if, say, a six-hour round trip was required."

I unfold my canal map of Britain and stare at it helplessly. "She could be living anywhere. It may be impossible to find her."

Millie says, "On the other hand, it may be a lot simpler than you think. Go back to her disappearance. You said Alison's changed identity meant she'd have no track record and could no longer get a job as a nurse. That's not strictly true, you know."

"I suppose not. She could pretend to be a novice and go through the motions of being trained all over again."

"No, she wouldn't need to do that."

"The employer would want references. They'd want to see her qualifications."

"Not if the person *offering* the job and the person *taking* the job were one and the same person."

I tell Millie she's talking in riddles; I don't understand what she's getting at.

She says, "Sunrise Refuge! Remember the newspaper article which said they needed a manageress for the new centre? Within a few months of that article, Alison's husband gets murdered, and she disappears. Suppose she became, under an assumed identity, the live-in manageress of the new premises, an employee of her own foundation. Those places for battered wives must be well hidden. The ideal place to vanish."

I feel a light has been shone on their scheme but I still have doubts. "Millie, I think you're right. The only thing is it might have been a stopgap measure. Alison could have moved on from there."

"She could, but look at the advantages. And it fits in with them having to use Teresa Lewis. You told me a newspaper report said the centre was to be on the south coast. The north-east was simply too far away for her to be absent for so long.  A refuge like that is a 24/7 operation, demanding all her time. I'm guessing Peters goes down on visits. That's when they planned Johnson's murder."

"Then, if we find the refuge, we find Alison?"

Millie points to the canal map. "Here's where we're aiming for. We can't get all the way there by water. We can get within twenty-five miles or so."

I ask, "If the refuge location is a closely guarded secret, how are we supposed to find it?"

Millie smiles at me, "I have a simple plan for that."

## Chapter 54

## South

Unlike my first escape, not long in the news, the second has fascinated the general public. The papers are full of speculation as to my whereabouts. I have become a modern-day Lord Lucan — some British holidaymakers even spotted me sunbathing on a beach in Sierra Leone! Predictably, the online conspiracy theorists are having a field day: my escape was planned by the British government; the CIA are involved; I'm under royal protection, due to a dead relative who once groomed the Queen's corgis; the police lied about my re-capture and had to employ a David Buckley impersonator to pretend a second disappearance. And now, the involvement of a mystery woman has been thrown into the mix, a gift to the tabloids, greatly adding to the romance of my escape. It's unfortunate the observant Jane Magee met Millie in person. An accurate photo-fit is now in circulation, and I'm waiting for the tabloids to pick on Millie's natural assets, since an artist's reconstruction of my narrowboat with its former prominent painted logo has also been issued. I anticipate the headline "Brazen Buckley Beauty Bares Bountiful Breasts on Barge".

Annoying having to keep below deck but we have the capable Richi and Geraldo to pilot the boat. Without them, I am sure we could not have travelled this far without being apprehended. In his capacity as official lookout, Tozzy has been shouting down into the cabin whenever the river is clear for us to come up for air. I only hope some enterprising local isn't observing our progress through powerful binoculars.

When we arrive at our destination, I will be faced with the problem of needing a new disguise. At the time of my recapture, Jane Magee and Forster saw me as bald-headed John Edwards. The circulated police photos have almost certainly been revised to show me both with hair and hairless. Millie suggests I grow my hair again, but cut it and shave my head to look like average balding guy of my age. Her suggestion does nothing for my vanity, but I see the sense. I will remain out of public view until the transformation is complete.

At Leicester, we leave the river for the narrow canal network. Even in these safer waters Geraldo and Richi's superior experience shows at the locks, which they manage together with impressive coordination. They are aided by Tozzy, who has become their apprentice. He seems a natural for boat life. I hope that through it he might find a way out of the stranglehold of petty crime and permanent unemployment.

Millie's keeping quiet about her plans. I sense she wants me to experience a period of calm after the trauma of recapture and being locked alone in a cell for two months. All she will tell me is that Sunrise Refuge, where we hope to find Alison, is situated on the south coast in an unknown location close to the town of Brighton.

#

Peters has been thinking. He's been thinking a lot. How did Buckley locate Teresa Lewis? Peters' contact with her had been minimal: three restaurant meetings, rehearsals at the drama studio. In any case, all that happened before the night of Johnson's murder, before Buckley got involved. Subsequently, a handful of phone calls. No way Buckley could have intercepted those. Someone must have seen him with Teresa, someone whom Buckley knew to seek out.

Peters tries to look at it from Buckley's point of view. Buckley believes Peters to be responsible for Johnson's murder but to prove it he has to establish motive. He's probably already guessed Peters was under threat from Johnson; he wants to find out why. Problem is: Johnson's dead. But one of Johnson's cronies might know something. Buckley doesn't lack for resourcefulness or courage; he has the audacity to join Making Sense. There he meets the person who saw Peters and Teresa together. Why would that person have an interest in the case? Suppose they were being paid to be interested. A detective agency? Unlikely. Johnson wouldn't risk exposing his underhand activities in that way. Must have been a secret job: one of Johnson's political minions, set to spy on Peters and his affairs. Do as Buckley did. Join Making Sense. Find the people closest to Johnson. Find the follower.

#

Jane Magee relishes her trip to Brighton. She goes there regularly, partly for work, partly to meet up with an old friend, a woman of a similar age to herself, whom she's known for at least thirty years. There's nothing the woman wouldn't do for Jane, nor Jane for her.

Jane will leave her daughter, Alison, in the care of her husband. She hates to be parted from her. An only child is always precious. But she'll be glad to get away from the Buckley debacle, the embarrassment of her prisoner absconding twice in quick succession. And she's deeply concerned about the consequences of the escape for the Peters situation. Yes, Brighton will provide a welcome break.

#

"We know the refuge is in the Brighton area," says Millie. "Their number's in Yellow Pages. The closest we can get by water is either Godalming or Tonbridge."

Richi spreads out the waterways map on the cabin table. "Tonbridge is out of the question. We'd have to go up the Thames to open sea, round the Isle of Sheppey and back in at the Medway. I've done it in a yacht but you'd be insane to risk it in a narrowboat."

I say, "So, it's Godalming. We go down the Grand Union, then follow the Thames to the River Wey. How do we get from there to Brighton? As you know, I'm nervous of public transport."

"I'll be hiring a car," Geraldo replies.

I ask, "And when we get to Brighton, how do we find out the address?"

"We don't need the address," says Millie. "We only need to meet the proprietor. I'll phone up and play the battered wife. I'll suggest a hotel where I could meet Alison in the bar 'without my husband finding out'. When she gets there, she'll find out too late she's been tricked into meeting David Buckley."

#

Peters shows his ID at a council house door in Scunthorpe. "Is your son at home? I've good news for him."

259

Tozzy had warned his mother not to give away his location but this man isn't the law and he seems to her to be a helpful sort of official.

"He's gone to the south coast with some friends, having a holiday on a boat."

Not catching on to the significance of what Tozzy's mother has just said, Peters continues to probe through casual conversation. He says, "I didn't know he went sailing?"

"He doesn't. They're on a canal."

Now Peters is keenly interested. "Do you know where they are now?"

"He phoned me last night. Said they'd arrived in Surrey. God – something."

Peters takes out his notebook. "Could you give me his mobile number?"

"He left his mobile behind. Can't afford to top it up."

Peters smiles pleasantly. "The place wasn't 'Godalming', by any chance?"

# Chapter 55

## Death as a Necessary Evil

Peters has decided to commit murder for a fourth time.

Johnson? Johnson deserved to die.

Teresa Lewis? He felt sorry for Teresa but, with the choice being her life or his, what else could he do?

Buckley? Buckley's become too much of a threat. How to kill him and get away with it?  Use the method he used in Norfolk — a murder disguised as a suicide. Regrettable. He could have avoided it. She didn't need to die.

Peters has already decided on the expert opinion he will give at Buckley's inquest: "Driven by his obsession, David chose to end his life the same way as Alison."

# Chapter 56

## Convergence

Approaching London, I'm seeing the place from an entirely new perspective. Hampton Court is particularly impressive when seen from the river. Viewed through tall wrought-iron screens, a spectacular formal garden of clipped hedges and topiary leads down to the wide frontage of the baroque palace. Of course, three centuries ago, the Thames was its principal means of access and therefore given the building's best face.

At the small country town of Weybridge, we turn off the Thames onto the Wey navigation system. We tie up while Millie and Richi go shopping. They return with several bags of groceries, and a book Millie has found in a charity shop — another copy of "Vanished" by Laurence Thompson.

The boys start the engine and cast off to continue our journey southwards, whilst Millie and I sit at the cabin table down below, deciphering Alison's letter to the professor. The limited language of the decoded text contains no specific facts. I guess it's not easy finding the precise words you need from within the pages of an eighty-thousand–word novel when you are composing the message in a situation of extreme duress. Alison uses the phrase "danger to my life", and she begs the professor to "make contact through my friend in London".

Millie asks, "Do you think that's the woman she visited the night her husband got killed?"

I reply, "Samantha Massey, mentioned at the inquest? Strange she gives no address."

"We'll have to assume the professor knew it. Or, as a mental health nurse, she might have been contactable through an agency."

I suggest we should take advantage of being close to London to try to locate Samantha Massey ourselves, in the hope of finding out key information relating to this critical period of Alison's life. Millie says not. She's wary of any delay; we can use Samantha as a fallback option, should the Brighton scheme fail.

Our conversation is interrupted by Geraldo calling down into the cabin it's safe for us to go up on deck. Considering the proximity to London, we find we're passing through a rural backwater, with very little density of housing, just a few riverside pubs and old lock keepers' cottages. For a short while, the river runs parallel to a motorway, then through Guildford town centre, where I once again make myself invisible below deck. Otherwise, this is as unspoilt a stretch of water as any we've encountered on our journey from the north east. Eventually, we arrive at Godalming, where an old military canal branches off towards the coast. It's under restoration, so we can't go down it. Instead, we arrive at a bridge marking the point the waterway ceases to be navigable. We can go no further and tie up at moorings nearby.

Next morning, Geraldo hires a car and he and Millie set off for Brighton. After so many disappointments, I ought to be more philosophical about this latest endeavour to locate Alison but I am frustrated by having to remain down below till their return. Early afternoon, they come back, reporting having located a suitable hotel bar for the meeting. Millie made a phone call to the refuge, masquerading as an abused wife. The manageress agreed to meet her at five o'clock. She told Millie to look for two women sitting together, both early fifties, blonde, dressed for a night out. Apparently, they dress that way in case an abusive male should discover his partner talking with them. Easier to pretend the contact is merely social when dressed for the part.

Our plan is for Geraldo to remain in the car, ready to drive us at a moment's notice, while Richi, Millie and Tozzy will come inside the hotel to act as look-outs, and to assist, should a quick escape be necessary. Such precautions are advisable. Peters will have warned Alison to be on her guard. Everything depends on the impression made by Millie. Did her phone call come over as genuine, or has her impersonation of a battered wife already sounded alarm bells?

We prepare to depart to beat the traffic and be well in time for the five o'clock meeting. Before leaving, I check in the mirror my new look as "average guy, early-fifties, going bald". At the last minute, Millie announces she's not coming with us, that she will stay to look after the boat. I can forgive her lack of enthusiasm. She may have just organised the end of our relationship.

#

Jane Magee's daughter will be back home from school by now. Jane can't wait to video-call on her laptop, to show her the fabulous Brighton hotel she's staying at. She can grab a few moments while she's waiting for her taxi. Then she realises why she can't do that. She'll give a quick phone call instead. Afterwards, she has to text Brian Peters.

#

Magee's text message throws Peters into a state of indecision. He'd not seen Jane for a week and had no idea she'd been planning to go to Brighton. He can play it two ways: tell her what he knows and get Buckley arrested, or proceed with the other plan — Buckley's demise. Peters has searched the river without success. He'd look a fool putting the police on Buckley's track if his information were incorrect. Furthermore, uncomfortable questions might be asked about his interference with police business. He'll stick to his original plan.

The narrowboat, *Millie*, has eluded him. Have they departed already? Or have they abandoned the vessel and hired a substitute? He's seen a few hire barges of the type companies rent out for family holidays. He's trained his binoculars above deck and below deck. No sign of Buckley. Soon it will be evening.

Moored on the opposite bank, a boat named "Wanderer", painted a uniform dark blue. Peters observes it through binoculars. Down in the cabin the lights are on. Peters had considered Maureen to be well endowed but this young woman cooking in the galley is something else altogether, exactly as Jane Magee had described her.

#

We arrive at the hotel at a quarter to five and send Richi ahead to reconnoitre. Ten minutes later, he returns. "The bar adjoins the reception area. The two blondes are there, sitting on high stools, high heels, party dresses, showing off their legs. Nice-looking women."

265

"Anyone else in the bar?"

"An elderly couple sitting at a table. That's all. It's early. I checked the corridors and the other reception rooms. The place is clear. I don't see any trap. Just in case, I'll wait in sight of you. Tozzy can keep watch at the main entrance."

We leave the car and enter reception through swing doors. Richi points out the bar. He whispers, "Good luck."

I approach two blondes of a similar age, sitting at the bar talking to each other. One of them looks in my direction. After the trick of Teresa Lewis, and the debacle in the graveyard at March, I have lost all confidence in my powers of recognition. I ask gently, "Alison?"

The other woman turns to face me.

**PART 6**

**SECRETS**

# Chapter 57

## Jane Magee

Jane Magee loves her job but she would give it all up for her daughter. A mother's instinct to protect her child is stronger than anything. For years, circumstances had conspired against her having a baby. She knew a woman in Brighton who'd been unable to get pregnant and had given up on having a child, so when Jane eventually conceived, she felt a sense of guilt, that she had a duty to dedicate her life to this precious gift. She resigned her post. Her superior in the police force said that they were very sorry to lose her; she could have her old job back at any time, as soon as she felt able.

Working for the police was a million miles away from Jane's self-image. A friend fixed up the interview. A thoroughly nervous Jane attended, expecting to be told she was unsuitable for the role. Against all her expectation, she got the job. She thrived at it, steadily working her way up the ranks to eventually become Detective Inspector.

Only when her daughter had reached school age did Jane feel confident about going back to full time work. Her old police borough no longer had a vacancy, so she had to commute to a town twenty miles away. It was there, in her new job, with everything going so well, that she met the man at that party, a social occasion for politicians and legal people to get to know the local law enforcement team. Jane knew she was making a big mistake but she could not help herself.

Disguised as a prostitute, Jane Magee's staking out a seedy hotel. Peters arrived five minutes ago to meet a woman, so it's safe for Jane to go in now. The hotel desk clerk looks up briefly from the magazine he's reading. He's seen Jane before, many times. She takes the lift. She didn't need to ask the desk clerk the room number. She already knows it.

The thick carpet of the second-floor corridor absorbs her footsteps. No click of high heels will warn the room of her approach. She knocks on the door and assumes the voice of a Polish maid: "Room service!"

Peters opens the door and ushers her inside. They kiss, as he lifts her skirt, pushing his hand inside her panties, feeling the wetness between her legs.

Jane says, "A week's too long. I need you all the time."

Peters loosens his tie. "Get your knickers off. I'm going to fuck you like that, dressed like the tart you are. You know, if they ever discover what you've been doing and throw you out, there's always another profession; I mean high class stuff, where the big money is."

"That's not funny!"

"Sorry. They won't throw you out. We have it all tied up. Anything new to tell me about Buckley?"

"Pleasure before work, Brian. We'll talk about that afterwards."

## Chapter 58

## Martin Douglas Horner

The fates arrayed themselves against Douggie Horner from the moment of his christening. The vicar intoned the name "Martin Douglas Horner" like a judge pronouncing sentence. In trouble at school, sent to borstal as a teenager, numerous convictions for petty crime, many times Horner sincerely tried to go straight but always his past caught up with him. The gold bullion job was supposed to put an end to all that. One final gamble. Afterwards, he'd retire from crime, buy a fleet of vehicles and set himself up with a taxi business.

Not the best planned robbery. The police quickly arrested the main perpetrators, though the gold remained safely hidden and they failed to identify Horner as a member of the gang. Pity they failed to identify also the volatile, knife-wielding Creeson. Solicitor Warby would be alive and the gang would have their money. Now Creeson's dead, his body found floating in the Thames, and Douggie lives in constant apprehension of a similar outcome. Though maybe his luck's changing. The job at Brown's boatyard and his temporary lodgings in Hunstanton are keeping him safe, away from his usual haunts in Kings Lynn. He's good with his hands. They taught him carpentry in Borstal; they even gave him a certificate of merit, so he's pulled out all the stops to impress his employer. No way can Douggie afford to lose this job. Not because of the money, not because he couldn't get other work but because of what he knows about Peters.

In his previous job, a bit of part-time taxiing, Horner picked up an attractive blonde in the centre of Kings Lynn. She asked to be taken to a house in an expensive neighbourhood on the edge of town. The following day the blonde hailed his taxi again. They both laughed at the coincidence. She acted as if returning home after a shopping trip. Douggie knew otherwise. The guarded replies to his casual friendly banter told him this woman was on an assignation, probably having an affair.

Horner met the woman a third time in very different circumstances, when he and Creeson accosted her after the inquest. Next thing he knew, he was reading about her suicide in the newspaper. Douggie saw his opportunity. Identify the lover and blackmail him. Squeeze him for the money needed to buy a little place in sunny Spain and retreat into the cover of a business, running an English-speaking taxi service for tourists. Douggie correctly guessed his blackmail target lived at the very same house where he had twice dropped the woman from his taxi. A few enquiries revealed the house as belonging to one Brian Peters — a married man. Douggie tailed him from the house to the boat shed on the river, to the boat, and to the blonde.

Douggie marvelled at her nerve. True, she'd made up her skin to look a lot darker, and slightly altered her hairstyle, but, no doubt about it, the woman was alive. She and Peters must have contrived to share the loot. Did they take the boat to a house along the coast where they'd stashed the money? Douggie hoped to pick up information at Brown's yard. Inevitable before long he'd meet a customer who knew of the boat and where it made landfall. A couple of "customers" denied him that opportunity, police officers arresting him for his part in the gold bullion robbery, a crime which cost him more than a decade in gaol.

On his release, Horner tried hard to stay clean. The temptation of a safe haven in the sun eventually overcame him, however, and he risked returning to Kings Lynn. Like Buckley, nearly a year later, Horner figured out the place to trace Peters would be the local hospital. Unlike Buckley, however, he'd no instinct for inspiring confidence. The first nurse he talked to obviously intended to give nothing away. The second blurted out Peters' location in the north-east almost out of fear; she was glad to see the back of Horner.

Douggie wasted no time moving north. As soon as he had fixed up lodgings, he scanned the newspapers for job advertisements: the only thing he could find, a politician wanting a driver. The first day of his employment, Horner drove "Honest Jack" Johnson down to London for a political rally. They had to return to the north-east that evening for a social event. Time had been taken up with a press conference — Johnson's outrageous comments inevitably made good material for selling newspapers — and they arrived back late. The exclusive event being held in the private reception rooms of a hotel, Douggie made his way to the public bar, hoping to get food. There he recognised Peters, in intimate conversation with a dark-haired woman. Douggie returned to the car to lie in wait. A few minutes later, Peters and the woman left the building. Abandoning his employer, Douggie drove off in pursuit.

# Chapter 59

## Johnson

Johnson was none too pleased, on leaving the evening reception, to find both his car and his newly appointed chauffeur vanished. Only a cryptic text message: *Emergency took car*, stopped him reporting a theft. Next morning, he accosted Horner, "Your excuse had better be a good one!"

When he'd applied for the job, Douggie had made no secret of his criminal record. He'd appealed to Johnson, saying he was getting too old for crime; he wanted a steady life. Now he admitted he had come north to find Peters. He told Johnson what happened at Warby's office in Kings Lynn. He explained how Peters must have taken possession of the gold-bullion robbery proceeds through Warby's widow. He proposed that, if Johnson agreed to turn Peters over to the authorities, he was willing to share the reward still on offer. Johnson would get money for free and Horner would get the essential advantage of anonymity — if the gang knew he had betrayed them, they would track him down and certain death would follow.

As a cautious lawyer, Johnson knew things wouldn't be that easy. How could he explain to the police the source of his knowledge without revealing the identity of his informant? Furthermore, the story sounded tenuous at best. Did Warby's widow know about the money? Why would she give it all to Peters? If her suicide was faked, then wasn't it more likely the money would be in *her* possession? He asked Horner for six months to decide the best way to claim the reward. Privately, he had already decided on an alternative plan, a much more lucrative plan.

Just like solicitor Warby, solicitor Johnson had over-stretched himself financially. And, just like Warby, the prodigious bullion haul turned him to dishonesty. For Warby: theft; for Johnson: blackmail. He decided to squeeze Peters for a share of the loot. However, he needed to be careful. Suppose Peters hadn't received stolen money. The attempted blackmail of an innocent man would turn against him. It would be himself under threat of prosecution, not Peters. He needed a second reason for blackmail, a kind of backup plan.

Douggie had told Johnson of his following Peters and a dark-haired woman to a hotel. An hour later, the woman left the building alone and drove off in her car. Who was this woman? Douggie had tried to follow her but an articulated lorry got in the way at a junction and he lost her. Would the exposure of her identity seriously compromise Peters? She might have been simply a casual girlfriend, or a one-night stand. That she left the hotel alone so soon after arriving, suggested otherwise but Johnson wanted to be sure. He would put Peters under surveillance. He chose Tozzy as his agent, a judgement well justified by the energy and persistence Tozzy applied to the task of identifying actress Teresa Lewis. The mysterious woman with the black hair proved to be more elusive, however, and Johnson began to get impatient. Eventually he decided to bluff Peters into an admission of guilt.

Johnson sent Peters a note, suggesting they meet at the cottage one evening when his wife would be out, so that they could "talk privately". He enclosed a back-door key, with the suggestion Peters should let himself in, because, "it's best you not be seen calling at my front door." Johnson hoped the melodrama of the key would alert Peters to the danger he faced, softening him up for the blackmail.

At their first meeting, Johnson began by saying he knew all about Peters' love affair with the "dark-haired beauty", as he referred to her, and how damaging it would be for both of them if made public. He could tell from Peters' reaction that his bluff had hit the mark. Having thus cemented his backup plan, Johnson moved on to the gold-bullion accusation. At first, Peters ridiculed the suggestion, his denials so vehement, Johnson began to think Horner's story might not be true after all. But then he had an idea. He told Peters he knew there was more at stake than money and it would be "unfortunate" if his name and address were passed to certain interested parties. The threat of violence collapsed Peters' resistance. He asked Johnson what he wanted in return for a guarantee of safety. Johnson said he wanted money, not Peters' own money, only the stolen money. He wanted it all. It didn't belong to Peters, so Johnson felt no crisis of conscience in taking it from him. But, he said, he felt sympathy for his predicament and would allow him to pay in monthly instalments, delivered in cash to the cottage, always on a night when Johnson's wife would be out of the house.

On one such occasion, they agreed a time of nine thirty for delivery of the following instalment. Johnson urged Peters to be punctual, telling him he would be returning home for only half an hour before being picked up by his chauffeur, as he was flying out to join his wife in Paris for a holiday. Peters noticed Johnson always wrote the name "Brian" by the date and time in his appointments diary. He suggested a pseudonym for anonymity. "Why not the name of that columnist who's always abusing you: David Buckley?" Johnson laughed, saying he was glad Peters retained a sense of humour. He duly entered the name.

On the fateful evening, Johnson arrived home to be confronted by a burglar dressed from head to foot in clown costume and mask and wielding a pistol fitted with a silencer. The clown spoke in a curious harsh whisper. He ordered Johnson to turn and face the wall. Johnson did as he was told; he didn't want to get hurt. The last words he heard were, "Welcome to your death!"

# Chapter 60

## Maureen

When Alison gave Peters a box containing her most treasured possessions to take to Maureen, she didn't know she was setting off a chain of events that would lead to murder.

Alison had resigned herself to sacrificing her home but no way was she willing to sever all ties with the past. She collected together her photo albums, her mementos of her student days, and all the things that reminded her of Greg, including her favourite silver bracelet, a Christmas present, inscribed with the name "Alison". Items capable of being duplicated, like photographs, would have to be copied and the originals returned to their place. The police weren't stupid. Should they search the house after the suicide and find a total absence of family memorabilia, it would surely raise their suspicion.

Peters organised the copying. After the supposed suicide, he planned to take the mementos to Maureen. Peters recognised Maureen as being the weak link in his scheme. He must convince her of her friend's safety, or she might cause trouble. Peters had himself suggested to Alison that Maureen look after her possessions. He had not yet met Maureen, though Alison had spoken of her many times. Significantly, Alison had never spoken to Maureen about Peters.

Maureen had finished with her last patient of the day, a rather tiresome child with a super-precious mummy, when her secretary came in to say there was a man in reception. She had a knowing smile on her face. Maureen wondered why. The handsome specimen waiting there, expensively and immaculately dressed, introduced himself as a consultant psychiatrist. He explained he'd been sent by Alison and asked that they might talk in private at an intimate little pub nearby. There, he outlined the true circumstances of Greg's death, the business of the missing money and the reason Alison's life was in danger. He showed Maureen the late headlines in the local evening newspaper, which had already picked up on the story of a woman's clothes and car abandoned at the beach. He reassured Maureen of her friend being safely in hiding, pending starting a new life under a changed identity.

Maureen felt a certain amount of unease that Alison should send this man, whom she had never heard her speak of, to convey this troubling information but her overwhelming reaction was one of shock that her friend had been forced to take so drastic a course of action. Peters could see he would need to work on Maureen, that she might not be reliable, that she might convey her misgivings to others. He suggested he take her to dinner the following evening, when he would give her the box of Alison's things for safekeeping. Privately, he had no intention of letting go of Maureen until a hundred percent sure of her mental state. That dinner marked the beginning of many social meetings, finally developing into a full-blown affair. They made love out at sea on his boat; on hot summer days in the sand dunes along the coast; in expensive hotels when it rained; once on the couch in her surgery waiting room in the middle of the night.

The copies of Alison's possessions Peters gave to Maureen weren't the only ones in existence. He had thought it prudent to make a backup set. He copied not only photographs but also family audiotapes, and many documents, including Alison's diaries. The latter fascinated him. A day-by-day account of her experiences as a trainee nurse, her attendance at left-wing rallies, her joining the university drama society, the cultivation of a close friendship with a student playwright named David Buckley and explicit details of her subsequent relationship with Buckley's professor. You could reconstruct someone's life from material as detailed as that.

# Chapter 61

# The Body on the Beach

DC Fisher sat alone in the waiting room. He never liked visiting dentists, even when strictly on official business. The sight of the attractive young lady who entered in a white coat made him forget his unease. "Miss Ross? My name is Detective Constable Fisher." He showed his ID. "We're hoping you can help us identify a missing person."

"Miss Ross is on holiday this week. I'm her stand-in. Is it the body washed up near Hunstanton?"

Fisher said, "We've visited all the area dental practices. Miss Ross is the last on our list. Could you check whether she has amongst her patients an 'Alison Warby'? If so, we'd like a copy of her records."

Winding the clock back to the previous morning, we would have seen an elderly couple out walking their spaniel through sand dunes adjoining the beach. The dog raced down to the sea, as dogs of that type are inclined to do. The couple had walked on a quarter of a mile before they noticed their pet had vanished. They saw it in the far distance sniffing at an object close to the water. It wouldn't come, even when called, so the husband went off with the lead to retrieve it. He came running back to his wife, breathless. "A dead body! Call emergency on your mobile!"

If we could wind the clock back to the depths of the night, we would see a motorboat anchored offshore at high tide and a man in a rowing boat approaching as close as he could to the shoreline and tipping a heavy object out of a sack into the water. His intention: to position the body so as to leave no trace how it arrived there. He'd chosen this spot because it he knew it to be popular with bathers and walkers. Within a few hours, someone would discover the corpse, its skeletal wrist, exposed by the falling tide, still sporting a silver bracelet engraved with the name "Alison".

## Chapter 62

## Susie Gibbens

Resemblance: the key to the whole thing. The catalyst for all that followed.

From a distance you might have confused the two women, due to their similar hair. Close up: no way! Alison Warby and Susie Gibbens did not look alike. For one thing, Susie had dark skin, a consequence of spending most of her childhood in India. Not facial resemblance. Bodily resemblance. The two women were of identical height, similar age and of remarkably similar physique. Peters should know. They'd both wrapped their legs round him; he had his hands all over their breasts; felt the width of their hips; explored the fold of their buttocks.

For Peters, the threat of death eclipsed the threat of divorce and financial ruin. How likely the gold bullion gang would fall for the suicide trick? Simply a matter of time before the criminals traced Alison and discovered her association with himself. For them to abandon their search they would have to be convinced she had died. Only one way to do that — produce a body — not just any body — a body that experts could verify as incontrovertibly Alison's.

Peters wasn't thinking all this when he called at the surgery to pick up Maureen. He'd had his mind on more carnal matters. Over dinner at a riverside restaurant, Peters joked with Maureen about her career. He said, "If I were a dentist, it would seriously damage my love-life. I'd be thinking 'I can't go out with *her*. She hasn't got perfect teeth!'"

Maureen laughed. "Then you wouldn't want to go out with my patient I saw you fancying in my waiting room this evening."

"Her teeth looked alright to me."

"She needs a major job done on a pre-molar. A very bad accident as a child. She's had one damaged tooth fixed. She wants an estimate for fixing the other."

Peters said, "It won't be cheap, then?"

Maureen replied, "She's flush with money because of her divorce settlement. She told me she's celebrating the expulsion of her adulterous husband and living on her own again."

What is it that pushes a person over the edge from being a potential murderer to making a commitment to murder? In Peters' case, could we say fear, or greed, or a deadly combination of both, or the challenge to his ego, devising the perfect murder plot? His train of thought went like this: seduce Susie; murder Susie; store the body; wait for decomposition; dump the body on the seashore; swap Alison and Susie's dental records at Maureen's surgery.

Peters knew that when a body is sufficiently decomposed to invalidate other means of identification, dental records can provide a last resort but only if they are distinctive. It's not that Peters hadn't already considered the idea of a substitute body. Stealing from the morgue had been one idea, searching for an Alison look-alike on online dating sites, another. Both schemes brought serious disadvantages. Susie provided a living combination of seduce-able Alison body double together with distinctive teeth. And to start police on the right track, Peters could put on the corpse's wrist Alison's inscribed silver bracelet that he'd kept from the box of mementos passed to Maureen.

Essential for his plan, he needed access to the records. He dared Maureen to meet him for sex at her surgery late one night, as an excuse to be given a door key and be told the key code for the alarm system. The following evening, he returned alone. He already knew his way around. Several times he had called to take Maureen out to dinner and had observed her putting away patient records in a filing cabinet. He also knew where she kept the blank stationery he would need for falsifying substitutes. Susie's address he obtained from the records. He followed her from her house one morning to the factory where she worked. Peters deserved his reputation for being a fast mover. Within days of his contriving to run into Susie near her workplace, the couple were making frequent trips out to sea for sex on his boat.

At the right time, he would dump Susie's body on the beach, gain entry to the surgery after hours and replace the genuine records with forgeries. Important that Maureen should not be present when the police called; a stand-in should hand over the documents, unaware they were fakes. The opportunity came when Peters had to fly to Copenhagen for a medical conference. He would invite Maureen on the trip. On returning home, she would be presented with a fait accompli. Why wouldn't she go straight to the police? Because of the overwhelming consequences of exposing two major crimes: her best friend, Alison, would go to gaol; Peters would go to gaol, and Maureen would lose the only lover she'd ever had.

Peters has done his research. He knows how long a body must remain submerged in order to decompose beyond recognition. Only teeth and jewellery will be left as clues to identity. At his request, Brown's boatyard modified his boat, adding a bracket directly underneath. On a trip down to London, he commissioned the construction of a metal cage, to be towable underneath his boat. The newly found riverside boathouse suits his bizarre purpose, with its own mini dock, and doors that can be closed onto the world. Peters will sail in at high tide with the body inside the cage under the boat. As the tide recedes, the weight of the boat will force the cage down deep into the river mud. The mud will aid decomposition, cover the rotting corpse and hide the smell. Come high tide, the rising water will pull both boat and cage from the mud, making it available for another sea trip. Peters will make frequent trips, the caged body submerged in the water, while he enjoys sex with Maureen in the cabin up top. For how long? For several months; as long as it takes to prepare the corpse.

The last boat trip for Susie. Peters feels regret that he has to do this but then it's one life: hers, against two lives: his and Alison's. They anchor offshore and make love in the cabin. Afterwards, Susie swims in the sea. Peters is thinking of the time Alison emerged from the water and he joked, "Welcome to your death". This time there's no joke. This time it's for real.

The criterion for the perfect murder is met, one committed by a murderer who doesn't exist. How come the murderer doesn't exist? Because there is no murder;

it's a suicide, and, if you don't have a murder, you can't have a murderer, can you?

## Chapter 63

## Samantha Massey

Samantha Massey's offer to Alison had been unequivocal: "Live with me in London for as long as you need. We can pretend you're my latest girlfriend."

Alison accepted without hesitation. From previous visits, she knew her friend's flat would make a good hiding place, and she knew well the lesbian bar scene of Samantha's social life. Last time Alison went to London, the night of her husband's murder, she'd been out on the town with Samantha and her latest pickup, bi-sexual northerner, Jane. Although Jane with her thick black hair was prettier than Samantha, there was no disguising she played the 'man' of the relationship. Alison liked her. She felt a similarity between Jane and herself; they shared the same energy and drive, as evidenced by Jane's ambition to become a police detective.

The relationship didn't last long. By the time Alison moved in with Samantha, Jane had already got promotion and moved back up north. Samantha said, "You realise I'm the one who wears the skirt. I know you hate wearing trousers but you're going to have to dress in jeans and change your hair. Why don't you cut it short for the time you're here? Not for my sake. A lot of people come to London. It would be bad luck if you were seen by anyone you knew. And there's one other thing — you don't mind making out with me when we're in a bar or at a party? My friends know I'm uninhibited. It'll seem weird if we never kiss in public."

Alison replied that she liked the idea of playing a role, of becoming a changed person. In the future, such a change might have to become permanent.

One morning, the two women sat at their kitchen table, having coffee together, recovering from an all-night party. Samantha asked Alison what she intended to do with the Brighton refuge project, now she had supposedly died. Alison explained that, although the new building was ready for occupation, the interviews for a manageress had been on hold since the time of Greg's murder. Samantha said she had a suggestion to make. Would Alison consider giving *her* the job? She was well qualified for it, with her work amongst people suffering from mental trauma. And having herself in charge would give Alison a permanent place of refuge any time she needed.

Thus it was that Alison Warby went to live in Brighton, as a "battered wife", under an assumed name, being cared for by newly appointed manageress, Samantha Massey.

# PART 7

# RESOLUTION

# Chapter 64

## Stalking Millie

Peters sweeps his binoculars along the length of the narrowboat named Wanderer, its lights on, its curtains open. As far as he can tell, Millie's the only occupant. He quickly crosses the canal bridge and cautiously approaches the mooring from the stern end. As a boat owner himself, he remembers to step gingerly on deck; a sudden movement in the water might alert his target. He needn't have worried. There's a huge difference between the inertia of a fifty-seven-foot steel-hulled river craft and a tiny wooden sea-going pleasure boat. As he carefully opens the cabin door and slips inside, he hears the ring-tone of Millie's mobile. The call distracts her attention. She's unaware of Peters stealing softly up the corridor. He slips behind the curtain drawn across the shower cubicle and waits for Millie to finish her conversation.

As Millie cuts the call, she feels a draught. The outside door to the back bedroom has blown open. Funny; there's hardly any wind today. She locks it closed, just in case. She turns to see a man standing behind her. In panic, she tries to get the door open but a hand is placed over her mouth and another grabs her by the throat. Millie struggles. Does she struggle! She's a big girl.

The man says, "I'm not going to hurt you. My name is Brian Peters. I'll let you go if you agree not to scream."

Millie stops struggling. Peters releases his hold. "Unlock the door and leave if you wish but please hear me out first."

Millie steps outside, pressing the quick dial on her mobile.

Peters says, "I don't advise that! He's going to need medical assistance. Don't frighten him off coming back here."

She cancels the call. "You know what's happened?"

"I listened in to your call."

"He's found her."

Peters claps his hand to his forehead. "Fool that I was to underestimate Buckley once again! I thought Godalming had been chosen simply as a hiding place. It never occurred to me the real target was Brighton. Had I known, I would have forewarned Jane and she could have prevented the meeting taking place."

Millie says, "We have witnesses to the encounter: three friends. One of them was employed by Johnson to follow you. We can prove a connection between you and Johnson, so, no more make-believe!"

# Chapter 65

## The Consultation

Peters asks if there's any alcohol on board. He says he can do with a drink after a thoroughly exhausting day searching for their boat, culminating with the catastrophic news of the discovery of Alison.

Millie senses they have him in their power. She leads him through to the lounge and proposes making Irish coffees. Peters sits observing her, saying nothing. His penetrating gaze makes her feel like she's one of his patients. Eventually, he asks, "How did Buckley figure out Brighton?"

Millie replies, "He found a newspaper article reporting the second refuge. It was my idea you had hidden Alison there."

Peters smiles. "Really! So you're a young lady with brains as well as being a most attractive creature. He's lucky to have you. He'll certainly need you now."

Millie hands Peters his coffee. She's made one for herself also. Strange, in her imagination she'd built him up as a tyrant. In reality, an amenable person, enhanced by his film-star good looks. She rather likes him. She has to keep reminding herself she's socialising with a criminal schemer and serial killer. She says, "He knows now he can't have her. Is that what you meant about his needing my help?"

Peters sips his coffee before speaking. "In my professional opinion, Buckley never recovered from his obsession. The treatment he received merely suppressed it, enabling him to lead a successful life. A man like him, a nationally known name, with a substantial salary, no negative personality traits. Why no lady friend? Why a reclusive life in the suburbs? In his mind he was saving himself for *her*."

Millie feels a rising anger at this callous display of scientific detachment. "Thanks to you, his obsession was revived and she betrayed him."

Peters replies, "We had no choice. We did it for the sake of the child. Now you've found Alison, you know her to be happily married with a child, which is why Buckley can't have her. The child is *our* child. The husband doesn't know it. Probably he's sterile, which is why Alison hasn't conceived again."

"Why didn't you marry Alison?"

"Once we'd solved the problem of giving her a new career under a new identity, we were living hundreds of miles apart. The plan was I would get a new job so as to be near her but then something happened she said she could never forgive me for."

"You started to see another woman?"

"Alison didn't know I'd planned for a body to be found."

A sudden chill comes over Millie. The dramatic turn of events had put out of her mind a fundamental unanswered question. With Alison now confirmed alive, whose was the body on the beach? A question they had considered before, many times, though never that the body had been obtained through murder. She's relieved to hear a car pulling up by the canal bank. She peers out of the window. It's not the car she was hoping to see.

Peters asks, "Do you mind if we close the curtains. I prefer not to be on public display."

Millie pulls closed the curtain directly behind Peters. For the moment she feels safer leaving the others open. Is he the type of killer driven by rash impulse, or does he act only after cold calculation of the risk? She's unsure. Better keep him calm; keep him talking. She asks, "Would you like to tell me about Greg Warby?"

Peters replies, "He stole money from a criminal gang. They murdered him then pursued Alison for the loot. She'd no prior knowledge of her husband's crime. I helped her search her home and we found the cash. A fortune, though it wasn't anywhere near what the criminals demanded. Fearing Alison would meet the same fate as her husband, I dreamed up the suicide idea. We hid her in the refuge, with her friend Samantha appointed manageress. At that time, we'd not officially opened for business, so it gave us cover for Alison to have plastic surgery to remove a tell-tale blemish from her lip. A surgeon friend of mine from my time at Oxford did it. A first-class job. No trace of it now. Had he realised the true importance of the tiny mark on her skin, he might not have offered his cooperation. When we split up, Alison insisted I take half the money. Ten years later, we met in Brighton "for old times' sake". The inevitable happened and she got pregnant. I didn't see her again for another five years, then we started to meet whenever we got the opportunity. We've not been able to keep away from each other; that's the problem. My knowing she has regular sex with her husband, and her knowing I cultivate a long-standing affair with a female colleague, only increases our lust for each other.

Millie asks, "What John and I, sorry, David and I, haven't fully worked out is where Johnson fits in."

Peters stands and peers through a gap in the cabin curtains. "What time are they expected back? I gather my follower is your companion 'Tommy', or is it 'Tozzy'? I shall be delighted to meet him."

Millie replies, "Soon, I expect. Tozzy told us Johnson asked him to find out about a woman. He observed you meeting with Teresa Lewis. Tozzy followed her all the way to Liverpool. That's how we found out about Teresa but Johnson said no, it was another woman…"

Peters interrupts. "You think he was blackmailing me over sex. You're wrong. Johnson played for higher stakes — the stolen money. What I'd feared most had come to pass: one of the gang had found out my affair with Alison. He guessed the suicide to be a fake but, since he'd no idea how to find a supposedly dead person, he set about finding my good self. He finally came upon me last year when he was working as chauffeur for Johnson. Lucky for me he'd fallen out with the gang, or I wouldn't be sitting here talking to you now. He knew there was still a reward on offer for information — it was the biggest robbery of its kind at the time you see — but he feared for his life to betray the gang directly, so he told Johnson, proposing a deal whereby Johnson would turn me in and they'd share the reward."

Millie says, "Johnson got greedy and started to bleed you for the stolen money?"

Peters replies, "Johnson's star was on the rise but he'd over-committed to his cause. He faced bankruptcy, with all the damage that would do to his reputation. He admitted as much, saying that by relieving me of my ill-gotten gains, he would in fact be purging me of my sins, putting my money to use in the service of a noble cause. Alison and I knew there'd be no end to the misery. About a third of the loot was missing. We never managed to find it, but, as far as the criminals were concerned, as far as Johnson was concerned, we were sitting on the full value of the stolen gold. Even when he'd bled us of all we had, he'd still be pressing for more."

Millie goes to the galley to prepare more Irish coffee. "So that's when you decided to murder him."

"Understand we did it for the child. *Our* child. There's nothing Alison wouldn't do for the child, even the extreme of betraying her friend from college."

"David figured out your plan when I went to live with him. He had a sudden realisation of how you'd cleverly contrived to set up his illness as the scapegoat."

Peters laughs. "I thank him for the compliment, but he wasn't an immediate choice. What happened was this. Johnson insisted I deliver the blackmail money on particular evenings when his wife would be absent from home. He gave me a door key so I could enter and exit unseen by a back alleyway. Unwittingly, his careful arrangements prepared the way for his death. The key provided the required covert access; the absence of the wife made it easy to carry out the murder. But we needed a way of putting the police on a false scent, of throwing suspicion in an entirely wrong direction. We toyed with the idea of a honey trap, with Alison luring a stranger to the cottage through a sex advertisement on the Internet. Our victim would arrive to find Johnson already shot. Naturally he'd flee the scene but he'd be traced through his mobile phone because Alison would have used Johnson's house phone to make contact with her victim. Unfortunately, anything like that seemed too crazy, an obvious ruse to frame an innocent man."

Millie says, "Whose idea was it to make David the suspect?"

"That's when Alison had her stroke of genius. She said, 'How about if I play myself, but pretend I'm married to Johnson. I invite an old friend to visit, someone I haven't seen for three decades, someone who's publicly declared his dislike of Johnson, someone who's publicly admitted to having suffered serious mental illness? Now a crazy set-up will work to our advantage. They'll assume murder due to insanity. There'll be no need for further investigation.'"

Millie interjects, "But you couldn't use Alison in person."

Peters nods his head in agreement. "We understood the risks of using a substitute. Barring that, we convinced ourselves we had the perfect scheme, especially as the police would be turning to myself to convince them of Buckley's disturbed state of mind."

"What happened to the man who betrayed you to Johnson? Aren't you worried he'll talk?"

"I admit he's the Achilles heel of our scheme and might need to be dealt with but he's vanished without trace, so we're guessing he thinks the bullion gang murdered Johnson. He'll be too petrified to show his face again."

A car pulls up outside. Millie says, "They're back. I'm going outside to tell John you're here. He doesn't need another sudden shock. One final question: Why are you admitting all this? It makes it easier for us to hand you over."

Peters says, "You can't hand me over without also betraying Alison. I'm relying on Buckley not wanting to harm her, even after all she's done to him. He'll agree, won't he? For Alison's sake?"

**Chapter 66**

**Whiteout**

Up till now, I have described the events I was involved in, as they occurred, from my starting point of sanity, through my belief that I might be slipping back into insanity, to the regaining of my sanity. I provide no such guarantee for the events immediately following the revelation of Alison. They are lost in a kind of white haze. I know only the shock of recognition, the shock of all hope lost for a sexual liaison and, worst of all, the shock of knowing the extent to which she had coldly calculated my fate.

I have no recollection of returning to my boat, only of being roughly manhandled by three medical orderlies who drove me by ambulance to a mental hospital, where they locked me in a room with bars on the windows. A doctor visited three times each day and a pretty nurse tended to me constantly. They gave me injections against my will, with the orderlies pinning me down on the bed. Millie tells me there was no such hospital; the medical orderlies were Geraldo, Richi and Tozzy; the nurse, herself; and the doctor, Peters. He'd obtained a month's leave from his job, supposedly on grounds of over-work. The hospital of my imagination had been a six-bedroom cliff-top holiday home on the Sussex coast. They'd chosen it for its isolation and because it had a utility room with barred windows. The injections, I had not imagined. They had found it necessary to heavily sedate me.

During my gradual return to normality, Millie fed me information piece by piece, for fear of overloading my mind and causing a relapse. I learnt first that Peters was

304

no longer a threat. With three independent witnesses to the discovery of Alison's identity, he knew the game was up and his only option to put himself at our mercy. Later, Millie described to me how Jane Magee's team were to be manipulated towards gradually winding down the hunt for Johnson's killer. Finally, she explained the plans for our future. A property had been found, backing onto a canal, part of a Victorian country estate that was being broken up and sold off in lots. The walled kitchen garden, together with the gardeners' cottages and outbuildings, would be purchased and gifted to us as our refuge.

We have been here five years. I cultivate the garden and the greenhouses, well away from the general public. I work alone but I don't mind. I'm used to limited social interaction, and I'm by no means alone. I have Millie. Our narrowboat is moored on the edge of our land. There's access to it down a lane from the main road. We've refitted and repainted it as a farm shop where Millie sells our produce. Our modest income keeps us secure and happy.

It pained me to think of my house in Lancashire, empty and uncared for, gradually reverting to a state of overgrown ruin. Tozzy's mate and girlfriend now occupy the property as squatters. The owner would need to take legal action to evict them, but I'm not going to do that, am I? They proudly send pictures to Millie on her mobile. They're keeping the house and garden in really good order.

Fergal Flanagan called back as promised. Tozzy's friends told him I'd sold up and gone abroad. Last I heard, he'd obtained them a floating shell of a boat and was helping them restore it. He's infected them with the canal bug. We're told they have plans to bring the boat down south on a visit.

Tozzy's been working full-time for Richi and Geraldo. His political convictions have evaporated, now that he enjoys the dignity of satisfying work. Still a problem with his use of the English language though, which he is constantly reminded to moderate in front of customers. His bosses jokingly threaten to send him for elocution lessons.

Pleased as I am with how things have worked out well for Tozzy, for his friends, and for Millie and I, there remains the main issue. The story must end, as it started, with Alison. There is still much to tell.

# Chapter 67

## For the Love of Alison

What happened to Alison, and to Peters?

Alison lives nearly two hundred miles from us. She can visit only infrequently. She always comes alone. We meet within the privacy of the cottage. We must never be seen together in public. Reminiscing about happier times, catching up on our lives without the context of deception, has gradually returned my feelings to a state of peace.

Peters put up the money for our market gardening enterprise. Keeping me safe provides a reciprocal guarantee for his own safety. Once a month he visits his "special patient", as he refers to me. I enjoy our sessions, though sometimes I think it is me who should be psychoanalysing *him*.

Why make a Faustian bargain? All I need do to prove my innocence is turn Peters in. My two escapes from custody and Millie's aiding and abetting, I would expect to be pardoned, in view of the extraordinary conspiracy against me. I might even claim generous financial compensation, not to mention enjoying the fame of celebrity, getting invited to chat shows, writing the best-seller of my story, and, best of all, resuming making a political contribution through my newspaper column.

A mother's love for her child may lead her to any lengths. The prospect of a life-sentence for her, of the father receiving a death sentence, drove her to a desperate plan. I will not destroy Alison's happiness by destroying the happiness of Alison, her child.

# Chapter 68

## Inquest

Jane Magee lies on the hotel bed, naked but for the lingerie she knows drives Brian Peters wild. She's enjoying the afterglow of being comprehensively used. Gentle lovemaking, she reserves for her marriage. Peters supplies the animal lust she craves.

Peters emerges from the shower. "Damn nuisance the case review time being changed. Lucky you checked. Would have seemed suspicious if we'd both missed the meeting. Our colleagues are police officers, after all."

Jane unhitches her stockings and slides them down her legs, slowly, knowing how much she's teasing him.

Peters says, "I suggest you do that behind closed doors or you might find yourself missing the meeting anyway."

She smiles, gathers up her clothes and enters the bathroom, leaving the door open. She says, "I'm going to recommend the Johnson case officially be declared cold, now that five years have passed and there's still no sign of Buckley. You can back me up by saying in your opinion there's every chance he's drowned himself, as Alison did. That will give me the ammunition I need to convince the chief constable."

Peters stands at the bathroom door, watching her shower. "Do you think they'll buy it? After two dramatic escapes, they know Buckley's a pretty resourceful character. He's become a legend in the media. They'll be making a TV movie about him next."

Jane turns off the shower. She hands Peters her towel. "Dry me!"

Peters engages with the ritual they perform after sex. His favourite part: applying the towel to her most intimate areas. Then he'll watch while she dresses. Maybe her husband watched her dressing this morning — though not the way she dresses for Peters.

Jane says, "If my colleagues knew the extent of Millie's involvement, we wouldn't be able to persuade them of David's death. Amazing how she worked out about the refuge, though she didn't know about Samantha, that *she* was the manageress."

Peters glances at his watch. "You leave before me. I'll follow on.  Buckley told me Samantha was mentioned briefly in the newspaper report of Greg's inquest. Could he have attained his goal more quickly by tracing her first, do you think?"

Jane pulls up the zip fastener on her skirt and grabs her handbag and car keys, ready to leave. "How could he have found her? In any case, the vital clue was buried in her past life. No way could he have known about Samantha's northern policewoman lover, Jane, and how she became my role and character model for the future."

Peters laughs. "Ironic! What's Buckley's most distinguishing visual feature? For a man of over fifty, his total lack of baldness. What does he think to do to disguise himself? Go to the other extreme. Shave his head. And there he is chasing round the country for a good-looking blonde. Did he not think the first thing Alison would do was to dye her hair the opposite — black? Look what else he does. Goes in for horticulture; pilots a barge all over the country; masquerades as a retired private eye, a solicitor, a mature student, a photographer, a white supremacist, a bus station tramp And he thinks Alison, with all her acting talent, a woman he once knew as a consummate mimic, who could do voices to order, and with all the strength of character he knows her to have, will go into permanent hiding, that she won't invent a completely new persona in which to openly pursue a new career,

Jane says, "I nearly caught myself out in the hotel on the way to meet Samantha. I was about to quickly video-call home before the taxi arrived, then I remembered I was wearing my blonde wig for old times' sake. Millie's a remarkable girl. I sensed she had special qualities, the first time I met her on the boat. When David finally recovers from his obsession, he'll realise he's got by far the better bargain."

Peters opens the bedroom door to check the corridor is clear. "You do yourself an injustice, woman. Look at all the good you've done over three decades through your Sunrise Refuge project."

# Chapter 69

## Epilogue

Millie and I sit cuddled up together on a sofa by the fire. We're in a particularly happy mood, due to the influence of my aunt's well-matured homemade wine, of which we still have three bottles left, and because our friends, Richi and Geraldo, are on a week's visit. They've travelled down from Ely, by boat of course. Although they have visited several times, Millie always banned them from referring to the events in which we shared. Only now has my nurse and guardian given permission for discussion.

Geraldo asks, "When did you realise you were being set up?"

"Peters admitted it to me at our first interview. I was half-crazy by that stage. He thought he could frighten me into a plea of insanity. Instead, he gave me a glimmer of hope I could escape my predicament."

Richi holds out his glass for Mille to pour more wine. "Your intention was to plead 'not guilty', wasn't it? If you'd lost the case, you'd have got life, or Making Sense's threatened death penalty."

"Peters would have had no problem with the latter outcome but he had to deal with Alison. Neither of them could have foreseen that the very day they chose to murder Johnson would be the very day his party would announce their death penalty campaign. Alison was horrified when she found out I might end up being hung for her crime."

Geraldo interrupts. "But at what point were you *sure* it was a set-up?"

"When I found the evidence that Peters knew Alison twenty years previously, not only the documentary evidence, but also the eye-witness accounts of their going out on his love-boat."

Millie says, "When John first told me the story of the trick they'd played on him, it was obvious the details didn't add up."

Richi says, "The whole 'Mr Clown' thing?"

"No. That made sense. If it was a set-up, they pulled all the strings and could play out the action any crazy way they liked."

"Alison being alive when she'd been proved dead?"

"That was *John's* focus, because of his obsession. What I wasn't happy about was where *real* people got involved, namely the police. It was all a bit too pat: the precisely timed discovery of the body, their certainty John would return for the gun, their immediately taking the trouble to examine Jack Johnson's appointments book, where common-sense would have told anyone a murderer would not make an appointment in his own name. It was like they knew in advance the murderer would be a crazy man."

I say, "Millie told me she believed Peters already knew how the police would react. Of course, what we didn't know until Brighton was he had an insider accomplice."

Richi says, "You must have had a lot of interviews with Jane Magee during the investigation. You never guessed for one moment she and Alison were one and the same?"

"Subconsciously I think I knew. Once I remember, Jane came into the interview room and it felt like Alison had come in. Then, at every meeting I felt at peace, even when she was grilling me over the murder charge. The problem was she and Teresa Lewis both being such accomplished actresses: Teresa's accurate take on how a fifty-year-old Alison might look and act, plus of course the faked-up lip blemish; Alison's becoming the character she had adopted, the convincing northern accent, the efficient police-chief manner, and of course the lip blemish gone, thanks to skilful plastic surgery. Over twenty years she'd grown into the skin she'd put on, becoming an entirely different person. She'd even developed a set of facial expressions I don't remember from the past; like a puzzled look she'd give me any time my story didn't make sense."

Geraldo grabs the wine bottle and tops up our glasses. "No point keeping this till tomorrow is there? It's so ancient it'll decompose to something lethal by then, if it's not already lethal. So, if Jane Magee hadn't been on hand to influence events at the cottage, or if you hadn't returned there as planned, their whole scheme would have collapsed."

"Millie thinks so but I disagree. Peters was too sophisticated a schemer not to have covered all eventualities. The name in the appointments' diary would still have led the police to me; they'd have me on CCTV at the railway; I'd have stuck to my clown story, believing my innocence to be my guarantee of protection, but my fingerprints were on the gun, remember; the outcome would have been no different. Lucky that Peters *does* think of everything, or I don't think Millie would be with us today. He told me, when he saw Millie alone in the boat his first thought was to kill her, wait for Tozzy and me to return, kill Tozzy, and once again contrive to pin the blame on me, for a double-murder this time."

Richi says, "That's chilling. To think of Millie alone with him, in peril of her life. Insane!"

"He dropped the idea for a perfectly sane reason — he'd no knowledge of my accomplices, or whether Millie or Tozzy had confided in friends. Also, the people I'd interviewed when on the run. Might some person unknown to him, seeing the TV coverage, come forward with evidence simultaneously clearing my name and implicating himself?  And then there was Tozzy's mother — a major mistake his talking to her face-to-face — he should have just telephoned. What set the seal on matters was when he sneaked onto our boat and listened in on Millie talking on her mobile to a 'Richi' and a 'Geraldo' about the events in Brighton. He realised then he was a thoroughly beaten man; that his best protection would be to offer to become our friend and ally, appealing to my reluctance to take any action which would also harm Alison."

#

 Next morning, we wake with terrible hangovers; the last time we'll risk drinking my aunt's ancient wine. Millie drags herself down to our post box, which we fixed on the canal side of the old kitchen garden wall. She returns with a letter, postmarked the north of England. It's my birthday. Apart from Millie, there's only one other person who knows the date.

314

# Chapter 70

**The Fatal Flaw**

Millie calls out from the kitchen, "Would you like black coffee?"

I give no reply.

Millie comes into the room. "John! What's the matter? You look terrible! Is it Alison? Is she OK?"

"She's sent us a warning. The chief constable's ordered a second case review. A new team of detectives; Alison's not involved. Although they're sticking to the conclusion my evidence was a fabrication, they've decided to look more closely at the only part of my story proved to have really happened — the phone calls that morning from the mystery caller. They're wondering whether the phone number trying to reach me had called any other numbers that day. Alison says Peters gave Teresa Lewis an unregistered mobile with strict instructions to only call my office and not use it for any other purpose. She was to turn off the phone and bring it with her to Johnson's cottage."

Millie gives a gasp of horror. "Don't tell me! She rang a friend."

"No. She did exactly as he asked. After she'd spoken with me, she switched the phone off and put it in her bag. But, in her hurry to catch her train, she forgot to put in her own mobile. The train broke down. She panicked, thinking I'd arrive before her, and totally forgot the phone prohibition. She used it to ring Peters."

Millie says, "Are you sure? The address book on the mobile would have been empty. Or did she have Peters number in her diary?"

I say, "That was the fatal flaw in Peters' scheme. Teresa, the actress, skilled in learning lines, didn't need an address book or a diary. She'd already committed his number to memory."

# Chapter 71

## Last Word

Millie says nothing. We're both in a state of shock. I hand her Alison's letter. "See what she says. The police have obtained a second number. They expect to identify the owner of the mobile."

"Why didn't Peters tell us all this before?"

"Alison hasn't been able to ask him yet. He's travelling in Slovakia. He's put his phone off."

"If she hasn't talked to him, how does she know what Teresa did?"

"You'll see she admits it's all conjecture. Alison knew the train breakdown nearly scuppered their scheme, and she knows now from this case review the precise time of the second call, which fits with the time Teresa would have been halfway through her journey. Why else would she use the unregistered phone at that moment, and who else would she ring but Peters? Alison thinks he was so distracted setting up Johnson's cottage that he answered without checking the caller ID. Teresa was already late so he automatically assumed the caller was herself. When he heard her voice, why would he assume anything other than she was calling from her regular mobile?"

I take Millie's hand in mine. "Looks like we'll be torn apart after all, for aiding and abetting a killer. Hopefully we'll get mitigation for circumstances. I'm hugely concerned for Alison. This will destroy her."

Richi comes downstairs nursing a hangover, followed by Geraldo. We explain the business with the mobile phones and hand them the letter to read.

Richi says, "You're safe, though, aren't you? What do you think, Geraldo?"

His brother laughs. "A sort of poetic justice on the actress's part, one of the skills Peters chose her for, bringing him down with such surgical precision!"

I ask, "Why surgical?"

"Because the phone number points to him alone. Nobody else is incriminated by it and he's not going to admit to accomplices."

Richi adds, "If he betrays you two, or Alison, the full details of the Johnson conspiracy will come out, plus he'd be gifting the prosecution with multiple witnesses, including Geraldo and me, willing to testify he's also admitted murdering Suzie Gibbens and Teresa Lewis."

"You're saying his best tactic is to claim ignorance of the caller and let the police try to figure out a connection?"

Millie says, "With DI Jane Magee involved, we know how well that will go for them! Probably why her letter says to wait for developments."

#

Millie's been going down to our post-box each morning to intercept the post as soon as it arrives. Today she comes back with an envelope postmarked Bratislava. Inside, a picture postcard of a medieval church, with the handwritten message:

*"Disappointed to be given so little credit. TWO unregistered phones purchased, one for the lady, one for me, to be used for ALL contact between us, so none traceable.*

*P.S. Won't be seeing you again. Further treatment unnecessary. Regard yourself as officially cured. Well done!"*

# Afterword

Like my first novel, *The Secret Resort of Nostalgia*, which was shortlisted for the 2017 Yeovil Literary Award, the beginning of this novel is partly autobiographical. As a student at the University of Birmingham in the late 60's / early 70's I formed a friendship with a fellow student named Alison. After college, we lost touch, but I did hear from a mutual friend that Alison had married a solicitor, which seemed at the time a curiously respectable act for an unconventional sort of person like her.

Decades later, when looking for an idea for the inciting incident for a stage play entitled *Here Be Clowns*, I remembered my friend and her surprising marriage. From that starting point, I developed a play with a good beginning and a good middle but I couldn't think of any ending that would work well on stage, though I could think of several endings suitable for a novel. So, the play, *Here Be Clowns*, became the novel, *For the Love of Alison*, based around a man's obsession for an 'Alison' (a fictitious character having little in common with the original, apart from being both blonde and gorgeous).  I wonder where Alison is now and whether one day she might read this book.

Find out more about the author and his novels and plays at the publisher's web site
https://www.businessassistant.biz/novelsandplays.htm

# Acknowledgements

Firstly, to my wife, Hossanah, our daughter, Melina, and our son, Muhsin, for reading the novel and making several useful suggestions. Secondly, to my friend, John Daly, for once again being willing to work through first drafts to give feedback. Also, to Doug Watts (Jacqui Bennett Writers Bureau) for his, as always, helpful professional critique. And to my friend and business colleague, Marcus Bolt, professional graphic designer and fine artist, for the front and back cover design. Last but not least to my dentist for filling me in (no pun intended) on the circumstances of identification of dead bodies through dental records. Slightly disconcerting that immediately after our conversation he proceeded to double-check my own chart was fully up to date.